HIGH

RISK

Adrian O'Donnell

For my beautiful wife Jo, thank you for all the help and support you have given me whist writing this book.

And to all the scary people I have met during my career who inspired me to write this story, I thank you all!

CONTENTS

THE PRISON

It's the worst part of inner London nestled in rural
parts
My only protection sharp wit, smooth tongue and
kind heart.
Adult bodies with childish minds intent on causing
harm,
Trying hard for 12 hours a day to maintain some
type of calm.

Another day, another fight, graceful orchestrated
Violence,
Punching, stabbing, the victims lay in
Silence.
Not an eye raised nor head turned by today's well
thumbed script,
Normal every day working life, tales from a London
Crypt.

Everyone's worst nightmare packed under a single roof.
Gangland brutality is everywhere, that's the petrifying
truth.
What did granddad do at work today, and tell us it
was cool?
I had to fight five kids today to get them out of
school.

Every day is manic, threats at every turn,
Violence is their business, a real going concern.
Why should I have to wish that I manage to make it
home?
Someone wants me damaged again, lost teeth or
broken bone!

39 hours every week, a coconut in a government
shy,
Inner city gangsters and a 60 year old mum square
up eye to eye.
A prize fighting baby sitter, a dad or a lads' last
hope.
Every day for 12 long years, how ever did we cop

PROLOGUE

Tony lay on the broken prison bed listening to the sound of a busy local prison shutting up for the night. It was still early, around eight o'clock, but that was how the routine ran here. "Numbers B wing?" a shrill shout requested.

"One hundred and seventy six!" came a distant reply slightly lost in the hum of a hundred tunes emanating from the confines of the locked cells.

This had been a good couple of weeks for Tony and early release was certain. Promoted to the number one wing cleaner, a trusted position that gave him unsupervised access to all parts of B wing, he just had to ensure that it was clean enough to keep the staff off his back for the next few days. In line with his newly elevated status, he had a cell to himself, a relief after months of sharing a cramped cell with any undesirable chucked in with him. He stared at the photos stuck on the stark cell walls, held in place with toothpaste as had a thousand other pictures before.

Two weeks and he'd be out, seeing his family for real, breathing the fresh air never smelt in jail. No longer would he be surrounded by badly painted walls, a floor showing burn marks from a million cigarette butts, the stale stench of tobacco and a stinking steel toilet which no matter how many times he cleaned it, the brown stains from previous use remained and the stench of urine oozed from the grubby floor. A line crafted from string stolen from the Wing office spread across the cell ceiling, tied at one end to one of the thick bars protecting the window and the other end to a nail that had, using some unknown implement, been banged into the wall above the empty bed next to his. It was the only way to dry his few items of clothing after they were scrubbed in the steel sink, all a long way from the comforts of home he was so looking forward to.

This part didn't worry him so much, but the faceless metal door that sealed him inside of this putrid space, worse than any public toilet, was hateful. The fact that it could never be opened from the inside was soul destroying. The only way to get out of that cell was if a screw unlocked you - bad enough when you were supposed to be unlocked, impossible if it was not your turn. Still, at least he didn't have to share this room with anyone else.

The chaos of men making last minute deals, drugs, phones, tobacco, or as it was better known 'burn' had melted away. The junkies had swapped prescribed tablets and other medications, mainly methadone which was always ready available, in their constant quest for sleep. Tramadol was also a crowd pleaser, he had never known so many young, fit people needing pain relief, and the endless depression of a night time locked up with only thoughts of separation from loved ones was the ideal moment to melt away into a drug induced release.

The hum of prison officer chatter came from a central area where staff congregated waiting for the last door to be locked and prisoners accounted for. Weekend plans, football scores, latest conquests, all were regular topics of conversation before they all went home to the needy wife and screaming kids. These snatched clips of conversation always made Tony smile. He longed to hear these sounds of home, he was determined his life would be different this time and that he would never return to this hell hole!

Drifting off to sleep a short while later, the sound of shuffling feet and jangling keys whipped him back into the present. The door opened and the harsh light from the wing landing swept across the darkness. An officer who looked about sixteen years old turned on the main light and started a monotone explanation, the type he had already given ten times that evening as he found beds for the latest influx of new prisoners to the wing.

"The wing's full, you'll have to share your cell tonight" he explained as Tony blinked in the sudden harsh light.

He didn't bother waiting for a reaction as he briskly said "In here" to the man standing just outside the cell door.

Tony looked up as the door clanged closed. A tall, athletic man stood with his back to the door, he didn't speak but just looked around the cell as though surveying a new bed sit for rent before carefully placing a book onto the top of the small empty broken locker between the two beds. He sat on the side of the empty bed staring at unseen things before rolling onto his back, gazing up at the flaking paint on the ceiling. A chilly breeze rolled through the small broken window making Tony regret the time he had smashed it with a broom handle to get more air into the stuffy cell one hot summer night.

Lighting a thin roll up and inhaling deeply, Tony blew a cloud of smoke towards the nicotine stained ceiling. He looked over trying to work out any clues as to who his new cell mate was. He didn't look like a junkie and seemed at ease with his surroundings, implying he had served a bit of time inside.

He guessed the guy was six feet plus, not an ounce of fat and a close shaven head that failed to hide a long jagged scar running from front to back. His arms showed brutal scars from years of cutting, all seemed old and healed but the razor blade had cut deeply across both forearms. He could have been any age between twenty and thirty, the pale skin was tight on his face making him look gaunt. He smelled of prison, no fancy aftershaves or antiperspirant, another clue that this guy may have been transferred in from another prison.

The man still said nothing, just hummed a gentle tune as he lay on his back with his eyes closed. Tony had shared many cells with a host of people during his past prison sentences. This guy was different, he seemed confident, almost self assured. He exuded the kind of atmosphere experienced when an important person enters the room and the power seeps out of them. Hard to explain, just different. Tony turned on to his side to face the newcomer, propping himself up on his elbow to get a better look.

"How ya doing mate? I'm Tony" he offered.

No response, just a continued humming of an operatic number. Suddenly the song finished and the man's eyes snapped open as he turned his head, catching Tony by surprise. Tony found himself looking into eyes which were deep and black, soulless and cruel.

"I don't like sharing a cell with anyone and I don't like the pictures of your shitty family, take them down".

He fixed Tony with a gaze, "Now!"

"Listen mate, leave it out, I'm home soon. I don't need trouble. I'll try get you a cell on your own tomorrow, I'll speak to the screws, I can sort it". Tony found himself gabbling in his panic to appease the man.

"I don't need you to sort anything; I am capable of sorting everything out by myself just fine. You can speak to your screw friends, but I don't think they can help you!"

The undertones of menace in the man's voice had Tony jumping from his bed and carefully taking his photos down before placing them into his drawer. Fuck that, a nutter, just what he needed he thought as he rang his cell bell for the last time.

Footsteps approached the cell and a tired old night officer looked through the observation panel. Tony stuck his face close to the panel and hissed

"Boss, this bloke is high risk, and he shouldn't be sharing."

The officer closed the flap, "Go to sleep son, it's not an emergency. Keep your bloody finger off the bell!"

9

Resignedly Tony turned to climb into bed but was surprised to see the man now standing against the back wall of the cell staring directly at him. He felt the last of his courage evaporate.

"Honestly I don't need trouble" he pleaded. I will move in the morning, just give me a break, I'm home soon."

The man didn't respond, he just slowly closed his eyes, lips moving silently as if in prayer. It was the most unnerving sight Tony had seen.

A shiver swept up his spine as he climbed under his thin prison duvet. I can make this till morning, then I'm out of this cell he convinced himself as he finally fell into a shallow restless sleep.

Tony woke. He wasn't sure what had stirred him but as his eyes acclimatized to the dark, he looked across the cell and saw the stranger's empty bed. What the fuck? Before he could waste any more time on contemplation a hand came from nowhere and clasped itself tightly over his mouth, followed by the glint of a razor blade as it cut into his cheek and straight through his right eyeball. No screaming, that was absorbed into the powerful grip, then a cold calculated draw of the blade across the throat. Tony didn't even have time to plead for his life, death was quick and callous. His unwelcome roommate then took his time, putting in eight hours hard work with a teeny weenie razor!

The six thirty morning roll check would never seem the same. The same tired old officer from the previous night attempted to look into Tony's cell but the observation panel had been blocked with newspaper. Unable to see in he called out angrily. "Uncover your panel!" and receiving no response, he jammed his keys into the lock with impatience. He was tired and needed to get home to bed, it had been a long boring night shift. The door opened into the dimly lit cell. He could see one bed was taken, the tall man laid on top of the covers smiling. The other bed was empty.

"What's going on with you two?" He demanded, "Where the fuck is your cell mate?"

He looked down, suddenly noticing a sticky mess on the floor, the dark oozing pool seeping from under the empty bed before spreading its reach across the floor. Blood splattered across the walls and ceiling merged into finger painting and writing as murderous messages adorned the cell walls.

"Find him yourself, and mark my homework officer. I am sure that you will be impressed …oh, and don't forget to tell his family". The man then took a long deliberate drink from his plastic cup savouring the moment, the prison tea warming his stomach.

The door slammed shut followed by the chaos of clipped orders, boots pounding along the landing amidst shouts from other cells as prisoners were awoken by the turmoil within their wing. Then silence, five minutes of beautiful calm before the tinny crackling of the prison officer's radio broke the trance. Scuffling feet and hushed whispers brushed under the cell door before it burst open revealing the silhouette of staff formed up like an American football team ready for action, crash helmets glistening in the bright landing lights and a small plastic shield held purposefully by the lead person protecting the team.

"Stand up and place your hands on your head!" Instructions were yelled from one of the officers as adrenaline filled the cell.

"You really have no need to restrain me!" The man sounded more matter of fact than scared – he was someone who knew the system.

"We will do whatever we need to do; we just need you out of the cell now."

The man eyeballed the officer behind the shield, "Come and fucking get me then!"

A voice from behind the staff barked two words "Get him!"

Instantly the three staff entered. They were dressed in black overalls and helmets with visors protecting their faces. All had shin guards and heavy black boots with thick black leather gloves completing the look. The officer who came in first held the shield in front of the top half of his body while the others sheltered behind peering for their target. He jabbed the shield forward causing a second of distraction before staff peeled out from behind and pinned the prisoner to the bed before twisting his arms up behind his back so high that he had no alternative but to lie there yielding to their efforts. He was dragged to his feet and pulled out of his cell, bare feet banging off every step encountered, tracksuit bottoms half falling uncovering light blue prison boxer shorts before being frog marched into a segregation cell, a cell with nothing in it whatsoever apart from the four bare concrete walls. Roughly handled by the staff as they stripped off his blood stained clothing and placed them in bags leaving him with nothing more than a rip proof blanket, he smiled inwardly. This had been a good night.

11

As the cell door clanged shut, he settled himself on the floor with his back to the rear wall, and gently hummed a distant tune while working out his next move like a chess grand master. He was close to checkmate although his opponent hadn't even realized the game had begun. Like a first day at school he had established himself and soon all would fear him. But this was just the start, the start to a long path of vengeance. There was one clear target ahead, and it didn't matter how long it would take before the ultimate trophy was gained. All in good time he thought, and that was something he had a good deal of. Some more work needed, more fear to be spread, more widows to be made, and more children to be left fatherless.

After an age, a face appeared at the observation panel of the cell, "Martin, how are you? Are you ok?" This was the kindness he had waited for, someone who thought that by using his name implied they were friends. Someone who thought he was still human, someone who could be helped. Now for another chance to show them what he was made of.

"Yes, but I just need to talk to you. Can I talk? I can't deal with what I've done, I need to talk." Martin Heard looked up pleadingly before dropping his head into his hands in what looked like despair.

"I just feel like ending it all, I have nothing left to live for" he continued.

The door opened to a sea of officers dressed in overalls and helmets standing observing, whilst a small man in a suit stood behind them.

Martin looked back up; "Can I talk boss?" He pleaded again.

The suited man walked past the officers and into the cell, just as Martin had hoped. He felt the razor blade sitting in the cheek of his mouth and moved it slowly with his tongue. The suited man didn't know what had hit him as Martin, moving as quick as lightening, sprang from the floor like a panther, grasping an arm and in one move had him in a headlock slicing the blade deep into the Governors right eyeball. The blade now sat to the left side of the man's neck, he gave it a tweak causing a small cut from which a trickle of blood ran down to his white collar before merging with the thick mess coming from the empty eye socket.

"Now fuck off behind that door, or this man is dead" he calmly ordered the supposed protective team who had frozen with the horror of what had just occurred. The officers shoved each other in their panic to get out and the door slammed shut. Martin had his prize.

"Right you little bastard, I think that you belong to me!" Martin commanded forcing him onto the floor.

The man whimpered and crawled across the floor before curling into the foetal position unable to focus as the blood streamed into his remaining eye. The pain was intense and cut through his brain.

"Stand up you spineless bastard" Heard ordered him and grabbing hold of the waistband of the man's pin striped trousers he pulled his pray into a crouched position as the torrent of blood started to turn the cell floor into a macabre skating rink. Throwing him back onto the floor Martin chuckled with delight as he pulled the clothes off the sobbing man, knowing full well that the staff would be watching through the observation panel in horror.

Soon he had him almost naked, wearing only a red pair of boxer shorts and again Martin laughed. He looked at the observation panel once more and could make out a wide pair of panicking eyes. Making a slashing motion he smiled rejoicing at his own creativity.

"Look boys, look at the state of this white skinned, flabby, pathetic little man - I may even take his other eye out! He showed everyone the razor before pushing his back firmly up against the cell door. In spite of being manic in his behaviour, an element of rationality remained in his head.

"Now, I know that these doors can open both ways. If I hear you removing the anti-barricade bolts, I will kill him immediately. Understand?"

A voice came from the other side of the door confirming that they understood.

The watching Officer, so terrified of the events he was observing, froze unable to even report what was happening. He had a front row ticket and was hypnotised by the brutality.

"What is your name Governor?"

"Roger" the poor individual replied with what was to be his last spoken word.

"Come here Roger, we need to cuddle up a bit tighter". He pulled him in between his own legs.

In the blink of an eye Martin punched him hard in the back of the head causing him to black out briefly. He came to, a thumping pain growing across his head, stars buzzing around his eyes. Martin had taken hold of his tongue yanking it forward so hard he could feel the muscle tearing. The blade was brought to Roger's face scraping his top lip and running slowly down his teeth before hacking the bloodied tongue from the open mouth and tossing it towards the rear wall.

The scream of pain and flow of blood was sickening. However this just seemed to spur Heard onto more action. Now in a full blood lust, nothing would stop the torrent of violence. The depravity of the attack was relentless, staff banged at the door pleading with him to stop. Stop? He hadn't even started!

Rolling him over on to his back, he slashed aside the unfortunate governor's boxer shorts and sliced into the small limp penis that had tried to shrivel out of the way, hacking it off and throwing it towards the tongue at the back of the cell.

In a final almost ritual ending, Martin sliced the unfortunate man's white flabby stomach wide open. Roger died on a blood soaked stinking cell floor with help standing less than four feet away. Martin sat with his back to the door panting with exertion. The naked man lay dead at his feet, his body cut open and every bit of him exposed. Martin had considered cutting the head off but his enthusiasm had ebbed and he was bored. Besides, there was a limit to what he could do with one small razor blade.

He stood and walked a few paces, sliding on the pools of blood congealing on the floor. He looked around at what he had created and felt relief rush through his body.

Wiping the blood from his face he shouted,

"Boys, come and get me!"

It didn't seem to take very long for the wheels of justice to turn in the case of Martin Heard, double murderer.

He stood in Court Number One at The Old Bailey, looking around at this working museum of law, where the very fabric of the country seemed to emanate from this one, large court room.

If he hadn't been standing in the dock wearing yellow and green overalls stating that he was a prisoner proudly across the back, he may have enjoyed the scene. If it wasn't for the beating that staff had given him after the murder of their colleague, he may have felt a little less sore.

The barristers had pondered how this man could have turned from a petty criminal with minor convictions of theft, assault and drug offences with a few years inside behind him, into someone capable of such depravity resulting in violent attacks and murder to such a horrific degree

The question that nobody bothered to ask Martin was why had he killed these two seemingly innocent people? He would have told them if they had bothered. He would have been very clear about his intentions on that one day in HMP Barnside.

Firstly, he despised pathetic petty criminals; they had stolen his possessions for far too long while living on the streets. They didn't deserve to share the air he breathed; poor pathetic Tony was just in the wrong place at the wrong time.

The second reason was far deeper and a great deal more personal to Martin. Every adult who had materialised into his life under the guise of a kindly care home worker, priest, politician visiting the poor parentless children or even the cute little TV celebrity who popped into your room to boost viewing figures and then popped into your pyjamas when the camera stopped rolling; everyone who showed kindness eventually hurt him.

All these past horrors had resulted in Martin Heard, the petty criminal who had graced the courts on numerous previous occasions, but what turned him into a cold, calculating killer was having the one thing in his life which meant something to him being torn cruelly from him.

What motivated Martin made him a dangerously damaged individual.

The Judge in his summary of the case was almost understanding of Martin. It seemed that society had allowed him to slip through the net. He needed to be punished for the horrific acts but he also needed help. He would never be released from custody in whatever setting it may take. However it was felt that Martin Heard was not capable of presenting any defence. He was suffering such mental illness that confinement and treatment within the secure mental health setting could and would be the only option. He would be committed to life imprisonment without hope of release. The judge did however hope that he could make some form of recovery over the coming years. Very touching! Martin thought his face looked familiar and he wondered if he had ever visited a particular children's home in Bristol during the early 1970's.

After sentence was passed, he was bustled down the wooden stairs by a number of eager prison staff and into a solitary cell.

"That's you fucked, murdering bastard! That Governor you butchered was a mate of mine, hope you rot!"

The door was slammed shut as he was left to contemplate the rest of his life in confinement.

But unknown to all those concerned, on this very day Martin Heard's life became focused. It suddenly developed a real purpose. For in the evidence bundle, which he studied while waiting in the small legal room in the belly of the court, sat a small printed email. It read –

For the attention of Mr Jackson Edwards QC.

<u>PROTECTED DOCUMENT</u>
Attached are the details requested in relation to the child of Martin Heard.
In confidence information.
Born 23rd December 2007
Name Tom Heard
Fostered 23rd December 2007
Foster Address. Mr Terry Davies. 163 Horn Clear Close, Dudley
Case worker, Mr Chris Byfield

<u>Not for the attention of the defendant</u>

CHAPTER ONE.

10 years later

Stephen Byfield sat eating toast in the large country kitchen of his Cotswold cottage. Tanya, his wife of five years breezed in and kissed him on the forehead.

"Have a lovely day sweetheart, I'm taking the children swimming this morning, and then popping out for lunch with a couple of friends. We'll all be home around four, I'll e-mail you later to see how your day is going."

Stephen smiled as he saw the twins jumping up and down with excitement; they loved the swimming pool and sliding down the elephant trunk slides.

"I wish I could come with you, sounds great fun!" He swallowed the last of the cold toast and washed it down with a gulp of tea. "I just need to get the prison working properly; I can't take my eyes off anything at the moment. The instant I think that it's sorted out, something else goes wrong, and it's going to take some time to get right. But I can't wait for some time off with you all!"

He kissed Tanya and then grabbed both children in a big hug.

"Listen to me monsters, I don't want you getting mummy's hair wet!" He then winked at both of them; the children shrieked with laughter before charging off in a quest for more double trouble.

"Have fun sweetheart and I'll see you this evening, hopefully not too late" Stephen told Tanya as he popped his plate and mug in the dishwasher, kissed her good bye before grabbing his bag and dashing out of the door.

Climbing into his new gun metal grey Audi A5 convertible he drove through the winding country lanes on the way to work with the roof down. The sun glinted through the leafy trees and formed a geometrical pattern across the road as he contemplated that the day was too nice for work, but work could not wait. Of all the drives he had taken to work in different prisons, this short five mile trip was the best. All leafy, country roads, no traffic and he could enjoy his brief touch with nature before the cold confinements of a concrete prison.

The formidable walls could be seen from more than half a mile away, an intimidating sight, even for the newly appointed Governor. He swept into the car park and backed the Audi into his reserved space. He could get used to this VIP treatment! The gate area was a buzz of activity.

"Morning Governor, roll of six hundred and eighty nine" he was informed as he approached the gate.

"Morning and thank you" Stephen replied to the information that they were nearing full capacity. He walked through the sliding gate and past the metal detectors and smiled to himself. The first time he reported for duty, the alarms had activated. He had forgotten that he had his phone in his pocket, a real basic error. Staff had not let him forget that one; he had put it down to nerves.

The new biometric key system was in place. Stephen scanned his finger print and took his keys. The new key machines were easy to use, it recognised a finger print, opened the machine door, and the keys that he could take were indicated by a green light. All he had to do was pull the keys from this contraption and go to his work place. Clipping his keys onto his key chain he headed out of the gate area.

A brief walk across a courtyard, designed in 1878 for horse and cart and Stephen was sitting at his large wooden desk. A computer and phone sat on the left hand side, a photo of the family stood proudly on the right. A separate phone sat in the centre. This one was red, a direct line straight to him, with the number only known to a few. When this rang, everything else stopped. It meant business, normally serious business.

This position as governor of Marwood prison was special, Steven had been given the chance to take over a badly managed establishment where recent audit scores showed deep concerns and Her Majesty's inspectorate had reported that it was a dangerous sewer of a prison. Damning words and the last Governor had been moved immediately with the stipulation that this must never happen again. Stephen knew this opportunity could be the making of him but what he couldn't foresee was how close it would come to breaking him! He switched on his computer and began preparing for that morning's leadership team briefing.

CHAPTER TWO

Martin Heard sat rocking on the bed of his high secure mental hospital room in the High Dependency Unit. He ran his fingers through his short hair and traced the scar across his head with a filthy finger.

He had been held in the Unit since he was caught bribing two new staff into bringing mobile phones and drugs into the hospital. He hadn't wanted either item but this had been a game which he enjoyed playing. During this sentence he had mastered the game of manipulating staff and he had become a champion in his field.

This time he had decided that he would make the staff earn every penny of their poorly paid job, starting a dirty protest, the most obnoxious type of protest known to the unit. Excrement covered every inch of the walls, ceiling and door, messages written by stinking fingers spelling out the injustice of the penal system. The smell was horrendous to anyone passing. Martin didn't care, he loved chaos and he loved the control that chaos offered him.

The clank of a hatch sliding open at the bottom of his "Dirty protest" room door signaled the serving of his lunch.

He looked down at the plate. The trusted patients who delivered the food to the doors had performed their latest stunt. One of them had defecated into the stew. The staff had not tried to stop it.

"Eat up old son, plenty more where that came from" they shouted and laughed as they walked past the watching staff.

A young male nurse opened the observation panel and stared through the toughened glass. He was smiling knowing full well what had just happened. Grabbing the plastic plate Martin took handfuls of the food and pushing it into his mouth with filthy fingers, he ate every scrap and licked the plate clean. Throwing it at the door before sitting on his bed he smiled and shouted "Fuck you!"

It was a repulsive show of protest, but one designed to show that he was unbeaten.

"Heard, get to the back wall of your room" a harsh voice bellowed from the corridor outside. He knew what came next. The door was flung open and a sea of uniformed staff stared at him from underneath their blue riot helmets. An old scratched Perspex shield protected them from whatever he could be bothered to throw. White overalls protected all from the decorations.

A large red fire hose appeared over the shield and the power of the water jet blasted him back into the filthy wall. This was spring cleaning in secure hospital style! Stepping inside, the staff hosed all those hard to reach areas before exiting as though they had just conducted the weekend car clean. The brown waste in the drain channel outside of the room told the true story as the water seeped away. Martin lay on the floor smiling, it was time for the anti to be raised!

Four hours later the same young nurse came back to the door. Martin could hear him talking to someone as he approached. "Let's see how much shit this dirty bastard has managed to put back on the walls!"

For the past few weeks it had been a pattern of behaviour. The more the staff cleaned, the more it got messed back up.

The observation panel opened and the nurse exclaimed "Bloody hell, Heard. What's wrong with you? Constipation?" The room was in pristine condition.

"Afternoon, you win! Can I have a shower and fresh clothes?" Martin requested calmly. The silence that followed was deafening. It was almost a sound of disappointment. The footsteps thudding their way back to the nurse's station resounded before muffled chatter became clearer as it approached the room door. The observation panel was opened again. This time an older face looked in. Martin remembered him as being the lead nurse with sadistic tendencies who enjoyed administering injections to calm rebellious patients down. Job satisfaction and a good day usually involved some poor sod having a very bad day, but today it would be this nurse's turn to have a bad day; the timing just had to be right.

Martin had walked the route a hundred times from his high dependency room to the decrepit Victorian shower room. Thirty eight steps and he reached the gate. Seven paces past the row of metal sinks on the left hand side and then into the shower cubicle on the left. It had to be this cubicle.

The joy of the dirty protest was that no one would follow him into the shower. No curious little nurse to see him remove the razor sharp tile he had prepared on previous visits, and the five discarded flat Perspex hand sizes mirrors - the type used for patients to shave - before hiding them in his clean towel.

'So easy, you thick, fat nurse. However will you explain this to your thicker fatter slut of a wife?' he thought as he contemplated his next move.

Looking over the stable door of the shower, Martin could see a disinterested group of staff, elegantly dressed in the fashion of the day, riot clothing. This pathetic protection always made them feel safe from harm but of course he knew better!

Quickly drying himself with the small white towel Heard dressed into clean clothing, picked up the towel and walked the seven steps back to the gate.

"You done old son?" a voice emerged from under the nearest blue helmet.

"Yes, all done. I just need a nurse to check out my finger. I think I broke it during the shower you gave me in my room".

The gate swung open and after twenty seven steps back towards his room he heard the magic words -

"I'll have a quick look". It was the thick fat bastard nurse.

The sound of heavy footsteps eagerly overtook the riot team and outside his room Martin Heard turned, grabbed and pulled. He had his prize! Kicking the cell door shut Martin looked down at the lead nurse. He had fallen backwards onto the bed.

"Stay still and you may live" he advised him before turning his attention to the waiting masses and giving a clear message-

"Come near this door and I will carve off his face!" Dropping the towel onto the floor the murderously sharp shard of tile was revealed, six inches long and as pointed and sharp as a dagger. They did exactly as ordered as the five Perspex mirrors were jammed quickly into the door housing wedging it shut which made it impossible for them to force the door open and rescue their terrified friend.

Martin now turned his attention to the lead nurse.

"What a turnaround in fortunes Mr Bell. For the past few weeks I have been surrounded by my own shit. Now you are up to your neck in it!" Grabbing the towel he cut it in half and roughly tied his hands behind his back with one strip before gagging the man with the other.

A face appeared at the door as a hostage negotiator eagerly and crudely tried to made contact. Martin ignored every word. There were no demands and nothing that he wanted. In this little room he was again king!

"Let me tell you, Mr Bell," Martins voice was calm and flat, "I have dreamt of this moment for weeks." He stopped for a second as the negotiator again feebly tried to sway the balance of power. Beneath the gag, the nurse tried desperately to say something totally unintelligible. Martin stared at him for a second before roughly pulling the gag out of his mouth.

"It's George Bell, call me George." The nurse had read Martin's notes and knew what had happened to the last person trapped in a room with him. His only hope was to try to get Martin to see him as a fellow human being.

Martin pulled the gag back into place before continuing;

"I even had a walkthrough of my plan last month...... *George*," adding his first name with an emphasis. "You must remember, I asked you to check on my foot. You were very keen to help. That was the point at which I decided that you would be the perfect victim – it is all so easy! I am a criminally insane person..... *George.* You put needles into my arse on a daily basis. The reason that I enjoy hurting people is explainable apparently. You believe that I am unwell!" He stopped and smiled at the now sobbing man.

"You, *George,* on the other hand, enjoy hurting people for different reasons. It is your career of choice." Again he stopped and looked at the sweating negotiator trying to talk through the door. "You have made a living from our pain."

He then whispered. "Sorry to spoil the ending to this story, *George,* but you die a horrible death!" Sighing deeply he dropped his eyes to the floor before adding

"I have practiced this as well.... *George.* You will die in front of the prison video camera as they film my surrender. The crowning glory for the silly little bastard chatting at the door will be to see your throat slit open!"

He again turned to the door. "Ok, say what you want, I'm listening."

Two hundred meters away in the command suite where all situations were overseen, the senior management team sat glued to the CCTV feed updated from the scene of the incident.

The facility manager, Mandy Johnston sat listening to the debrief from the outgoing hostage negotiator.

"Ok listen in everyone, we have an update from the scene."

The room fell silent.

"As of five minutes ago, the perpetrator Mr Martin Heard has asked to surrender". She looked down through her notes. "We have a surrender plan in place and this has been agreed with the Gold Commander from Head Quarters." Mandy was glad she had a higher level to back her up should this all go pear shaped. Everyone knew what Martin Heard was capable of, his sadistic notoriety had not dimmed over the years.

She took a sip of water from the glass in front of her on the large wooden boardroom table.

"Do we have sufficient staff to take the surrender?" she enquired?

"Yes Mandy, they're all in the staging post ready to go" one of the team replied.

"Excellent. The plan will remain as it is. We will take Martin Heard out of the room first. Ambulance staff will then enter and deal with George. Heard must be kept confined securely until the escort staff arrives with a secure van and police escort. He will be moved to the High Security Estate within the public sector prison service this evening."

Bill Chapman nodded. "It's all in place. All evidence including CCTV and video will be seized by the police and used during any coming court case. We are ready to go."

A voice came over the radio net.

"He is ready to surrender. Permission to take the surrender?"

"Granted. Codeword Highgrove, I repeat, codeword Highgrove." Mandy sat back in her chair her heart in her throat as she watched the CCTV coverage from outside of Heard's room.

A swarm of people were congregating around the room door. They had all heard the codeword to go. She gasped as the key went into the lock. "Good luck guys", she muttered.

"Ok, Martin" said the Negotiator. "We are ready for you to come out. Just remember that you must do all that we ask. Move back to the far wall. When we open the door I want you to walk backwards into the shield that will be blocking the door. We will search you, take you to another room and then have a doctor speak with you. Do you understand?"

Martin nodded.

"Firstly though, we will need you to remove whatever you have stuck into the door frames. We need to be able to open the door without breaking it down."

Martin moved towards the door and dislodged the mirrors before retreating back to the far wall. The key entered the door lock and turned. Slowly the door was pushed open. George's eyes were bursting with fear; he knew the next lines in this grizzly script. He tried desperately to warn the staff that this was a trap. Words that just wouldn't leave his mouth. Sweat poured from his face as he tried to get up but his legs failed him. Fear had taken over.

Looking out at the sea of faces and the red light of the recording camera, Martin sprang forwards grabbing George Bell by the hair. Yanking his head back he produced the weapon and plunged it deep into the mattress a few inches from the petrified man's neck.

With his face pressed close to George's ear he hissed, "That is how easy it is to die in my world.... *George*" before walking backwards out into the waiting shield. With a last salute he winked at his victim as the poor man emptied his bowels on to the mattress beneath him.

His time of leisure within the High Secure Mental Health facility had come to a crashing finale.

CHAPTER THREE

Terry stood in the centre of the old Victorian prison. He loved this place. The five wings spread out from the central office like the spokes on a bike wheel, with Terry as the cog.

He gazed around his little empire, his job was to manage these wings as well as the segregation unit - as duty governor, today it was all his! To his rear stood A wing, four landings in the old Victorian style shown in countless prison dramas. All the newly received prisoners were housed here. Joined onto A Wing the reception department was shoe horned in, an ugly pimple on a cows arse type of building, a haphazard bunch of rooms, none of which were fit for purpose, but it was all they had. In this building all prisoners were processed on arrival. On the opposite side of A Wing sat a self-contained, fourteen cell unit known as segregation. This was where prisoners who misbehaved or were incapable of mixing with others were housed - nobody wanted to be there, either as a prisoner or staff member. It was a barren place where only the very basic of privileges were offered. Four staff worked in this area full time. The only time out of cell for anyone held there was minimal, a quick daily shower, thirty minutes walking around a small exercise yard completely encased in mesh -more like a cage than an exercise area - and if allowed, a quick phone call to authorized people. These were the families who were security cleared to receive calls. These phone calls were monitored and checked for any coded conversation. The only benefit for a prisoner in segregation was that a Governor visited every day and this gave room for them to complain, an opportunity rarely missed.

Then to Terry's left sat B Wing. This held one hundred and seventy six convicted prisoners ranging from trivial offences to murderers - B Wing did not differentiate between who was who. A gas meter thief could be sharing a cell with Ronnie Biggs, or whoever his counterpart these days was. This wing was still in the old Victorian style and held together with paint and toothpaste –a total dump ready to fall down at the slightest sign of unrest.

Directly in front of Terry sat C Wing, a new building refurbished at a cost of six million pounds only four years ago, holding one hundred and fifty five remand prisoners all waiting to find out what the courts would reward them for their misdemeanors. Again, a hot pot of different cultures and criminality, it was also the wing suffering most violence. Staff would say that life on here for both prisoners and anyone working there was chaotic. Numerous staff had been hospitalised over the past three months, and lots of prisoners badly hurt, an area best avoided if you got the chance to swerve it. Terry was aware that many staff were hesitant to work on C Wing and he needed to work on a plan to sort it out.

To the right sat D Wing. This held vulnerable prisoners, or as commonly known the "nonces". Mostly sex offenders, they were the lowest of the low in prison society, and if given the chance these people would be badly hurt by others. There were one hundred and sixty four of these filthy animals, mostly elderly paedophiles who had been caught with their pants down watching child porn.

And then behind Terry and to his right was E Wing, long term heavy duty prisoners. This held only twenty of the country's finest Category A prisoners, those who needed the most secure conditions to keep them tucked up safe and sound and away from society. E wing was new and high tech. Staff enjoyed working in this area, plenty of kudos working with dangerous people, but high staffing levels evened out the danger.

And finally, set in a discrete unit, on its own little plot of land, was where the most trusted prisoners lived, the category C and D. These guys were low maintenance, and this an area favoured amongst the staff. One hundred and twenty nine places, all short term sentences and due out in a few months. Or that was the prison plan in principle, where the inmates should be housed but, like everywhere the problems came with overcrowding. The prison was often full to bursting, every bed was needed which often resulted in prisoners ended up on wings where they should not. Not ideal, but just a fact of prison life in Marwood, every day was a jigsaw of individual pieces being placed together to find the best fit available. Terry was interested to see how the new young governor would go about improving what seemed to be a hopeless situation, too few staff, looking after too many prisoners in a building which was way past its sell by date. He would do all he could to support him but was glad he didn't have the unenviable responsibility.

Although Terry had met Stephen as part of a full management meeting he had not had the chance to sit down on a one to one.

He wanted to get to know him a little better, find out what made him tick and, more importantly, find out what he expected from the managers. Every governor was different, but if you read them wrongly it would make life very difficult at a later date.

He walked down the administration corridor and saw that Stephen's door was open. As he got closer he saw Stephen sat at his desk and Terry hardly had time to knock before being asked to come in and take a seat.

Stephen pulled up a chair opposite Terry at the small table in the office. At thirty years old, he was the youngest Governor in the prison services history to manage a high security prison, a fact not lost on the local press. A full page article had appeared in the Marwood Argos and this had annoyed him as the photo shown of him included his family. Tanya had become so upset that all later editions of the paper had this photo removed, replaced by the usual shot of him sitting at his desk - not a great start to life dealing with the country's worst!

"Hi Terry, I have been meaning to get together with you and introduce myself properly, forgive me. It has just been manic" Stephen began, smiling warmly at his senior manager.

They seemed to click instantly. Stephen had been impressed with the leadership Terry had shown and by the respect he had earned from all members of the prison which had been evident in Stephen's first few days in charge of the prison. They chatted for twenty minutes or so before they were interrupted by the red phone.

"Sorry Terry, I need to take this call, area office have been hounding me for hours, catch up later in the week" Stephen apologised as he stood up to answer the phone. Leaving the office shutting the door gently behind him, Terry was impressed by this man and thought maybe the place had a fighting chance after all.

Stephen finished the call slightly irritated that it was not important business and he had ended his meeting with Terry to take it. Looking up at his clock, he realised Tanya should be heading home soon, she had really struggled with him taking up this new role and although supportive as always, the local papers had tested her to breaking point.

It had taken Tanya a few days to calm down from the press invasion, especially as this was the second time police protection had been needed. The first time was as a result of London's biggest gangster family wanting Stephen and his little family dead. She didn't enjoy the promise of a painful death, and although she had managed to survive threats to the family before, she was always desperately worried that she and the two children would be harmed. She hated this aspect of Stephen's success. Tanya, a beautiful woman at twenty eight years old had trained as a nurse, but had given up this profession to raise a family. She always dreamt of picking a career up again when the children had grown up, but this was a bit of a way off yet with the twins being only three.

When the paper had popped through the letter box on Thursday, she had opened it to be greeted by a picture of herself and her family smiling out of the pages under the caption "Youngest Governor takes on our toughest criminals." She couldn't help the tears rolling down her face as she contemplated the risk this could pose to them all, but especially the twins. She loved Stephen and was proud of what he had achieved, but she didn't want to spend her life looking over her shoulder when out or worrying about who was at the door when the bell rang. Her face stained with tears, she couldn't hide her fear from her husband.

"Please sweetheart, you promised that we would be safe, you promised my parents that you would protect us all, remember?"

Stephen appeared so practical at times, so matter of fact about the dangers. "Yes of course I'll keep you all safe" he'd promised. He had taken no time in phoning the editor, berating him for his irresponsibility and having the picture removed and replaced with the desk shot. Tanya had remained unhappy, but knew that this was one of the down sides to Stephen's job. Prisoners who didn't like decisions he made often made threats against his family in retaliation.

Security around Stephen and his family was always tight. During his meteoric rise to the top he had upset a few heavy duty criminals, and most notably the notorious Brood family. The head of this 1990's drug dealing family had been safely sat in a severe personality disorder unit in HMP Monkton where Stephen was a young Deputy Governor. Stephen had gained information that Kevin Brood had corrupted a number of staff and was running a very profitable prison drug market. He smashed this little business at a cost to Kevin and the Brood family of over half a million pounds. The Broods had promised that Byfield blood would flow, hence the police protection.

The ring of Stephen's personal phone line snapped him out from his domestic thoughts;

"Hello Stephen!" It was Julia Matthews, the Deputy Director of Custody, his new boss.

"Hi Julia, how can I help you?"

"Stephen, we have a prominent prisoner coming to you at Marwood. He was sectioned ten years ago but the staff at the secure hospital have decided that he is fit to return to the prison population, or rather Martin Heard has decided! It would seem that this man remains a handful and is now our problem. Are you aware of him?"

"Yeah, slightly before my time, but I've heard the stories!"

"Whatever you've heard, double it! This man is a cold hearted killer! He is a prolific self-harmer, serial hostage taker, double murderer whilst in custody but the worrying part is that he appears to be motivated by revenge on abusers. Ten years in custody and we haven't even scratched the surface with him. Oh and by the way, he is not to be underestimated, he is incredibly intelligent! Stephen, I want this man in the Segregation until we know what he is thinking, and one more thing, don't make any mistakes, this man is lethal. The recent report from the mental health team back at the hospital states that he is a psychopath. He enjoys killing, but strangely gets the most pleasure from killing anyone who has crossed him or, and get this, shown him any kindness! He's an odd ball. I have a full report from the secure hospital which I'm sending over to you as we speak…it should be there now."

Stephen let out a laugh, "We sure have many of those! Odd balls are our speciality! No problem, I'll ring you when he arrives. Trust me, no mistakes". Julia rang off just as his computer beeped and the e-mail appeared. Stephen opened the attachment and took a sip from his coffee as he began to read.

The report was dated six months ago. It was compiled by a senior consultant at the hospital. Stephen knew him and although they had not met, he had read a number of books and articles which he had written. His opinions were often controversial but readers of mental health journals seemed to worship him.

Scanning through the initial blurb he quickly focused on the meat of the report. It was painful to read, burning into Stephen's consciousness. Such brutality against a child, such hate and so many failures outlined Heard's life, all of which left them with a murderous time bomb on their hands. He read on.

Martin Heard was born to a drug addicted mother. He was almost feral, often having to empty kitchen bins or beg strange men visiting the house for food or drink. Instead he was given alcohol or cannabis. It is thought that even at the age of four he may have been drug dependent.

The life story of this child was simple. Strangers showed him kindness, then bestowed friendship which quickly turned into horrific sexual abuse. A conservative estimate presented by Health Care Professionals suggested that he had been the subject of abuse for three years. He had sexual diseases and emotionally had shut down. He was five years old when taken in to care.

As he matured in to adulthood, this abuse had triggered a horrific reaction. Any individual either male or female showing kindness was an enemy. The only way to prevent further harm and pain to himself was to eliminate that person, quickly and ferociously. Scare anyone else from hurting him; show the world that he was no longer a child that could be hurt.

These feeling grew and festered. Numerous placements and spells inside establishments fed the inner beast. He couldn't wait to escape and he soon did. The streets became his home. Staying on the streets in a drugged state seemed the solution. Every solution however had another problem gathering pace behind it. The problems overcame him giving way to severe personality disorders. But apparently not so ill that he needed further help from the Secure Mental Health Estate. They had reached the end of the road. It would appear that Mr Heard was bad, not mad.

Stephen sighed. How often would he see that statement? Normally it just meant that there was nothing else they could do. The only thing not recorded was what the report really meant which was of course; "Here you are, your turn, let's share the High Risk!"

He summoned the team, head buzzing with thoughts about what he would say to them, wanting to ensure they were under no illusions as to the danger this man posed to the smooth running of the establishment.

Ten minutes later the entire Marwood senior management team sat looking at Stephen, all trying to calculate what this news meant to them. Terry Davies knew exactly what it meant, Duty Governor this weekend and in charge of the Segregation, Terry was going to have double helpings of Martin.

"For Christ's sake, two years left in this job and I get Hannibal Lector to share it with!"

Terry was a fifty three year old former Royal Marine who had served in the prison service for as long as anyone could remember and had seen and done everything. He stood at five foot ten and had short cropped hair which to his disbelief was greying at an alarming rate! He prided himself on keeping fit, but was finding this a struggle as his fifties marched on. Still proud of a good chest, muscled arms and a thirty two inch waist although he could feel size thirty four just around the corner. He was proud of his Yorkshire roots, and against all odds had kept the accent, even though he had lived in the west midlands for twenty plus years. Marrying late in life, he had found an absolute soul mate, someone who could understand him and his ways. In short he was content at last and was happily anticipating the next phase of his life.

Everyone burst out laughing; Stephen acknowledged the humour and continued with business.

"Well done Terry! This guy will be here sometime this evening. I want every orifice scanned, I need him stripped clean, into sterile clothing and straight down to the block. No property at all, he can have a shower, some food and nothing else. From what I gather he has not made a phone call or had a visit for ten years, so no dramas. Brief all of the staff, he will be an eight person unlock with a dog handler present. This man has history Terry, he massacred a Duty Governor just for the fun of it! No risks, present no opportunity. Any nonsense on his part let the dog introduce himself. Any questions?"

"No boss, I'll go brief the team, and get extra staff arranged for the multi staff approach. If I think of anything I'll phone you." Terry got up to leave.

"I am at home all night, ring me when he arrives, and again when he is located in the segregation unit. Take care Terry."

"Yeah ok boss, let's not get too sentimental, he's just a prisoner, no dramas. I've been playing with these people for thirty years!"

Terry walked away but his heart beat a little quicker as he thought about what lay ahead. The remainder of the day flew past into the evening and he was sitting writing staff appraisals when his radio came to life, "Victor One phone 3208". He knew that this was reception.

"Boss, just had a call from the escort, they're here in ten minutes".

"No probs, I am on my way!"

Terry already knew this, the escort staff had kept him in the loop over the past two hour trip. It would appear that our man Martin had slept the entire journey. Hopefully the hospital had given him some type of medication to sedate him. All the indications showed that he was a total nightmare, in fact Terry had spent the past hour reading the case notes, an hour and he had only reached the first six months. He had never come across a man presenting such violence, such self-harm and such cunning. Four staff had been sacked during Martin's time in the secure hospital, all of them seemingly falling under his spell, all of them smuggling items in for him. Worryingly one tried to help him escape. The plan came to nothing, but somehow Martin Heard had ended up with a copy of a key.

I can't wait to meet our man, Terry thought, bring it on!

He walked through to reception, it was now ten thirty and everyone else was locked up. He breezed into the holding area.

" Evening everyone, where is my boy then?"

The reception officer smiled,

"Oh yeah, he's here all right, him and his property".

Terry looked, there was one book sat on the desk.

"Is that it?"

"Yep, one book, the bible!"

The staff pointed towards the holding room.

"All that preparation and he's been easy, not an ounce of fight! Didn't say one word! Typical Governors, making everyone worried for nothing!" the reception officer joked as he opened the cell door flap

A tall wiry man stared through the reception cell observation window. Terry was looking into the eyes of a man who was about to change his life, and more worryingly Terry sensed it.

It had been a long day. Terry was feeling hot and sweaty in his suit, the shirt collar rubbed on his neck and he just wanted to get this job done and get home.

"Okay everyone, no slip ups. Search him, strip him and let's get him banged up".

"Okay boss, let's shower him here and we could also feed him. That will give us less disturbances in the segregation when we get him down there."

"Whatever works, let's just get it done" Terry agreed.

The process was so smooth that before Terry knew it, he was part of a gang of staff moving the prisoner to the segregation block. The central character was in the middle, maybe six feet one, white, around mid thirties but showing the prison grey skin colour. He had cropped black hair with a scar running from the top of his head to the base of his neck which Terry thought looked surgical. His heavily scarred wrists were cuffed and his long muscular arms were showing signs of years of cutting. A faded tattoo interwoven with scars showed a death's head, both the skull and bones made more sinister by the vein like markings of the scar tissue. This man was watched like a hawk during the one minute walk to the segregation. The hush of the wing was shattered by shouting and whistling and the rhythmical thump of cell doors as they moved through. Everyone knew that something special was happening, the prison jungle drums had informed all that this notorious killer was joining them.

The contingent arrived at the assigned cell where once inside Terry faced the heavily guarded man for the first time.

"Okay Mr Heard, I am the Duty Governor and you are in the segregation unit at HMP Marwood. Do you have any questions?"

"Just the one question Governor. Who will live the longer, you or I?"

A shiver passed through the bones in every member of staff who witnessed that one sentence, delivered by a man who would take a life in a heartbeat.

"Probably you mate" Terry replied without missing a beat. "It's my anniversary tonight and I'm spending it with you. I might not even manage to make it home and to bed!" Terry had heard it all before and wasn't particularly fazed.

The staff laughed but Martin continued to stare straight into Terry's eyes, both men unblinking. A chill descended and the laughter stopped. Never were the staff so happy to see the door to that bleak unfurnished cell close.

Terry phoned Stephen. It was late, around midnight.

"Ok boss, all is good. He's in the cell tucked up for the night with no dramas so see you in the morning".

No dramas yet thought Terry, but he had a feeling they were in for a bucket load of those!

CHAPTER FOUR

The morning operational meeting had the normal buzz; Stephen sat at the head of the table and called the meeting to order.

"OK Terry, you were Duty Governor yesterday, can we have your feedback?"

"Yes boss, it was a good day. We unlocked 687, locked up 700, twenty two at risk of self-harm, seventeen on anti-bullying measures. Roll check lunch and tea were on time, and all staff got away from duty five minutes early. Receptions were late and we didn't get out until midnight. We had one late one in, Mr Martin Heard. He located straight into segregation, he was quiet all night but I get the feeling he could be a challenge."

Terry's natural instinct and years of experience had set his warning sensors flashing during his first encounter with the infamous Mr Heard the previous evening.

"Yes I'm afraid that you might be right Terry. By all accounts we need to be on our guard with this one. I want all operational managers to stay behind after the meeting."

With that, Stephen moved the agenda along to cover any other expected issues for that day's running of the prison.

The rest of the meeting was uneventful, just the normal day to day business and at the end the staff melted away just leaving Stephen and the six operational managers.

"Okay," started Stephen, "This is going to be a difficult period for us. I have given this some thought and I would like the following things to happen.

Firstly, every interaction with Mr Heard will be filmed via the body worn camera. This guy is known to be manipulative and we don't want him accusing any of you of making promises he can hold against us.

Secondly, Mr Heard will be a multi officer unlock. There will always be a minimum of six officers present on every occasion he is unlocked. You have all read the reports of what he does to anyone he gets alone, so let's not give him that opportunity again. Remember, he is a Category A prisoner, the highest status. Let's not forget the basics of dealing with these types of people, no move away from protocol.

Finally, you do not give him anything without agreement from me first. No deals for behaving well and certainly nothing agreed or given to him in order to pacify him. This man is super dangerous, he can kill, he can corrupt and he will have your job if you allow him the chance. Any questions?"

"How long is he with us Stephen?" Martha, the Head of Offender management asked.

"He is here until ministers decide otherwise, it's that sensitive, Martha. Let's all do our jobs and stay safe, no risks. Who's today's Duty Governor?"

"I'm afraid that's me" said Martha, "God help me!"

She took the radio and changed the identity of Duty Governor, "Hello M2PX, this is Martha Boswell taking up call sign Victor One, test call over."

"Signal good Victor One and identity noted. M2PX standing by."

CHAPTER FIVE

Martin Heard sat in the far right hand corner of the small white cell, no furniture, blank walls and a small high window that didn't open. There was a typical thick blue metal cell door, an emergency cell bell located to the left hand wall and a dirty little light switch that turned on a strip light fitted high on the ceiling. This cell was different to the standard cell. Outside of this cell door was a small entry way and then another cell door, double skimmed. They were taking no chances of him getting out through there! The floor was a grubby nondescript anti-rip lino. As a nice decorative touch to the back wall, there was a splattered palm print, most probably blood although other bodily secretions were a possibility. He sat there quietly summing up his surroundings. These people were serious with multiple staff every time the door was opened and him being stuck in the segregation unit with just his bible. He contemplated his options, should he give them a special play time, or should this be a different game he thought? *Fuck it, let's play first and see what they've got!*

The thump of Martin's head against the door certainly got the attention of staff, that and the blood oozing from the cuts.

"Pack it in you idiot, stop it or we will stop it for you!" A couple of officers sat in the segregation office, door open so they could see and hear everything going on which wasn't a lot with Martin being the only occupant of the unit.

Music to Martin's ears, *let's get this on*, he thought.

A few more smacks of his head against the door was enough. A radio call went out for extra support to allow the multi officer unlock and a few minutes later the door flew open. There they were puffed up, shield and helmets in place and ready for battle. *Best not disappoint* thought Martin.

He caught the top of the shield and smashed it into the throat of the first officer. The others pushed forward, followed by the inevitable struggle. Martin had performed this dance many times and he knew the steps all too well. The next two officers were pushed back, and then the ultimate prize, he managed to grab a riot helmet and pulled the officers head towards him. The smell of a lunch time drink violated Martins senses. He could feel the officer's panic and saw the wide, wild eyes.

"Tut tut officer, lunch time drinks make you sloppy!" He fixed his eyes on those of the terrified officer and pulling the edge of his helmet Heard wrenched it off his head. With his teeth pressed tight against the officer's right ear he whispered so that only he could hear "Next time, buddy, it won't just be your helmet I remove but your head!" The rest of the unlock team looked on, their fear palpable.

"Now boys, if you want your steroid popping buddy, leave my room, and take this with you."

Martin shoved the officer hard into his colleagues and they backed frantically out of the cell as the door shut loudly behind them. Martin knew they would be back in a minute, but they all knew it was one-nil to Martin.

The door flew open a second time but this time, Martin dropped to his knees with his hands on his head.

"Now, now officers, I am surrendering. I am offering no resistance so you know that you can't touch me, and as I am in special accommodation already, what the fuck do you intend to do? I suggest you go away and leave me in peace."

Yet again Martin had won. He knew the system inside out and knew the restrictions the staff worked under. He was already being held in conditions of the utmost deprivation so there was little else they could threaten him with. The staff made a clumsy attempt at searching him almost as proof that they did in fact have the upper hand, but Martin was just bemused. Hilarious to watch these oafs swallowing their own ego he thought.

The next few days were typical. Food spat in, sleep disturbed all night, no exercise, no showers, a double dose of sweet FA. Same old script, Martin knew the routine and knew what came next. These dumb bastards would try to suck up to him, try to tame him, and this time Martin would allow it.

Five days past, slow boring days, sun rise, sun set, nothing else - a living hell.

Suddenly; "Morning Martin, want some exercise?"

"Yeah, why not, can I wear some clothes?" The rip proof boiler suit he'd lived in for the last week was past its best and was beginning to hum its own tune.

A few seconds silence and then the magical words "Sure, I'll sort some out" were uttered by the duty officer. The cracks had started. He sat on the edge of his bed smiling and humming softly before the cell door was opened and he only counted five staff.

Martin stood on the covered yard, only ten foot square and caged in, but it was a start. He still had a number of officers watching, but he figured that they had lost a bit of their edge - he was winning. Another few days and the Governor would be down here to see him, he knew how it worked. Stage two would then kick in.

Friday crept up on Martin, he knew that this would be the day that the mighty Governor would appear, surrounded by his little army. This would be the start of the game plan and who knew how long they would play? Time didn't matter, only the final result was important, and he was after a resounding victory.

The first door opened loudly. It sounded like a royal visit with a number of shuffling feet, and the murmur of voices as the observation panel was uncovered.

"Mr Heard, the Governor is here. Do you have any questions you would like to ask him?"

"Yes, I do as it happens. Has the Governor enough decency to open my door to speak with me? I am not an animal!"

The door opened, a sea of faces looked in, and there he was, an adult Harry Potter lookalike, chubby face, short brown hair and little round spectacles. At around five foot ten, he looked a little overweight but was dressed perfectly. He sensed that this Governor had class and was well educated.

"Good morning, Governor. Martin Heard, pleased to meet you." he held out his hand.

"Put that away son" growled an officer with no neck. The hand was retracted.

"Good morning, Mr Heard. My name is Stephen Byfield, Governor of this prison."

Eyes locked as each man summed the other up, both convinced they had the upper hand but neither yet aware of how just deeply their lives would intertwine over the coming months.

With no further words exchanged, Stephen turned and left the cell.

CHAPTER SIX

It was after seven when the headlights of Stephen's Audi swept into the driveway of their cottage. The lights were on upstairs and Stephen visualised Tanya bathing the twins before bedtime. Briefcase thrown onto the floor of the hallway Stephen leapt upstairs, bounding two at a time.

"Where are my little tinkers?" Stephen yelled, "Where are those cheeky monkeys?" He could hear the giggles that only three year old twins could make and within seconds he was in the bathroom with foam on his nose.

How was your day darling? You look tired" Tanya asked as she wiped the foam off his nose with a towel.

Stephen gave Tanya a cuddle and kissed her on the lips, "Very busy, and we have a very naughty boy arrived. I will tell you all about it after supper."

Ellie and Harry both giggled, "Daddy's got a naughty boy, Daddy, have you sent him to bed?" Ellie asked as Stephen lifted her out of the bath.

"Yes sweetheart, he's in bed with a smacked bottom!" The twins laughed and danced around the bathroom.

An hour later, with the children asleep in bed, Stephen and Tanya ate supper together. Afterwards Tanya snuggled into Stephen on the leather sofa. "Is everything ok, darling?" She loved hearing about his day and it was nice to have some grown up conversation after a day of two three year olds and their endless chatter.

"Yes, very exciting. We have been sent a real head case who is going to cause me some sleepless nights. I'm not sure why they've sent him back to our care. I'm amazed they no longer consider him a mental health case."

Since the government had brought in their inspired idea of 'Care in the community' for patients with mental health conditions, Stephen and other governors around the country were both exasperated and saddened by how many of these people now ended up in prison as their illnesses went unmonitored and the inevitable crimes were committed.

"If they didn't think you were up for this, you wouldn't have been given this failing prison." Tanya knew that he was proud of what he had achieved but also had doubts sometimes regarding the responsibility he now held.

"I know, sweetheart. If I can turn this one around, there are endless opportunities for us."

"Just no more police protection" she pleaded. "Your antics busting the drug ring at the last place ensured we had the police on our door step for three months. This latest press release where our photo was shown added another two weeks to our guests' stay! You know I just don't want the kids frightened. I do trust you Stephen, and I know that you won't do anything that will get us harmed." "Darling, I would die protecting the family" he reassured her as they cuddled up and watched TV until they both felt sleepy. As they lay in bed, they chatted long into the night, discussing work, future plans and the children. They also spoke excitedly about the family holiday which was only a few months away. Two weeks on a Greek island sounded like heaven and was still a surprise for the twins. Stephen and Tanya were the closest that they had ever been and so secure in their life together that the prospect of another child was discussed before making love and drifting into a contented sleep.

They weren't the only people thinking of Stephen Byfield's future plans. Martin laid awake thinking and plotting.Rarely did he allow himself to wallow in the past, but for some reason tonight was just one of those nights. The harsh blur of children's homes cut into his thoughts, memories of a teacher telling him that he had no family. Martin had thought that all children lived like him and it wasn't until he was much older that he found out how wrong he was.The abuse on Martin continued when he was moved in to a children's home before he was five or six years old, he couldn't remember exactly how old he was. He could just recall how it made him feel special, loved, wanted. Once in care, he had been in the same home for as long as he could remember, for some reason it was never him who was picked by those wanting to adopt. It began in the time old fashion with one of the resident carers showing a particular interest in him, before starting to single him out for treats. An extra helping of his favourite food at meal times, choosing him to come and help in the small vegetable garden they had in the grounds of the home. This lead to the carer telling Martin he could come to his room for a story before bed time as he was such a good boy, and by the time the inappropriate strokes and touches led to more intimate acts, Martin thought this was what all men did and it was something they all had to put up with. It seemed that it didn't matter whether he was at home with his mother or in a place of supposed care, all men seeming to be the same. Eventually a video of his abuse was found by a cleaner and handed to the police but the abuse didn't end there. He was moved on to a further home where it just became more secretive and more violent. The more Martin fought, the harder the rape became, and the more evil the perpetrators seemed. Even self-harm and constant running away could not stop the pain. He learned that those in authority were the ones who inflicted most pain.

Eventually, having run away a final time, he found a friendship of sorts. Travelling fairground owners did not ask many questions, and a fifteen year old boy fitted in very nicely, able to help with the majority of tasks involved with constructing and dismantling rides every few days. The sexual abuse stopped but the fighting increased. Martin learnt the art of violence, frightening violence. So horrific were Martin's acts against local youths that even the fairground workers were glad to get rid of him.

At seventeen he wandered the country, pack on back, living rough. Theft, violence and a number of spells in young offender institutions followed and improved his skills. It also encouraged an unhealthy obsession for heroin, something that would haunt him for years.

In his early twenty's he had met a girl, both rough sleepers, both hooked on heroin. They stuck together through thick and thin until she became pregnant, not planned but very welcome. Both cleaned up from drugs and two days before Christmas a baby boy was born.

Martin was a dad, a proud dad. A dad with no home, no job, no prospects, a long criminal history and a past drug abuse problem. The girl was no better and with no home to take the baby to, so entered Mr Chris Byfield, Social Services, who in one fell swoop took their child from them and into care. The parents, not even having said goodbye, were back out on the streets, melting back into a heroin induced existence. His beautiful girlfriend took her life, dying on the floor of a multi-story car park with a needle hanging out of her arm, a shot of heroin so large it would have killed five people. Martin holding her lifeless head vowed vengeance, and now, ten years later, he was well on his way there.

CHAPTER SEVEN

Two weeks past and Martin lay on his bed, looking around at his few possessions, a blue plastic mug that was heavily stained by months of tea drinking, a white plastic knife, fork and spoon and a couple of books he had borrowed from the library, nothing too stimulating, the new Jack Reacher book and an older dog-eared volume in which the birds of the British Isles were documented. These all sat on top of a plastic moulded cupboard, unbreakable – everything in this cell was unbreakable in theory. If you put your mind to it, you could cause some damage to the water pipe but this only ensured the screws turned the water off and then you couldn't flush the toilet. There weren't many tricks Martin hadn't tried during his time spent either in Her Majesty's prisons or in the secure mental health units; his dirty protests, covering himself and his cell in his own excrement ended when he learned that staff were paid an extra allowance when he committed this act – why would he want any prison staff to earn a single penny from his efforts? He'd even tried food refusals – this lasted two days – again, a pointless exercise. Nobody really gave a hoot and he was the only one who suffered.

Self harm, however, was a different story. When that razor blade worked its magic, everyone sat up and took note. Nobody loved a dead body – especially when they were on duty! He thought back to a cold morning in October 1996, he found himself on a constant watch after playing a game with staff. He was considered such a risk of killing himself, that he was put in a gated cell, no cell door, just a barred gate with an officer sat outside watching, twenty four hours a day. He was given nothing, no clothes, no bedding – the only thing he had was a concrete bed with a rip proof mattress and a rip proof blanket to keep him warm. The area was sterile, well, almost – the staff had forgotten about his little trick with the blade, the blade hidden deep inside his mouth. For an entire day, Martin cut himself on the hour, every hour causing a sea of blood. The staff couldn't stop him. When they opened the gate, the blade went back in to his mouth and was hidden.

In desperation, the governor of that prison placed him in a body belt, a brown leather strap that went around the stomach with handcuffs each side. His hands were strapped to his sides, a rather unpleasant position to be in. This would be the only time that Martin had offered sight of the razor blade to anyone. He was going to use it, but knew he would lose it. That day, he stood in his cell, arms strapped to his side, chatting to the young visiting duty governor who felt that with Martin constrained as he was, he could risk talking to him inside his cell. Mid conversation Heard sat down on the bed, spat out the blade in to a handcuffed hand, twisted his body and in one quick movement, slit the young governor's stomach wide open. A truly remarkable feat, but the young duty governor wasn't so impressed. The reaction to the mass of blood sounded like poetry to Martin. The staff rushed in and he lost the blade but so what? He could get plenty more. It took him around half a day, the prisoner cleaning the floor in the healthcare unit brushed one under the barred gated cell and before the staff could react, he had managed to get it into his mouth and hidden. The cleaner was sacked, but so what - he had his prize! Self harm was a powerful friend but a tool Martin was going to keep for a later date. He reminisced about another fun game he enjoyed playing – hostage taking! While in another faceless segregation unit, many years ago in London, Martin had become friendly with a civilian library assistant. He was around mid-forties, very camp, and shared, or thought he shared, the same interest in books as Martin did. One day he moved a little too close for comfort and Martin grabbed him. He was bundled into Heard's cell and subdued in seconds before staff had time to react. Staff did try to negotiate with a prisoner in these situations, but in this case they went in to a complete panic which to Martin was great fun. He had, however, one golden rule – never to keep the hostage for longer than four hours. It became a bore after this time. In this case though, Martin made an exception. The sobbing librarian was securely tied up with a ripped sheet, his testicles were resting nicely on Martin's tabletop. Martin's blade rested on top of these, ready for carving – he had never seen anyone sweat as much as this man did. The normal boring negotiations started, what did Martin want, why was he doing it and other irritating distractions. That's when Martin thought *fuck it* and sliced the left testicle off. Although the pain must have been excruciating, the librarian didn't utter a word. "I want a fucking helicopter and a blow up doll, and if I don't get them, I cut again." Of course, he got neither, so he cut off the other testicle. This time, the librarian did scream. "I want a pizza and a back gammon set or I'll cut him again." What Martin did get was his cell door blown off its hinges and a squad of specially trained officers beating the shit out of him. "That was impressive, didn't save his testicles but very, very professional…well done boys, you're a real asset to the trade." Those words and barbaric actions got him transferred to yet another high security prison and many more months spent in segregation.

He rarely got the chance to take another hostage apart from the poor little bastard governor he killed in the cell ten years ago and the pathetic nurse which had resulted in his transfer back in to the prison service. The real prize, however, and something most coveted by Martin, was a bent screw, a member of staff who would do things for money. Smuggle drugs, phones – anything, he just had to pay the bent officer and it was happy hour! Martin had corrupted dozens, in fact, he had lost count. Some, he allowed to carry on trading, some who became tiresome, he shut down and when he shut them down, they normally ended up serving time themselves in prison.

Martin had learned the value of collecting evidence on every single one of them. Once he had hooked his fish, there was no escape – the hook just dug in, deeper and deeper. The sad thing was, people lined up to be hooked, he didn't even have the money to pay, they did it because he made them…Martin dominated people's minds, destroying them and they kept coming back for more. He loved this game; he loved the power he could exert. This made him strong, dangerous and irresistible to some staff. He was Her Ma'esty's weapon of mass destruction and he loved it!

CHAPTER EIGHT

Colin Method was the prison chaplain; he had worked within the prison for eight years. A happy go lucky plump, short, bald man, all staff thought he had a heart of gold. He did however have one very large skeleton in his cupboard, and it was starting to bang loudly on the door, very loudly.

He was a single man, no children and lived in a prison owned house. Colin devoted all his time to the church, either within the prison, or helping with the homeless within the Bristol area. Work much appreciated by all connected with him or the charity he served.

Occasionally Colin even managed to find accommodation for these desperate people. He was a well-recognised man and much loved. The homeless would ask if Colin was on duty, they would look for him as he walked the streets, just to chat, share good news, or just soak up the kind words offered. A good man, a saint!

Colin was a saint with a very tarnished halo. A saint who had demons riding on both shoulders, a saint with a very grubby secret.

Throughout the 1990's Colin had offered his services to St Mary's, a home designed to look after and protect children who found themselves in care. Children who needed protection and those same children looked towards the young chaplain to offer comfort. He offered comfort alright, he also offered entertainment to a number of high profile people, TV stars, judges and politicians to name a few. If you had a taste for abusing children, Colin was your fixer, ruthless, soulless and brutal. His holiness Colin Method could provide you with anything, any depravity, any age or sex, and for an additional fee he would film it. A saintly man he was not!

Rumours had recently spread, ever since the high profile court cases of 2013 where this home was placed firmly in the spotlight. Numerous perpetrators were now behind bars but not Colin, he was fireproof. The DVDs of some of the country's finest politicians were sitting safely in his locked safe. They knew that they were there, and Colin slept well knowing that they were there. What a glorious insurance policy, a real life, 'get out of jail free' card!

But although Colin felt safe, he couldn't stop feeling dirty; dreams of horror had taken over each night of sleep. That dreadful thing called a conscience had come home to roost, and boy was it roosting in Colin's head. He made work his life, his only reason to survive. If he helped every needy person, surely God could forgive? He just needed to keep helping, get more ticks on the list than crosses. Maybe, just maybe he could be forgiven, if not, what was the point? He just needed to keep trying to right the wrongs.

He considered the prisoners at HMP Marwood to be his parishioners and he was proud to visit all areas of his parish including those in segregation. He had heard of the notorious new prisoner they had down there and was keen for Martin Heard to become part of his congregation.

"Morning, Mr Heard, I'm Colin, the chaplain here at Marwood. How are you? I see that you have a bible, how refreshing!" Colin peered through the observation hatch on Martin's door, his shiny pump face beaming benevolently in on Martin.

"Good morning chaplain, yes I have my bible and my faith. I don't have much else I am afraid, travelling light!"

Martin patted the book he had placed strategically at his side on his bunk in full view of the door. He had heard the chaplain was due round that day and had plans for him. "May I call you Martin?" Colin continued, quite sure that he could help this misguided man see the error of his ways and accept God in to his heart. "Don't you think it's time that you came out of special accommodation, it has been a couple of weeks hasn't it?"

"Yes, I am ready; I have seen the error of my ways" Martin replied piously. "Can you help me, Colin?"

"Can you stop attacking staff, my son? You must be ready to repent of your sins, and accept that we are all here to help you. We are not the enemy, that is only inside you, and you must let go of your anger." Colin prided himself on his ability to be able to connect with some of the most violent prisoners and felt he had the ability to tame where others failed.

"I have chaplain, yet still I have an army each time my door is open. I have so many Christian things to discuss, but not in front of these gentlemen." Martin knew how to play the game.

"I will see what I can do" Colin promised. Martin stood by his open door hatch and watched the chaplain waddle off down the landing on his way back to the Governor's office.

Stephen was uncomfortable discussing this with Colin, he knew that the prisoner should not still be in special accommodation but didn't want to be told so by the chaplain. He eventually agreed to review the situation and Colin disappeared happy that he was on his way to saving another soul.

Later that morning the next piece in the jigsaw fell into place, Martin was moved into a normal segregation cell. This came complete with cardboard furniture and a metal bed screwed to the floor with a thin black foam mattress on top, absolute bliss. Martin looked forward to future visits from his new best friend.

CHAPTER NINE

Days turned into weeks that melted into months. Complacency had set in, staff on first name terms, multi staff unlock well gone, exercise periods and showers every day, and better still, as Martin was the only prisoner in segregation, he was allowed to clean out his own cell unsupervised for fifteen minutes while the staff chatted in the office. Obviously everyone had Martin all wrong. Sat in his cell with a kettle and TV, Martin smiled to himself. It was all so simple, almost time for his next phase as these idiots knew nothing. Even a basic check would tell them that this was how he operated, simple stupid lazy people, who thought that he was tame, a stupid error.

Colin Method trundled to the segregation unit for his daily visit with Martin, the past three had taken place privately in a spare office, and Colin felt at ease.

"Well Martin, how is your bible study coming along?" Colin asked as they settled themselves down on the two chairs in the office.

"Very well thank you Colin, I know so much about how the Lord works."

"Do you want to share this knowledge with me? I am intrigued!"

"Of course! Can I speak freely Colin?" Martin requested, leaning forward towards Colin in apparent earnestness.

Colin at once agreed, he really felt he was on the brink of a conversion!

"Well Colin, I do know something, I know who you are and what you are, I know that in St Mary's children's home you abused little boys! I know it all, so if you know what is good for you, and don't want to be sharing a cell next to me, you will do as you are told!"

Colin took a deep breath. "I don't understand, what on earth are you saying?" He blustered. "I think we are finished here!" and he jumped to his feet and started towards the door.

"Oh yes, Colin, I think you are finished!" Martin continued. "Think about what I've said. Come back tomorrow and I want some writing paper and a pen, a nice pen, understand?"

Colin said nothing, just left the office and scuttled quickly away, a man with a million thoughts buzzing around his saintly brain. He wondered how on earth Martin had discovered his dirty little secret.

Martin hardly slept that night, it was a high end bluff against the chaplain, and he wasn't sure would it work. Martin had no proof other than some stories he had heard from officers chatting away in their office on the wing. They called him a paedophile, and mentioned his time in St Mary's. It seemed as though his secret wasn't quite such a secret after all, although no one seemed to have the proof needed to make it public. It was more of a rumour which reared its ugly head every now and then. Martin didn't even know where St Mary's was.

The next morning his cell door opened. It was Colin, complete with paper and a lovely writing pen. He didn't talk, just shut the door and walked away. Martin didn't particularly want the paper or pen, although the pen would make a useful weapon, but he had hooked his fish!

Martin was beginning to find the segregation routine mind numbing, the IQ of the staff was low, and they had no imagination. Everything ran like clockwork, the same thing every day. He couldn't even play with their heads as they had no brains to play with, just muscles and they didn't seem to hold back in flexing those things when riled!

Martin was woken up at seven thirty each morning by the day staff. He was expected to get out of bed and tidy up his cell. He decided that if he were to continue with his plan for vengeance, he would need to comply with what was asked, but only for the moment.

The rest of the day followed the same pattern. The Duty Governor would appear at ten o'clock and conduct adjudications, the process by which the prison dealt with prisoners who broke the rules. These always took place in the segregation unit office. Just lately these proceedings had taken up the entire morning, so boring, but occasionally entertaining if someone didn't like the governor's decision. Then Martin would be audience to the shouted threats, the usual questioning of the governor's parentage, the pleas of innocence, that someone had planted the drugs in the prisoners cell...he heard it all as he sat quietly in his solitary cell. The adjudications were followed by the duty governor visit, every prisoner in the segregation unit was seen and as Martin was the only resident at that time, the Duty Governor was all his. He was always polite, always waiting for the next piece to fall into place. He'd learned over his years in the system that patience paid off. Some Governors could be manipulated, others were hard headed. All, however, had been worked out by Martin. He knew how every Governor ticked, knew when to push and when to allow the system to win, every person fitted into the plan. But the period of good behaviour was wearing thin for Martin and he was now bored. His opportunity to resolve this however, came sooner than he thought!

A shout and a crash in the office during the daily round of adjudications sounded positive. The staff had jumped on some prisoner who seemed busy telling the Governor where to stick his justice, and hey presto Martin had a neighbour. Play time!

Martin waited for him to calm down, waited until the moment was right, then, with his mouth close to his observation panel he began whispering to the unsuspecting victim. The whispering continued through the day and long into the night. The segregation staff could see that this poor man was looking confused, maybe upset. They couldn't put their finger on why, maybe it was the shock of segregation, but still the whispering went on.

Then it stopped, completely stopped. Silence enveloped the segregation unit, then a giggle followed by a long almost uncontrolled laugh. A cell bell was sounded, the cell bell of Martin Heard.

"Excuse me officer, I know that it is two thirty in the morning, however I am worried about the poor boy in the next cell and I'm sensing there is something not right with him. Can you look in on him?"

Confusion, chaotic movement, cell door opening and a hive of activity. Martin had heard it all before, nurses, officers, and the police and coroners. All the guests of a man who had strung himself from an upturned bed, a bed worked loose from its fixings and stood on end, a bed serving as a gallows.

Martin listened, peeping out of the crack of his door. What a clever powerful brain he had, a few words, some direction and a little bit of persuasion, all too easy. This cured the boredom, it satisfied Martin's love of death, and he didn't even have to raise a finger.

The next morning, the prison had a subdued atmosphere which often followed a suicide. Staff suspected, officers muttered in the office with the door closed, one foolish man even pointed the finger at Martin. But he just lay on his bed, his reply when questioned rehearsed.

"Nothing to do with me, you have had me locked in this cell twenty three hours a day! I am not David Blaine, I can't kill somebody that I can't reach! I know I am bad, maybe a bit mad, but I am not a magician. Now, when is lunch ready, all this excitement has made me hungry!"

Later on that day Martin Heard's cell bell sounded again.

"What do you want Heard?" The actions of the night before had left everyone on edge.

"The chaplain please, the suicide has messed my head up. Can you ask the chaplain to come and see me?"

The request was met with a grunt, could have been a yes, maybe a no - he would just have to wait and see.

Around thirty minutes later the cell door was unlocked and there stood a reluctant Colin, the child molesting chaplain. He had avoided Martin since their last encounter. Martin made small talk, he quickly asked the chaplain if they could speak in the privacy of the spare office and Colin reluctantly agreed.

Sat in the office Martin felt powerful.

"Colin, I have written a short letter to my poor old aunty, will you post it for me? No need for the staff to see."

Colin nodded silently and placed it into his pocket. He knew he had no choice.

"Good man Colin, one more thing for today. I want to move back onto the main wing. I want to play with the general population, please arrange it."

"Martin, that's not possible, I can't make that sort of decision!" Colin felt a fine film of sweat form on his forehead as he contemplated where all this might end.

"Arrange it" Martin insisted, watching Colin squirm. He found it amusing how easily he could control this man...what a pathetic individual!

Colin sat in the governor's office that afternoon. He tried so hard, he painted Martin Heard in such a good light, detailing how he had found God and had repented of his past wrong doings. Surely everyone should be given another chance he heard himself asking Stephen. Stephen Byfield was having none of it.

"Colin", he said once Colin had ground to a halt with his impassioned plea,

"You're too close to this, back off. Your decision making is flawed, and worse still I believe that you are been conditioned by this man. Back off before you get yourself in trouble."

Colin nodded, he was getting good at nodding. He left and took a long lonely walk back to the segregation unit. The staff were now used to the Chaplin visiting their sole inmate and knew he liked to talk to Martin alone. Colin was one of the few prison visitors who could insist on a confidential meeting with prisoners.

"Sorry Mr Heard, the governor is not interested in you leaving segregation, I couldn't persuade him." He felt anxiety creeping all over him as the words left his lips, "Sorry."

"Sorry? You are sorry, Colin? Step into my cell."

Colin now wished that the staff had insisted on accompanying him. He did as he was told, and stood just inside the doorway to the cell. What happened then was astounding, brutal even in this environment. Martin Heard pulled the Chaplain towards him, quickly and quietly. He undid Colin's trousers and pulled them down, silently pushing the cell door to. Colin's penis and testicles were fully exposed. Confused Colin wondered what was happening, he was half excited, but also afraid of staff seeing them. He need not have worried, they were busy having a conversation around a date one of them had had with one of the female officers the previous night, and how he had added himself to the long line of men working in the prison who had been there before him! Martin used his tongue to locate the razor blade hidden in his mouth, and spat it out in to his right hand. The blade was held firmly against the exposed testicles.

"Listen Colin, I tell you what to do, you do it, understand?"

Just like the Churchill dog, again, he nodded, his eyes transfixed by the shine of the metal as it dug slightly in to the top of his crown jewels.

53

"I want you to bring me a mobile phone, you will do this at tea time. I want it in my cell by six o'clock this evening, I don't care where it comes from, but I want it here at six."With that, Martin gave the blade a slight twist, causing a small nick in the top of Colin's left testicle. He patted Colin on his exposed buttocks, "Get dressed and get busy."

Colin, needing no further encouragement yanked up his trousers and was out of the cell before Martin had fallen lazily back on to his bed. He waddled off down the landing, the sting in his testicles leaving him in no doubt that he had to do what was asked or face being outed for the depraved individual he was. He knew how sex offenders were treated in prison, and had no wish to join them.

Martin sat in his cell thinking the Chaplain was useless. He had no say in anything that went on within the prison, he was not respected by bloody Stephen Byfield and therefore he was expendable. He needed to find a man or woman with influence, somebody that would help him fulfill his destiny, a destiny that was so close to him, a destiny that would end with the death of Stephen Byfield and his rancid family. Nothing could or would stop that happening.

At precisely five fifteen Martin Heard's cell bell rang once again. One of the two officers on duty in the unit ambled up to his door hatch.

"What is it this time Heard?"

"I need to speak to the head of security. I have something to discuss in private, but if they are not here within thirty minutes it will be too late."

Within minutes there he stood, Charlie Peters, head of security.

"Hello Mr Peters, I have some information which may be of interest to you."

As Colin Method trundled through the segregation unit half an hour later at five forty five on route to his destiny, he was met by Charlie Peters and two police officers.

"Colin, I hope that I have got this wrong, but we need you to come with us to the Governor's office."

He followed, feeling sick to the base of his stomach. He knew Martin Heard had tricked him but there was no come back, he would have to take what was coming. The short walk seemed to take forever, but suddenly they were there, in the harsh glare of the governor's office.

"Mr Method," said Stephen, "We spoke earlier about the care you needed to take in your dealings with Mr Heard. You appear to have ignored my advice and you continued to have contact. We now suspect that you intend to traffic a phone into this prisoner's possession, I just hope that I'm wrong?"

Colin did not speak; he simply placed his hand into his trouser pocket pulled out the phone and placed it on the desk.

"You might as well have this letter too, I had promised to post it." Colin placed the letter Martin had given him to post down on the desk next to the phone.

Stephen stood aside while the police arrested Colin.

"How did this happen?" Stephen wondered out loud. "How could such an evil man corrupt one of my staff?"

"Because he is smarter than you Stephen" said the chaplain, "And he will not be stopped."

The police studied the envelope.

"Shall we open this in your office, governor? It may be a security issue."

"Sure" said Stephen, "if it doesn't interfere with the case, go ahead."

The envelope was opened, the contents placed onto the table in front of Stephen. It was a thick wedge of paper which Stephen unfolded carefully and recoiled.

Looking at him was a picture taken from the local paper, the photo of Stephen and his family. Underneath were three simple letters, R.I.P. and the address, that of Stephen's Cotswold country cottage.

CHAPTER TEN

Colin Method was led out to a waiting police car; his exit from the prison had been a very hushed affair. Staff whispered about what may have happened, the rumours varied from drugs to phones. No one knew for sure.

He sat in the back of the car hands handcuffed to his front, such an undignified exit with the two officers in the front talking about things completely irrelevant to his plight. The truth was that Colin wished that he only need worry about the phone, even although he knew that would get him a prison sentence. He fully understood what would come next. A full search of his prison house would uncover a past life, a life full of pain, one that he wished to forget. One that was sitting in a hidden safe placed behind the false back of the built in wardrobe.

Maybe, just maybe they would overlook it, then, when bailed he could use this dirty library of videos to place some influence upon the great and the good of the judicial system. His video evidence of abuse included two high court judges, one police inspector and a host of politicians, not to mention the odd TV celebratory or two. He just needed to remind these people that he needed a hand, in which case the videos would disappear for good.

He sat looking out across the busy streets, at families walking from shop to shop with young children screaming for attention. Everyone was going about their normal safe lives unaware of the plight of the man in the car passing them. The traffic lights changed to red as they approached, the shrill beeps of the alarm, encouraging people to cross in the short time given. For a fleeting moment he thought of escape, of throwing himself out of the stationary car, but reality kicked in. The police could give him a five minute start and still catch him, they were fit and youthful, he was finished.

The car pulled into the secure compound of the police station, his door was opened and the officer seemed almost apologetic.

"Come on buddy, let's get this done so we can get you back home. This hasn't been your best day ever has it? I bet that bastard prisoner ate you up and spat you out!"

"Something like that officer, he is very unpleasant." Colin knew any sympathy towards him would be short lived if those videos were uncovered. He tried to be the grey man, hoping that no one would pay much attention to him or search too hard if they decided to visit his house.

"Just a couple of things we need to clear up." The desk sergeant addressed Colin as he stood in the reception area of the police station. "Our policy with the prison is that we need to search your house, and although I am convinced that it will be fruitless we need to do it. Can I have your keys please?"

These were handed over along with the promise that there were no other things to find. Colin almost felt his fingers cross.

He was processed and charged with smuggling the phone into Marwood, and was told that this could be a custodial sentence. He was also questioned about the threats made in the letter written by Martin Heard. The police seemed more interested in this. Maybe there was some hope after all and the focus would be on Martin rather than on him.

He was then placed in a prison cell. Colin had never realised what a depressing feeling this was and the reality of real prison life was kicking in. How could he have been so stupid? How could he let himself be manipulated by this one man?

After what seemed an eternity the cell door opened and a young officer invited him to join them in the interview room.

"Colin, we have searched your home and as you pointed out to us there were no other items of interest to us."

He let out a sigh and gave a told you so gesture to the senior policeman.

"Can I go home please? This has been such a long and tiring day." He half rose from his seat, ready for the agreement to release him.

The policeman looked up at him, "Yes you can, shortly. We still have a search team waiting at your home as we haven't entirely finished the job."

"What do you mean, not finished? You said that I have nothing of interest." Colin once again felt a sweat breakout on his plump forehead.

"We have found one thing of interest, your safe that was concealed in the wardrobe. We would really like to see the contents so if you could let us know the combination, we can check inside and be on our way."

"The safe only has a very rare bible within it and I would rather it not disturbed if possible. I am a man of the cloth, please respect this one wish." Colin had one last ditch attempt to save himself from the imminent fall from grace, but the inspector just looked at him.

"The combination please, sir?"

And his world collapsed, along with that of a number of high profile people. A few twists of a dial and the hand of fate would deal a deadly blow to some of England's finest.

Colin sat once again in the police cell. He looked around, staring at the bright light and barred windows. Was this how the rest of his life was intended for him? His parents would be horrified about his activities, the social stigma of having a sex offender within the family would kill them. His father was president of the University, captain of the golf club and had a filthy sex offender for a son!

Mother would never forgive him, he knew this. She devoted so much time to the church and was so proud when Colin was ordained, that she thought she would burst with pride. A tear fell down his cheek as he pressed his cell emergency bell.

"May I have one quick phone call? I need to explain to my parents what is happening, then I will give you my full statement. What you are about to find in my safe will stay with you forever, it has cursed me for the past few years."

He spoke briefly to his parents and asked for forgiveness. He hung up with his mother's sobs echoing in his ear and his father's stony silence saying it all. He returned to his cell having been told they would interview him again in ten minutes once they had finished processing the items found in the safe.

The young policeman unlocked the door as promised, "Come on old son, you have a lot of explaining to do!"

When he received no response, he pushed the door wider and saw Colin Method hanging from the bar on his window. A single strip of bed sheet had been tied around his neck and fixed securely to the bar.

Colin had seen this used by many prisoners over the years, his eyes were bulging and the sheet had cut deeply into the sides of his neck. His tongue drooped out and his bowels had failed him, all dignity gone along with his life.

The officer grabbed his cut down knife and sliced through the sheet, shouting for help at the same time. Staff responded and worked on the lifeless body. Death was pronounced twenty minutes later and so ended the life of another of Heard's victims.

CHAPTER ELEVEN

The senior staff sat in silence. Stephen was in full attack mode.

"This bastard has threatened my family, he has corrupted my staff and he has only been here for five bloody minutes. We must stop his games, not just because the threat is against me, but because he has run us ragged. Terry, what the fuck has happened to our careful plan? This guy has had unsupervised interviews with all and sundry, he is dictating what he does and where he does it. How have you allowed this to continue? Get a bloody grip!"

Terry apologised.

"Sorry doesn't cut it!" Stephen continued "Review the policy in segregation. Take away anything unauthorised and reinstate the multi officer unlock. I want the staff changed and a brand new team in place by tomorrow. I will not tolerate any further slip ups."

Terry left the office immediately, he wasn't asked too, but he just knew it was expected of him. Stephen was not a man to mess with, that was very clear.

Stephen sat back looking at the remainder of the team. His blood was well and truly flowing so they might as well all have some of this.

"You sit there and wonder why this place is failing; I look around and see why. You don't need a bloody degree to see what's wrong! Get out there and do your bloody jobs for once, be professional and manage your areas. Do what I bloody pay you to do. Any issues with that? Any questions?"

Stephen's glare dared any one of them to even try replying. No one said a word, they all just scurried out of his office with his reprimands ringing in their ears. They were under no allusion as to who was in charge, and not one of them was blameless. They had all allowed things to slip as time went on and Heard was seen to cause no trouble. They had all been lulled in to thinking his reputation was all hype. The stories of the horrific murders of ten years ago had probably been exaggerated and magnified over time. If anything, he was one of their calmest customers! That vicar was only a bloody civilian, they were professionals, most of them with years of experience in the prison service. It was not fair of Stephen to tar them all with the same brush.

Left by himself in his office, Stephen's anger showed no sign of abating. *Fuck them all, this is my family at risk* he thought. That man will be given no more chances to even think of threatening us. Who was he anyway and why was he hell bent on destroying Steven's family? Were the threats simply those of a prisoner with a grudge at his lack of freedom, or was there more to it than that? Stephen knew these were answers he would have to find if he were to have any peace.

CHAPTER TWELVE

Stephen and Tanya lay in bed, listening to the rain tapping away on the window.

"Are you ok, sweetie?" whispered Tanya, "You've been very quiet."

Stephen had deliberately not spoken about the day's events, very unusual for him, but given the circumstances, acceptable.

"Such a busy day, I had to give the team a good telling off, I think they were shocked!" he chuckled as he said this, "Is there any chocolate left in that packet?"

A guilty pleasure for these two love birds was the occasional very early night when the twins were fast asleep, TV in bed, lots of naughty snacks and a few cold glasses of fizz. Heaven! Especially the night before they were due to fly off on their much anticipated holiday.

Only this evening, all Stephen could think about was the photo and address. How the hell could he know? This was confidential information. Did he have someone watching them? How did he find out this information?

Stephen slipped out of bed, he glanced at the clock, it was only nine thirty in the evening and still very light outside. He peeped through the curtains and looked at the single track road outside. It was empty, as usual. For the first time since moving here, he wished they had more neighbours.

How would he tell Tanya this one? How would she take it? Would she leave him? Had the bloody chaplain given away his information? So many questions and not one damn answer.

Stephen thought it over for a while and decided he would tell her. Just not yet. No need. This man was a loner, and given the fact that he was locked away in the beating heart of a prison which he controlled, he couldn't and wouldn't hurt them.

"Nothing but a bloody terrorist" Stephen muttered under his breath still leaning on the window sill, head between the curtains.

"Sorry sweetie, I missed that?" Tanya called over from the bed.

"Nothing", Stephen replied as he climbed back in to bed and snuggled her back in to the crook of his arm, her head on his shoulder. "Just commenting on the cow boy builders that Dom is chasing on TV."

As a couple they were very well matched. Tanya had a private education, and her parents who had been with the Royal Navy for over thirty years had insisted that she attend a good school as a border. They then travelled around various ports and dock yards, Dad as a Rear Admiral, mum as a forces wife. It had worked well and Tanya had achieved good qualifications and a social network which, if she wanted, could open doors. Dad had passed away three years ago and she missed him dreadfully. Mum stayed in the house in Devon and was slowly rebuilding her life. It had been a long grieving period, but Stephen and Tanya had helped her through. She had in fact become a regular and very welcome weekend guest and occasional baby sitter.

Stephen on the other hand had managed to survive his time in a tough Bristol secondary school. He had however shown a great aptitude towards English, maths and history. He became the first Byfield to pass through university which had been great fun, and it didn't stop there.

After graduating Stephen worked for a children's charity. He was spotted by a former Prison Governor who suggested that he may have the qualities needed to be fast tracked into Prison management. This was Stephen's big break, his calling, and he had felt at home from the first day.

Stephen and Tanya's differences became their great strength, inseparable, and definitely unstoppable.

Tomorrow they were off on their two week break in the Greek islands and the timing couldn't have been better. Stephen couldn't have been happier to remove his family from the threats he had so recently received, and the break would certainly give him time to calm down and deal rationally with Martin Heard on his return.

CHAPTER THIRTEEN

Standing at West Midlands Airport Stephen scrutinised the departure board. Everything was going fabulously, even the flights were on time. The children sat in the burger bar, filling up on a big tasty burger, ice cream and fizzy drinks. This was the reward for two hours of good behaviour. Stephen and Tanya finished their meal and wiped their greasy lips. The tray and rubbish were dispatched into the bin and the Byfield family headed towards the departure gate.

But not before Stephen's phone rang. He sighed as he recognised the number, Area Office.

"Hi Stephen, it's Julia."

"Hello, Julia, lucky you caught me, we're boarding the flight in ten minutes!"

"Ok I'll be brief, but wanted to tell you first." This was always a preamble for something that Stephen wasn't going to like!

"I have been giving you some thought, given the recent high profile inspection reports, and the removal of your Deputy Governor just before your arrival. I have decided to put in a managed appointment. Normally I would have discussed this with you, however someone has become available at short notice. I don't think that your present team are up to managing Marwood in your absence, so this should support you."

"Ok, Julia, you've given me the hard sell, who have I been given?" Stephen knew this was going to get worse, just a gut feeling. An immediate appointment normally resulted in a bust up between a Deputy Governor and a Governor at another establishment,

"Paul Parker, Deputy Governor from Saltwood. He has a bundle of high security experience and is a solid manager. He won't take any nonsense in your absence; I think he'll be fine."

Paul Parker, fifty five years old, well known womaniser and a drunkard who Stephen had met a number of times during national meetings. Always the last to leave the bar, never far from the odd racist remark when very, very drunk which seemed to be every time Stephen saw him, and always opinionated. What made it worse was that in Stephen's view, most of his opinions were wrong!

Of all the people Stephen could choose, Paul Parker was the last on the list. To top it off, Paul had been in the running for the top job at Marwood, only Stephen had beaten him to it. Paul had not taken this well as pointed out in a number of emails sent to Stephen from friends once the news of Stephen's appointment was announced. Apparently Paul had been heard berating Stephen, as just "a fat Harry Potter who'd need more than his wand to get that prison on the straight and narrow!" At first this made Stephen laugh. Now Paul Parker would be sat in the same corridor as him, and running the prison while he was away in Greece - not a nice prospect!

"Ok Julia, can we chat about this in more detail when I return? Just a couple of points I need to flag up when I see you." Code for, *are you bloody joking? This man is from the Dark Ages, and the fact he has messed up elsewhere does not help me.*

"Sure, have a great holiday, see you in a couple of weeks." The phone went dead, and funnily so did Stephen's appetite for his new deputy. Secretly he had wanted Terry; he had passed the exams to hold the role and just needed a bit of polishing. Stephen could have managed that, no problem. Anyway, the flight was being called and he put thoughts of work out of his mind as they boarded for their holiday of a lifetime.

Paul Parker breezed into Marwood, all attitude and cheap suit as he strutted into the Governor's office. Stephen's personal assistant welcomed him, and tried to show him where the Deputy Governor's office was located. Not a chance, Stephen's office had been invaded. Photos of the family were thrown into the bottom drawer as Paul made himself at home.

"What's your name, not that I ever remember names!"

"Jane" she replied feeling very underwhelmed by Stephen's short term replacement.

"Two things, Jane, first, get the coffee on, and then get the rest of the team in here. Let's start sorting this shit hole out!"

Twenty minutes later the team gathered wondering what was going on. Paul sat at the Governor's desk, dictating to them as though they were children and he the new head master.

"Anyone who doesn't want to be here leave now, hang up your keys and get a job in Tesco's! I don't need you. If you decide to stay, do it my way. For the next two weeks it is Paul Parker's way, it has worked in the past, it will work again. Any questions?"

Terry raised his hand, "Has the boss been consulted?"

"I am the boss. I have been placed here because you lot can't do your job. When Stephen Byfield arrives back from sunning himself while the rest of us work, I will tell him what changes are in place. He won't argue with me, nobody does."

"He's allowed a holiday, he's a good Governor and I'm not happy with your style Mr Parker, it's rude and disrespectful!" The words had left Terry's mouth before he had thought about the meaning. It was met with a hush.

"I see where we are going. No problem, everyone back to work, and you" -here he pointed at Terry- "can stay where you are."

Terry sat like a school child waiting for a telling off, only this time, the school kid didn't take any crap.

Paul started in the manner Terry expected, "If you have a problem with me, Terry, speak up or fuck off. I know all about you and I don't rate you. I have still to hear anyone who thinks anything at all about you, hence you've been stuck in the same job for years."

Terry cut him off. "That may be the case, but I know why you're here. I know that you can't keep it in your pants, and I know that you're the most unprofessional arse wipe I have ever met!" The two glared at each other in a brief standoff.

Silence for a few seconds then a thunderous "Get out of my office!"

"Not your office mate, this belongs to a proper number one Governor!" Terry got up and walked out.

An uneasy standoff was the order for the rest of the day while the magnificent Paul Parker had the full tour of the prison. The poor Security Manager had to undergo an ordeal where every process and procedure was questioned and criticised. He was left feeling battered at the end of this onslaught, but as expected, Terry's areas of responsibility came under the most criticism. Apparently everything had to change and whichever idiot managed these areas needed performance managing. Terry had heard it all before.

Paul moved on to the segregation unit where Martin still remained the sole resident.

"What's your name?"

"Martin Heard. What's yours?"

"Mr Parker, acting Governor, why are you here?"

Martin liked this angle; he could work on this, divide and conquer.

"I haven't got a clue, boss. All I know is that I have been in here for months. I have behaved, I have even reported wrong doing. So you tell me, you're in charge, why am I here?"

"Not a clue."

Paul Parker looked at the staff, "Get him out of here today. Put him onto a wing. Let's get this place empty, it's no place for lodgers!"

"But sir!" The staff were quick to object remembering too clearly their governors fury over the lapses previously occurring with this prisoner.

"Are you arguing with me? Get him out, and do it now!"

On your fucking head thought the staff. As Paul strutted off the unit, they phoned Terry. Terry knew the implications of this decision. Did he try to talk to Paul Parker, or did he let the inevitable chaos happen should Heard be allowed out of segregation? He knew he couldn't risk letting it go so reluctantly walked back to Stephen's office where he knew he would find Paul.

"Paul" started Terry, "We can't let Heard out of segregation, he is a danger to everyone. He is a double murderer in custody including a Duty Governor who he massacred, and a serial hostage taker and a Cat A prisoner. Stephen is very keen that he stays in the unit where no mistakes can be made."

"All historic, get him moved." Paul hardly looked up from the paperwork in front of him.

"No, it's not right." Terry insisted, also still bruised from Stephen's verbal onslaught over the chaplain's unfortunate relationship with Martin Heard.

"Are you refusing?" Paul now looked up, his face hardening.

"It looks that way." Terry knew they could not remove Heard from the unit. He had to prevent this from happening.

"In that case, I am suspending you Terry, for insubordination with immediate effect. You will remain suspended until an investigation in to your behaviour has taken place. I already informed Julia this morning that you were acting in a mutinous way and refusing to toe the line. You are a bad apple Terry and I think that you need tossing aside!"

Paul had a smug look of victory on his face as he made a quick call. Shortly after, the Security manager appeared. "Please escort Mr Davies out of the prison" he instructed. "He will not be returning". Charlie Peters walked to the gate with Terry in silence. "Sorry about this mate" he said as he took Terry's keys off him, "I'm really not happy about this and hope it'll all be sorted when Stephen returns."

" Don't worry mate" Terry replied, "just keep an eye on Heard, we all know what he's capable of." With that, Terry turned and left the building.

CHAPTER FOURTEEN

Martin Heard stood on the B Wing landing smiling to himself. He looked at the innocent victims scurrying about the landings, his mind contemplating the disgusting filth fit for nothing but elimination.... "I could be a modern day super hero", he mused. "In fact the idiot in charge of prisons should present me with a medal. I could reduce prison overcrowding within a matter of hours! I wonder if he would like that prospect?"

Martin became tired of plotting destruction, he wasn't in the mood to kill today, but it wasn't far away. That little tickle of excitement was growing again and it would need a good scratch before long. Waiting and watching were Martin's forte and by the end of the day, his patience paid off. The fat black prisoner was dealing drugs from the shower, officers oblivious to the trading hidden under a cloud of steam, but business seemed good. He'll make a good itching post thought Martin as he watched the unusual amount of prisoners seeming to need a shower.

The fat man was a twenty nine year old named David Dunstone, serving a hefty sentence for drug dealing. In and out of prison since he was sixteen years old and before that in a number of care homes, a real product of South London society. Standing at six feet one inch and with a bull neck and head the size of a basketball, he was an imposing figure. His hands, the size of shovels, would often deal out justice while dealing out death.

He had developed a nice little side line inside of the prison walls where a cute little teaching assistant from the education unit proved very beneficial to his business. A promise of meeting up with her next year when released, for a life of champagne and excitement was all it needed. They had a little fumble around a few times, nothing serious, but she was as green as grass. Still living at home with mum and dad, twenty three years old and full of adventurous stories of a gangster lifestyle. In fact it was her who had suggested this lucrative trade. She would bring everything in, mostly concealed within the food for the cookery course she ran, and he would sell it. She didn't see one penny of profit, she just expected a large return on his release.

What she didn't know was that David Dunstone already had an arrangement back in South London which included five children to five different mothers. He had no intention of meeting this airhead when released, but she served a purpose. Plus he thought he may just get the opportunity to have his wicked way with her before too much longer.

He had lived a life of considerable comfort inside the prison. B Wing was his manor. He controlled the import and export side of the trade and to some degree people feared his power. He controlled the drug addicts with a rod of steel and would think nothing of introducing some poor unsuspecting prisoner to his wares. Violence was also never too far from the surface. This was how it had been through care homes, juvenile prisons, young offender institutions and now adult prison. Out of his twenty nine years on the planet he had spent ten inside her majesty's hotels. But David Dunstone would never see his release date and his business was about to be the subject of a hostile takeover bid.

Martin entered his own cell, like a conger eel disappearing back into a crack in the rock. All the little comforts were here, TV, a little white kettle and most importantly, his door unlocked for most of the day! What more could a serial killer plotting the vilest acts thinkable want? And a vile plan was indeed being hatched; there could be one less on the breakfast roll call tomorrow!

Drug addicts were desperate people, even in the wider world they would do most things for money. In prison a desperate little heroin addict would do absolutely anything, all for a couple of bags of the good stuff, and as an ex user Martin knew the buttons to push. He watched the showers, waiting for the moment, the moment he knew would come. There it was, there and gone in a second, but Martin had spotted it. The 'in debt' junkie, trying to score drugs from Mister fat black man, and instead got a blade held to his eye. Done and dusted literally in the blink of an eye. The frightened little junkie headed back, head down to his cell, passing Martin's open door.

"Oi, come here!" He looked up to see Martin beckon him in with a jerk of his head.

The junkie obliged.

"Do you want two free bags, no charge?" Martin asked as he pushed the cell door partially closed.

"Course I do! What you want in exchange? Nuffink is for nuffink." The junkie might have been desperate for his next fix, but knew there'd be a catch.

How very observant thought Martin. He stood aside "Step this way."

Martin had previously traded with Mr 'soon to be dead' drug dealer. The bags were shown to his little junkie friend and he was hooked in more ways than one. He would do anything for Martin, anything at all.

Martin lay on his bed as a few minutes later the sound of the alarm shocked him slightly but it was more in excitement than concern. He knew what was coming.

"All away B Wing!"

The prisoners on the wing were locked away quickly, all except one man who was in the process of been escorted to the segregation. *Oh my little junkie friend, I do hope your handy work was good* thought Martin.

The normal signs were there for all to see, the regular procession of officers, governor, police and coroner, the procession of death. Martin smiled, the policeman taking the photographs didn't.

A dirty drug dealer found in his cell with his throat sliced open. Who would have thought it?

CHAPTER FIFTEEN

Paul phoned Julia.

"Julia, you're not going to believe this, we have a death in custody. Looks like a drug deal gone bad. The dealer has had his throat slit and has died in his cell."

"Give me the details, victim, perpetrator and actions taken." Julia wasted no time on small talk.

"Victim was David Dunstone, twenty nine years old, known dealer. Serving five years for class A drugs, not for release until August next year. Perp is Tony Jones, known drug addict. He is serving life for the murder of a shop keeper in Wolverhampton two years ago. He's in the seg at the moment. He is also admitting the offence but he's off his face on something."

"Ok Paul, keep me informed, we'll prepare a press briefing. Once the police have done, get the place up and running again."

"No problem, oh and I have suspended Terry Davies."

"Really? I thought he was a good guy, Stephen spoke very highly of him." Julia was quite surprised at this news, she had heard nothing but good about Terry.

"Caught him briefing others to disobey my instructions. He is a destabilising influence and he is also a loose cannon. His attitude towards Martin Heard was a worry but I have sorted that out."

"How have you sorted it?" Julia had an awful feeling she knew the answer she was about to get.

"He is out of segregation on B wing. He had been held in the seg for a ridiculous amount of time, for no reason as far as I can see."

"The same wing as the murder?" she asked, already knowing the answer.

"Yes boss." Before Paul could say another word, the phone went dead. Julia was on her way over to the prison. She appeared at the door of the Governor's office. Paul was taken aback, and the look of surprise on his face gave her a clue that this man was uncomfortable with her arrival.

"Ok, fill me in with the details, Paul."

Paul explained what had happened; Julia sat there, coffee in hand listening.

"Couple of questions, Paul. Firstly, why is such a dangerous man as Mr Heard now located on a wing? We had a plan agreed where normal location was not an option."

" Yes Julia, Terry advised me that it was part of the plan to move him back into the normal daily routine as part of his rehab. I thought it strange, but ordered it to happen based on the strength of Terry's briefing to me after the morning meeting. I can move him back if needed?"

"Do it, do it now!"

Paul picked up the phone and spoke with the Duty Governor; Martin Heard was immediately moved back into segregation.

"Secondly, why the hell have you suspended Terry? This is above your limit of authority. Reinstate him immediately. I will commission an investigation, but I am not happy with your decision. Remember something Paul, this is a last chance for you, screw up again and it's the end. Have I made myself clear?"

"Perfectly" replied Paul.

"Phone Terry now, Paul, I want him back, and I want him in here before I leave. I need to speak with him."

Paul knew he had screwed up badly, damage limitation needed.

He phoned Terry from his Deputy Governor's Office.

"Terry, I have spoken to a number of people. It is clear to me that you are not the person responsible for this mess and I shouldn't have ordered you to take Mr Heard out of the segregation unit. I'm sorry. I would like you to return with immediate effect. Julia Matthews is waiting to speak with you."

"No problem" replied Terry. He knew, and more importantly Paul knew, this was a big deal, a real power shift, and on day one. Now that was speedy!

CHAPTER SIXTEEN

A fabulous white villa welcomed them at the end of a six hour air and coach trip. The cool blue pool looked too inviting to ignore and within a split second all four of them were in swim wear and jumping in, cases left abandoned on cool tiled floors. It was bliss! They all laughed and played for the next hour, dried off and finally after a bread, ham and cheese supper from the ready stocked fridge, and giving in to tiredness, Harry and Ellie fell into a deep sleep. Tanya checked the fridge and cupboards, everything that they could need was here, plus a well-stocked shop at the end of the road. Pure heaven she thought.

A full two weeks spread its arms out in front of them, every second to be shared and savoured. This was worth all the hard work of the past few months mused Stephen as already all thoughts of Martin Heard slipped from his mind.

This family was a tight unit. Best friends as well as husband and wife, Stephen and Tanya were good parents, firm boundaries but enough slack for everyone to have fun, and fun they had, nonstop. Even while the children slept Stephen was convinced that they were still smiling, and on one warm Greek night Stephen and Tanya decided that the time was very, very right to try for a new addition to the family, a decision put off recently by work pressure. After a couple of bottles of local wine and a day of nonstop sun all past pressures were released, and Stephen had no resistance from Tanya at his suggestion of an early night.

Two weeks swimming, eating, drinking, relaxing, cuddling and laughing came and went and ended with them looking forward to the next break. They returned on a Friday giving themselves the weekend before Stephen had to return to work. Sat on the plane with Greek sand still between their toes and so glad that they had the foresight to book daytime flights, soon the green fields of southern England became visible. Home sweet home thought Tanya, Stephen had different thoughts, darker thoughts.

On landing, his phone bleeped a number of times. He had turned it off during the break, an agreement he had reached with Julia for pure rest and no business.

The words he read as he stood in the baggage reclaim filled him with horror. What the hell had been going on? A death, in fact a murder, with a separate text from Terry explaining the events of the first day. There were numerous other texts stating that so many things within the prison had changed, all on the orders of Paul Parker. He stared at the screen, unable to comprehend how in the space of just two weeks so many things could have gone wrong. He looked into his contact details and found Julia's private number, he dialed, something he had never done before.

"Julia, it's Stephen."

"An expected call, Stephen. Well, where do I start? I think that before you go into the office on Monday we need to meet up. Can you drive over in the morning? We can meet at my house. Have you got the address?"

Yes, it is in my diary, what time?"

"Come over by ten, it's only a thirty minute drive, you'll be home by lunch. I may have left you a problem and we need to chat."

And so Stephen's holiday came to an abrupt end!

The following day, Stephen's car pulled into Julia's driveway. Surprisingly, the house was not as nice as Stephen's – thanks mum and dad he thought, as he sorted out his paperwork and rang on the doorbell. Julia appeared looking very casual in tee shirt and shorts. She looked very athletic, a fact not noticed before by Stephen.

"Morning, Stephen, come in. Coffee?"

He thanked her and took a seat in the conservatory, an airy room with French windows opening out on to a pretty garden. Julia didn't waste any time and the process of placing Paul Parker into the prison was discussed. As Stephen had thought, this was not Julia's idea. She had been told. It would appear that Paul had been less than discreet with the Governor's personal assistant in his last prison. The affair was uncovered and her forthcoming marriage was over. All in all it was a mess, and an abuse of position. Paul was lucky; he knew people, some heavy duty people that was for sure. However, this move to Marwood was his last chance, any more slip ups and he was gone, all favours had been used.

This was not the best kept secret within the service. Rumours had spread, but as normal Stephen had not taken a lot of notice. He was not one of the chattering classes.

More worryingly for both Julia and Stephen was the cavalier attitude to life in his new post, this man would need careful management. Was Stephen up for closely managing his Deputy Governor Julia enquired?

"I am, Julia, but I would rather not be in a baby sitting position. I have a big job, and to have to performance manage Paul will be a distraction."

Julia agreed that it wasn't the best solution, but both were stuck with it. "It is what it is, I'm afraid" Julia stated.

"It would certainly appear so" Stephen agreed resignedly.

Julia then spoke to Stephen, no answer required. It was clear that this was not Stephen's mistake, the service had faith in Stephen and he would be given time to turn this prison around. Julia would support him and where needed would defend him. It was also apparent that talks at extremely high levels had taken place. Stephen was still the man for the job. However something else was becoming clear, he was also the man who would manage Paul Parker out of the prison service.

Stephen arrived home and the smell of roasting pork greeted him as he opened the door.

" Hi, darling, great timing, ready to carve in around fifteen minutes. How did it go?" Tanya greeted him with a smile, her face flushed from working over a hot oven.

At times like this Tanya was the best person in the world to speak with. The advice she offered was always sound and sensible, especially on matters involving difficult staff. Some of the toughest decisions made by Stephen had been discussed with Tanya first, in fact on more than one occasion while speaking to a staff member, he actually used Tanya's words. It made him happy that everything was done as a team, even his own team were managed by Stephen and Tanya. Good thing nobody realised it!

While washing up the dirty pots and pans Tanya gave the best advice that anyone could offer,

"Sweetheart, go into work, be confident and take control of Paul Parker right from the start. Be honest, be firm and tell him that you aim to help him develop and restore his previous reputation. But also tell him that he has to be a team player. Any disruptive behaviour or maverick approaches to already agreed plans will not be tolerated. Any unprofessional behaviour will be stamped upon but more importantly any disloyal behaviour and you will deal with it."

Stephen nodded.

"This is a fresh start for Paul, make sure he knows that." Again Stephen nodded, it was great advice. He loved his life, what a wife, what a brilliant best friend. They were invincible when they worked together like this.

CHAPTER SEVENTEEN

Stephen arrived for work early, he was raring to go and he needed to put the prison back onto an even keel. He didn't know if it was just his imagination, but it seemed that the staff were honestly pleased to see him back at work. What a great welcome!

Paul was sat in his own office where he appeared to be working through a series of risk assessments.

"Morning Paul, good to see you. Meet up in ten minutes in my office, I'll get the coffee going."

"No problem boss, see you in a minute." Paul glanced up briefly then went back to his work.

Ten minutes turned into twenty. Stephen checked his clock and then phoned Paul's extension.

"Paul Parker speaking."

"Paul, come around to my office, we need to talk."

"Sorry boss, I am on my way."

Stephen could feel his nice warm feeling coming to an end as he heard a knock at the door; Paul had graced him with his presence.

"Come in Paul, I would offer you a coffee, but it's gone cold." The ground rules were then spelt out for Mr Parker and the meeting went amazingly well, just as Tanya had suggested. However Stephen did have one last parting shot.

"Paul, for the record, should I ask you to come and see me, you do exactly that. You do that when I ask, and not when you are ready. Clear?"

" Yeah, sorry, just getting to grips with things." Paul knew he had been reprimanded and he didn't like it. Bloody little upstart, who did he think he was?

The next meeting for Stephen was far more worrying. Terry knocked, "Come on in Terry. How's things?" Stephen greeted him with a smile.

"Well, where do I start? With the new Deputy Governor changing everything, or him suspending me? Can I sit down?"

A fresh coffee was made and Terry gave Stephen the complete feedback, warts and all. They were a good partnership and Stephen had learnt to trust him. The story sounded unbelievable, a tale of lies and deceit, dangerous decisions made and then blamed on others, all in all everything that unsettled a team.

"Terry, this is between us, nothing leaves this room" Stephen warned him.

"Of course, as normal boss" Terry reassured him.

"We need to keep an eye on this. Give me a list of everything that has changed and I'll review the decisions. I need that list before the nine o'clock operational meeting, can you do that?"

"One step ahead of you there boss, I have it here." Terry handed over the pages of notes he had in his hand.

The meeting was well attended, everyone who was anyone had turned up and there was a buzz of expectation in the room. Stephen was right, everyone was happy. Well, nearly everyone!

"Morning all" and Stephen got down to business. There was silence as he spoke.

"I am happy to be back. There are lots of things to do, and other things to get right. We have to be on it, no slacking. Let's get this right and our lives will get easier, I promise."

The staff looked at him, Paul looked at the floor.

"I see a few things have been changed around during my two weeks lying in the sun. Stephen made a point of emphasising this point just so that Paul knew what had been reported back to him. "I have reviewed the changes and on this occasion I wish to change them back to what I previously agreed. In one month we will review again and if I have got it wrong we will discuss it and go from there. The managers smiled and nodded. They knew who they'd rather work for.

"Please ensure that these changes are made at once and let's get back on track. Any questions?"

There were none, however Paul stayed behind.

"You made me look an idiot there Stephen."

"No Paul, you did that all by yourself. Close the door as you leave. Oh and by the way Paul, there will be no investigation into Terry, count yourself lucky it's not you under the spotlight."

Paul left. He seemed in a rush and Stephen thought he heard him muttering as he closed the door.

CHAPTER EIGHTEEN

The prisoner asked to speak to Terry. Thirty seconds in his office and a prisoner wanted a private chat. That must be some kind of record!

"Governor, I need you to help me out. Me and my brother have just been sentenced, we both got seven years and we need to get back to Liverpool."

Terry knew this family. A gang of five Scousers had been running a racket on the wing. They were tied up with the Brood family and they clearly had a member of staff on the payroll. The drugs found around the prison of late were in larger quantities than normal, two nine ounce bars of cannabis had been found that day. This stuff was coming in via a member of staff.

"Yeah, I know what you want and I think that you know what I want!"

Silence in the room, broken by a Liverpool accent.

"You want the bent screw!"

"Yep, I want the bent officer, and I want him caught with the gear, nothing else will do. Give me that and you get your move to Liverpool."

The prisoner stood, "Let me think about it and speak to you tomorrow." He left the office and drifted in with the meal queue.

After all these years, the thought of catching a corrupt officer still got Terry's juices flowing.

Terry knocked on Stephen's door; he explained the situation to him in detail. Stephen didn't seem surprised as they had apparently been aware that someone was smuggling drugs and phones in. He didn't give any names but just told Terry to report it through the security manager.

Terry felt a little deflated. He made his way up to Charlie Peter's office to discuss what he had gleaned from the prisoner. Apparently an ongoing operation was in progress and they were suspecting a staff member named Liam Selby. He had worked at the prison for seven years and had raised suspicions already. A number of traps had been set but he somehow always managed to avoid getting caught.

Terry was not surprised, he didn't like this officer. He always seemed to be talking to the known dealers, had recently upgraded his car and lived a lavish life style way above that of someone on an officer's pay Last month he had turned up for work with an unexplained black eye and reported that his home had been broken in to. This man was playing with dogs and sooner or later he was going to get fleas!

The following lunch time Terry walked back onto the wing and this time both Liverpool boys wanted to have a private chat. They had decided that Liam Selby had outgrown his use. They had chatted to the Brood family and had gained permission to hand the officer over to Terry. He would be wrapped up like a present at Christmas.

They sat in front of Terry and gave the car and registration number of Mr Selby. They also had text messages from him although obviously unwilling to hand over the phone. They described how he picked up the drugs, how he smuggled them in, and most importantly, when the next drop would happen.

The trap was set. The following Monday, Liam Selby would enter the prison with five phones, a large quantity of heroin, crack, cannabis, steroids and a small bottle of vodka. Terry was so excited he could barely contain himself but outwardly he kept his calm.

"Ok lads, say nothing. If on Monday this happens, you are gone, transferred by Friday. You have my word."

The information was passed to Security which caused a buzz to flow around the office. They had chased this bastard for ages and this could be the big break.

All weekend Terry was like a cat on a hot tin roof although he wasn't at work on Monday as this was his day off before another weekend duty. Monday morning dragged. He expected a call from work but nothing came. By eleven he could last no longer and phoned into the security department.

"Hi it's Terry, any news?"

"Nothing, he hasn't come into work, he reported sick." Terry was gutted, his day ruined.

Tuesday morning came and Terry went straight back onto the wing where both Liverpool lads were waiting.

"Sorry boss, he fucked up and some of the Brood boys gave him a hiding. He'll be coming in on Thursday with the stuff, honest."

Again this was reported, just not such a buzz this time. The week dragged, not just because Terry knew that he was working over the weekend, but because he wondered if these two lads were playing him for a fool.

He was in early on Thursday morning. Security had arranged for uniformed police staff to be waiting in the Governor's office, just in case Mr Selby turned up. The phone rang and Stephen turned to Terry who had joined them.

" Mr Selby has just arrived, show him into the office. And Terry, I hope that you're right, if we have messed up again this bastard will be fireproof."

Liam Selby was shown into Stephen's office and as soon as he clocked the uniformed officers he knew he'd been rumbled and attempted to bolt but there was nowhere for him to run to. The officers grabbed him and forced him over the table where he was officially cautioned and arrested. At that moment his world collapsed.

" Ok, ok calm down, let me stand up, I'm not fighting!" Selby tried to shrug the officers off.

He was allowed to stand. In his sports bag the drugs and alcohol were sitting in open sight, brazenly exposed to whoever looked. In the side pouch of the bag sat the mobile phones and steroids complete with syringes. What a disgrace, Terry thought as Selby was escorted out of the prison and directly to the police station. His car and home were searched and further quantities of heroin were found in his fridge. Phones were wrapped in cling film waiting for delivery and fifteen thousand pounds in cash was found under his bath. It was a job well done.

He made a full statement to the police and named another five members of staff who were involved. At the later court hearing he pleaded guilty and received seven years in prison.

The Liverpool lads moved to the prison near home, the Brood family moved onto their next corrupt officer and the staff named by Selby suddenly became whiter than white. It was amazing what good effect a high profile arrest such as this had!

CHAPTER NINETEEN

The Brood family had influence over vast stretches of the country having cut their teeth in Northern Ireland in the sixties, acting as a go between with Libya and the IRA. This had given them a great deal of kudos, and a little hard cash. With the entry of the SAS into the game the safer bet, and one which gave a greater life expectancy, lay in the UK, so they moved out and onto an overnight sailing from Dublin to Holyhead. And so the greatest gang culture since the Kray family was imported. They first made their name in England through the protection racket, charging pub and club owner's vast sums of cash to stop their buildings from burning down, or nasty accidents happening to the owners. But with the rise in the popularity of cocaine in the eighties, they formed a pact with a South American cartel. For a decade they had the selling rights to much of London, Manchester and Birmingham which had produced massive wealth and power so great that the family name itself could be sold. If you had a disagreement with anyone, for the price of five thousand pounds the Broods would help you settle the row. Such was the terror of dealing with these people that debts or feuds were resolved in minutes. They were a family to be feared indeed.

So from the simple roots of a mother, father and half a dozen children came an army. Led by a ruthless general, the grandson of the original founder, Kevin Brood was presently serving twelve years imprisonment for the selling of stolen gold.

The family business however was growing nicely and the prison drug ring recently smashed by one small man, Stephen Byfield, was growing again. The half million pound loss was still a scar that needed to be healed although the loss of money wasn't the part that needed healing. The fact that this man had damaged the family's honour was what needed redressing. He had left employees of the family in trouble; many prison officers carefully cultivated over the years had been caught and exposed as corrupt. The prison sentences they served had left them useless, the investment and time training them wasted, but this branch of the franchise was back on track.

In a brilliant moment of clarity, Kevin Brood had ordered that family members visit friends in every high security prison around the country, from which they selected five. They then made five exact replicas of these visiting rooms, even copying the tables and chairs. These studios were built in a disused barn where drug mules practiced the art of passing drugs without detection. Such were the skills designed here that the prisoner receiving the drugs just had to sit and collect, it was sleight of hand at its finest! Since the introduction of these practice areas only one drug mule had been detected which led to a highly successful return on investment!

The second breakthrough that Kevin had noticed was an own goal from the prison service, who were only recruiting staff from the local areas. This ensured that the Broods could terrorise local men and women who had joined the service, finding a few with a dodgy history and leaning on them. They flattered them with gifts, girlfriends, boyfriends or drugs and if that failed, they brutalised them. In one prison targeted by the family, the number of younger male staff suddenly developing broken bones shot up. This trend lasted a month with positive drug tests for prisoners going through the roof in the following months.

The method in which drugs could be smuggled by staff into some prisons was so simple it was almost routine. The officer would receive a phone call at home and he would be told to meet in a supermarket car park at eight o'clock that evening. The car park would still be busy so the deal was done in plain sight. The officer would sit in his car and someone would simply walk up, hand over a bag containing everything that needed to be taken into the jail and in another bag, two thousand pounds in cash.

If the officer did this only once a month he would double his wages. Once a month was not an option though, once a week was the norm which meant a lot of cash for all concerned.

Two staff worked together, one sat in the prison car park with a bag full of heroin, crack or cannabis and whatever else had been ordered, the other attended work as normal. If staff searching was happening that day he went directly to the office and phoned his car park friend. The drugs were then left in the car for later delivery. If searching was not happening, the bag was just carried in.

Once in, the bag was left in the cell of the prison drug dealer where it then became his problem. Those wanting drugs had to pay. This was also simple, the family and friends outside paid the dealers outside and everyone got a cut. A simple but profitable business.

Of course the staff would be caught over time, some quickly, some lasting years but there was always a queue of bent staff wanting to visit Tesco's at night!

CHAPTER TWENTY

Kevin Brood had resided in HMP Riverside for the past four years. So much wealth outside had not made a great deal of difference to him, still falling asleep in a shitty cell, still waking up looking at the metal door and coming and going when he was told. He hated this life and needed power, not just the power he commanded through paying people to hand out prison justice, not even the power to bribe the odd prison officer. He needed to get himself to an open prison and have the key to a room instead of a cell. Feel the wind in his hair and the sun on his back. Power to work outside of the prison and get the business back under his wing.

His big moment came when he asked to speak with the Governor dealing with allocation to other prisons, sounding him out about his prospects of moving on. Brood had fifty thousand pounds to spend on corrupting these people and he was ready to offer whatever was needed to get this move. He kept this up his sleeve for the moment, ready to play the ace card when he felt the time was right.

After speaking with the Governor for ten minutes he was surprised when he was told that he would do his best to help him out. Kevin could have fallen from the chair, a screw was going to help him out, and for nothing in return! He stood up and shook the governor's hand. "Thanks boss, I'm grateful."

He heard nothing for three weeks and just as he was beginning to think that he had been mugged off and was looking to find this lying governor and give him a bit of a reminder, Brood's door opened, it was him and he had kept his word.

"Kev, I sent your details to Blandford House, they have replied this morning and they'll take you."

"Fuck me gently" cried Kevin "I don't believe it!"

Nor did the governor apparently, they both laughed, "Don't let me down Kevin, I've put my neck on the line here."

Keven promised that he would be good, he repeated all the crap he needed to, he even managed to talk the governor into allowing him to go the following week. Just enough time to reclaim all his debts and put prison business into the hands of one of his boys.

"An open prison, so funny! I was ready to pay fifty thousand to get there and they have sent me free of charge! I honestly can't believe it!" Kevin was in full flow to his right hand man.

"I'm going to be running that place within the month; they aren't going to know what's hit them!"

The following week Kevin Brood stood in the grounds of an old manor house beside a sign saying 'Welcome to HMP Blandford House'. Prisoners were walking out of the house doors, car keys in hand and driving themselves to work in their own cars. It was unbelievable!

He walked in through the old oak doors where a member of staff was waiting for him. He introduced himself as they sat down and had a coffee. The rules were explained and Kevin was given his room key. Apparently a full induction would happen in the morning. He wandered up the stairs and saw a face that he recognised from years ago, some double crossing bastard he hadn't forgotten. Plastering a smile of his face, he strode towards his fellow detainee;

"Hello Ken, nice to catch up with you, I haven't seen you since Billy's funeral!"

Ken smiled and threw his arms around Kevin, "Mate, I can't believe that you're here! Don't fuck it up for yourself, this place is a doddle. If you struggle to do bird here, there is no hope! I work in the local Blue Cross charity shop, me for God's sake!" He rolled his eyes and laughed.

"Mate, I can do it anywhere. Now tell me what is going on and which screws are on the take".

It turned out that the officers were straight, all except the gym officer. He was as crooked as you could get, anything could be brought in, anything or anyone. He even supplied prostitutes on family days, whores disguised as girlfriends, coming in and shagging as many as they could before being turfed out at the end of the day. He made a good living from it and he needed to. It was a short lived existence normally, although this man had been at it for years.

Kevin met him on the second day at the prison, during his gym induction. He spoke to him while trying out the bench press, learning his name was Gary. He was a forty two year old body builder pumped up on steroids which must have been costing him a packet and which were more than likely funded through his dishonest nature.

"Gary, can we have a chat at some point? I need to go through some gym rules so I need to have a one to one with you in your office."

Gary wasn't having any of it. "Fuck you, you speak to me on the gym floor! You aren't anything special Brood, just another prisoner so don't expect any favours in here!"

Kevin's blood pressure shot up but then he calmed himself. Outside, that man would have been dead before he uttered his last word, but in here, patience was needed.

"No problem boss, I'll catch you later."

He turned and jogged out of the gym but he was livid. Kevin returned to his room and wanted to destroy the next person who came near him. He didn't have long to wait before there was a knock at the door. He opened it and there stood Gary.

"Don't fucking put it on me! If you want to do business I'm cool with that, just don't do it in front of anyone. If anyone suspects me I'm history, understand?"

Kevin nodded, "What do I have to do?"

"Give me a shopping list once a week, whatever you need I'll get. You pay me three fifty for a phone, drugs prices on application, anything is available. Then you pay me a thousand per month to be your personal shopper, any questions?"

"Do you do discount prices for cash?"

"Fuck you!" Gary turned and left.

Kevin produced his first shopping list the next day. He wasn't sure how this would go so he asked for some normal items, a couple of blue DVDs and as a test, a mobile. He set up a standing order into a private account for Gary, the first thousand was in there for him, plus an extra five thousand. This should get his interest!

Sure enough Gary came calling and Kevin could see his greedy little tongue hanging out. He had smelt cash and he was Kevin's new best friend.

"Kevin, we are going to be an unstoppable team! I have someone else to pay who just oils the wheels, but if I pay him, I can't be caught! Trust me, we're bullet proof!"

Kevin wondered who this person was, but let it go for now.

"Oh, and one more thing Kev, I've got a work place for you, a job in the local leisure complex! We're going to train you up to be a personal trainer, how's that?"

"Brilliant, when do I start?" Kevin couldn't believe he was going to be outside prison gates at last.

"I'll drive you over there tomorrow morning, around eleven, I need to do the PE classes first."

The next day, a moment that Kevin never thought would happen, found him sitting in Gary's car driving out of the prison, heading to Northgate leisure centre. This was a massive complex full of young mums keeping fit and old couples swimming or chasing a shuttle cock around. There were also a number of classes, Yoga, Boxercise, Aquacise, you name it, you got it.

"Gary, how exclusive is our arrangement?" he asked as Gary parked up outside the centre.

Gary thought for a minute, "Not exclusive Kevin, but not widely known, only people with serious cash need apply. I was told that you were coming, I picked you, you didn't select me, that's how it works!"

It was a good deal, only sensible people with real clout could join, no baby gangsters, so no mistakes. That's how Gary had lasted so long in the corruption game.

They visited the manager's office where Kevin was given a tracksuit and led on a tour. It all seemed good and the normal job description was handed to him with the usual warnings,

"We will give you every chance to improve, we can even offer you a job on release if you excel. Mess up however and you're gone."

Kevin nodded, "No problems, I'll give it my all."

An hour later he sat back in Gary's car,

"Well Gary, it seems that if I am very well behaved, I'll be able to give up my multi million pound a year industry and get a fifteen thousand a year job as a fitness guru! Makes me want to take the straight and narrow!" Gary burst out laughing,

"Yeah I did think that!"

"Gary, how long have we got?"

"Couple of hours, why?"

"Run me home, I'm only forty five minutes away."

The car spun around and the sat nav was set.

Gary sat in the driveway of the mock Tudor house. Kevin was upstairs giving his wife the good news about his fresh start. He gave her the good news three times, just in case she missed the first two announcements.

Deed done Kevin jumped back into the waiting car and back they went. This really was a fabulous arrangement; he could get very used to this.

He lay in bed that evening and felt the time was right to gain back some control so he turned the smuggled mobile phone on and dialed.

"Hello, don't talk, just listen to me. I have just met that prick Ken Crossley, he grassed us back in 2004 and he cost us a lot of money. He has forgotten but I haven't and I want him dead. He works in the Blue Cross charity shop in Blandford. I want him taken care of, grassing bastard."

"No problems, watch tomorrow's local news." The phone went dead.

Kevin walked around the prison the next day, he was getting his bearings and allowing others to see him. The Brood reputation went well before him and he was already royalty.

Ken Crossley didn't return from his placement that day, the local news reported that an armed gang had robbed the shop. Ken was shot in the face from point blank range and had died in a pile of unwashed second hand shirts, a fitting end for a dirty bastard. The police arrived at the prison and spoke with a few people. Kevin wasn't spoken to. He remained looking glum throughout the day, so glum in fact that the chaplain offered a memorial service just so Ken's friends could remember him. Ironic really when he was dead because Kevin could never forget him, he had a memory like an elephant. Anyone who grassed or ripped off the family was logged and indexed in Kevin Brood's mind. Filed under 'B' was Stephen Byfield who owed half a million and a heap of respectability.

CHAPTER TWENTY ONE

The small pub in the Kent countryside was an unusual meeting place for such a successful company to meet, an extraordinary board meeting called to discuss a threat to the business and bad debts.

The managing director sat at the end of the table in the privately booked snug in the pub.

The plates of food long cleared and the board members sat drinking chilled water. Alcohol and business never mixed.

"Gentlemen, I have a proposal which I would like to place before you. I will then put it to a vote as we do with normal business.

I do need to be brief as you will be aware I have somewhere else that I need to be this evening, I fear that they will miss me should I be late.

A threat has emerged to our operation, our enterprise within Her Majesty's Prisons has suffered substantial losses both through reputation and income which I estimate has cost us in the region of half a million pounds. For that I want blood, Stephen Byfield's blood. I want a thorough job so do your research and wipe him out for good. Show of hands please." He looked across the room "Unanimous! Excellent! See that it's done."

He smiled, took a cigar from his inside jacket pocket, left the pub and climbed into the back of a waiting car.

"Blandford House mate, and don't dawdle". Kevin relaxed as his chauffeur drove him home.

CHAPTER TWENTY TWO

The staff stood in the centre area of the prison, the drifts of prisoner disagreements could be heard coming from numerous windows. Some unfortunate prisoner who had borrowed too much tobacco and couldn't pay it back was getting it big time, especially when a voice piped up "He's getting out on Thursday." A volcanic eruption occurred, he owed so many people. The one shouting the most vicious threats hoped that he would be paid first, some even threatened to go to his cell in the morning and steal all his possessions...how ironic, resettlement at its greatest! Battle weary staff stood in a group listening, although they didn't care.... They would have dealt with it if they could have identified the voices, they were just too tired to bother. Anyway, the rule was always the same, don't borrow, don't lend, that way you'd be okay. Break these rules and on your own head be it.

Terry sat in his small office, listening. He was the duty governor again and in the prison and on call all over the weekend. It was now eight twenty in the evening and he'd been in the prison for over thirteen hours with still another few to go. Terry knew he had to wait till all new arrivals to the prison were processed and locked up safely in their cells. Then, and only then could he leave for home and his ever patient wife, Jo.

He was hungry and tired – today had been exceptionally busy. Juggling prisoners in and out of the health care department, depending on who had the biggest clinical need, was always such a difficult task. He wasn't medically trained and just had to take advice from the nurses on duty. Terry's role was to tell the prisoners that they were considered well enough to return back to the wings. Tonight's unlucky case questioned his decision. "But Boss, I'm still ill." "Never mind son, I have one far more unwell than you, so back up and move on"...and so the game went on. Terry's personal ground hog day!

Sitting listening to the prison buzz, Terry reminisced. He had left home at sixteen, he'd found work with a friend at a local wood mill earning only a small wage. The only benefits were that he was given free bed and board. He'd only moved twenty miles from home but it may as well have been a thousand miles. Rather than the old story of booze and drugs, Terry's friend was an excellent role model and a fabulous athlete. Distance running was his main love and slowly Terry began to become involved. This progressed to fell running in which mountain peaks in the Lake District were jogged up and down. By the time he reached eighteen, he could run a marathon in less than three hours. Terry also became addicted to rock climbing; he had a head for heights and brilliant body strength. It was also soon evident that Terry could have a fight with anyone and on most occasions come out on top. Even at eighteen he refused to take a backwards step if a grown man wanted trouble.

One sunny summer afternoon at the local village fete, a Royal Navy recruitment officer challenged Terry to join the Royal Marines. He jumped at the chance – what did he have to lose? So on June sixth, 1978, Terry arrived at the Royal Marine training camp at Lympstone in Devon ready to save the world. The training staff quickly saw that his natural aptitude for overcoming challenges along with a steely determination to succeed made him a first rate candidate but more amazingly for the training staff, Terry seemed to take teams of men along with him. He inspired people to achieve, a truly outstanding recruit.

He passed the training course with flying colours. No individual awards were on his mind, in fact, when spoken to by the training staff, he stated that he didn't want any individual recognition during the passing out parade at the end of training. The staff honoured his wishes but made it clear to him that he was the best recruit they had seen for many months. He did, however, accept the award for best shot as this was a truly individual performance. In Terry's eyes, the rest was down to team work.

Terry was posted to his unit and he quickly established himself as a good marine, gaining promotion quickly, and by the time he saw action in the Falklands, he was twenty two years old and a corporal. This was the first occasion he had tasted full on combat although he had been part of some smaller operations in Northern Ireland in which a number of terrorists were killed. The Falklands was a real war, he thrived in combat and marched proudly in to Port Stanley to claim victory. Thirty plus years later, he still refused to discuss any details of the action.

Selection for the Special Boat Service was an obvious choice after the realities of war. He wanted more of this action and life was a bit slow without the adrenalin shooting around his body like a high velocity bullet.

Then he met Jo, a truly stunning lady. They had met by accident one summer night and within a blink of an eye, his world had changed. He wanted her, he wanted to spend his entire life with this one person and she felt the same. They quickly wed and given the horrors of his occupation, Terry decided to leave the Royal Marines and get a steady job, one in which he could stay at home, raise a family and stay alive. Hence here he was sitting behind a desk in one of her Majesty's prisons, surrounded by the worst society had to offer. The very sad part of this story was that from the age of sixteen, his parents had no knowledge of where he was or what he had done. He simply said thank you, good bye and closed the door on the way out. He never saw them again. Parents addicted to cheap booze and hitting their son were not generally missed. They had been dysfunctional but somehow, by pure luck, he'd turned out okay. And that's the way it remained and till this day Terry didn't know if they were alive or dead, and nor did he care.

Random staff walked past his office as Terry typed away the day's events. Distant radios played shit tunes, but he had been listening to this rubbish for twenty nine years. He was immune to whatever passed as modern music. The empty coffee cup sat on the desk. Do I have a quick one thought Terry but decided against it; hopefully he wouldn't have time to drink one before he could sign out for the night. When his phone rang, it made him jump slightly. At this time of night, most communications happened on the personal radios. Then he realised it was an outside call. It gave a separate type of two tone ring and this only happened when people in the real world wanted to talk to you. He picked up the phone "Duty governor, how can I help you?"

"Hello, this is the prison escort company, we have a late one coming your way and he won't be there until around nine."

"You are joking? We don't accept after eight o'clock, you'll have to find someone else to take him. My staff want to get home." Terry put the phone down groaning inwardly, he knew what would happen next...five minutes later the expected return call came. "Can I speak to the duty governor please?"

"Speaking."

"You have just refused to take a late reception, I've spoken to your deputy director of custody, she says that you are taking him. Do you want to tell her you are refusing or shall I?"

Terry knew this would happen, it was an age old game of cat and mouse.

"Okay, you win, I'll take him, what time will you be here?"

"Around twenty minutes, and by the way, he's a handful. He's attacked my staff already!"

"Brilliant, that's just what we need, we'll be waiting." Terry hung up and walked down to the reception area to warn them.

The van pulled in around nine thirty. Terry could see that it was rocking on its wheels. Whoever was in there was not happy. The van door opened and a contractor walked out, hand cuffed to the loudest, ugliest eighteen year old thug that Terry had ever seen. The boy stood in reception and the hand cuffs were released. Terry looked him up and down.

"Now son, I hear you're going to give us trouble, is that right?"

The boy looked round at the welcome party. He didn't answer and just gave Terry an insolent stare. Terry had tried the nice approach; he was very tired and rather pissed off at the delay to him going home.

"Okay son, let me leave you with my orderlies in reception. If you don't know what an orderly is, let me explain. They are prisoners selected to work in the department. They are not allowed to return to their cells for the night until you are dealt with. The longer you fuck me about, the longer they stay at work".

The boy still remained silent.

"Give him his meal boys and have a chat with him."

The boy disappeared in to the holding area of reception with the orderlies. No one was totally sure of the process of what happened next as it never seemed to be witnessed. However, half an hour later a very polite young man with a red puffy face reappeared in front of the desk very apologetic. The reception orderlies packed their bags ready to go back to their cells with another night's work done.

The rest of the evening was uneventful which was a relative term within Marwood. The forty minute drive home had become a tedious experience, especially when Terry was at the tail end of a sixteen hour shift and in full knowledge that he was still on call for the rest of the night. Any incident within the prison would mean a phone call to him and another night's lost sleep. Still, only another seventy two hours of this, he thought, and someone else would pick up the radio.

Saturday morning came too soon. The sound of the alarm and Terry knew he was in for another hectic day. Staffing numbers had been slashed by the government and every day in the prison was a game of Russian roulette. Never enough staff to do everything and any emergencies meant that you were flying by the seat of your pants! Terry arrived at work and walked through the gates. He collected his keys and spoke to two custodial managers standing in the centre. These were two senior grades who were responsible for the daily running of the regime. They were Terry's eyes and ears.

"What's new boys?"

"Couple of lazy bastards have reported sick, we don't have enough staff again, plus we have a prisoner arriving from an outside hospital. We need a bed in the healthcare unit."

Yet again, the eternal problem. Time to find some other poor bugger to go back on the wings before he was well enough! This time Terry found someone suffering from mental health issues, a man that thought he was Jesus and could save everyone. He also thought he had Facebook directly linked to his brain and could speak to the judge as his Facebook friend! Terry thought that he was the least likely to kill someone or do something daft so "Jesus" was dispatched to the wings! Lots of willing disciples were waiting for his arrival, all too ready to take his loaves and fishes along with his tobacco and trainers.

Terry had a look at what else was awaiting him. Nine prisoners had broken the rules yesterday and he had the duty to punish these little bastards through an adjudication process. Segregation was filling up and Terry noticed that Martin Heard had four new playmates with him. His heart sunk when he thought about the prospect of speaking with all these winging prisoners in the segregation. At least Martin would keep him on his toes. He had seemed very secretive lately, since the chaplain had been sacked. He had obviously been talent spotting, looking for a new officer to corrupt. Terry suspected that he had found his target...Martin Heard looked like a man with a plan.

He phoned segregation.

"What time do you want me for the nickings?"

"Nine thirty boss, and we have nine."

"So I hear, and how are the residents?"

"All fine, still asleep I think,"

Music to his ears. If he got down to the segregation unit quickly the prisoners would be too tired to speak to him. He looked at his watch, nearly nine thirty, better get in there and crack on. The adjudications would be an all morning job, he just had to remember to do the cell visits first and he would save twenty minute talking about crap. The plan went splendidly, all prisoners asleep and even Martin didn't feel like talking.

Terry ploughed through the adjudications issuing fiery justice. Then a worrying call came over his radio asking Terry to report to the kitchen immediately. He quickly left the segregation unit and took a short cut through B wing. He arrived in the kitchens two minutes later. He was met with a scene of devastation. The mains water pipe had blown and water cascaded through the ceiling and over every electrical appliance that stood in its way. The freezers were on automatic defrost and all systems had shut down. The floor was under three inches of water and the ovens had stopped working. Worse still there were only four hours to fix the problem and prepare dinner for seven hundred prisoners! All Terry could do was laugh…if that's the worst thing that happened that weekend, he'd be happy! He phoned the maintenance manager and explained the problem. The manager panicked, shouting that if the mains were not shut down within the next few seconds the entire kitchen would be lost. There would be nothing he could do to save it.

Give me a break thought Terry. *He must think I was born yesterday.* His first action had been to isolate the supply.

"I've done it mate, the first thing I thought of so stop panicking!" Terry was lying. It just so happened that when you are standing next to something that resembles the Niagara falls and the main stopcock is about one foot away from you, self-preservation tells you to stop the flow of water. As for the electrical supply, water and electricity are not friends. Terry's new found maintenance buddy could just climb his little ladders and sort that one out himself. Fingers crossed with that one otherwise the meal time could be eventful.

Terry returned to the segregation. He had just given Martin another friend to play with. During the adjudication hearing a young prisoner had decided that Terry's parentage was in question. He had also suggested that Terry's arse could be used for sticking the adjudication paperwork up. What the poor lad had failed to remember was that Terry was an old campaigner. He had done his homework on the misguided youth and had discovered he was due for early release in two days time. Well, this was manna from heaven; Terry produced the said authority to release the poor lad out on the table in front of him.

"Um, seems you were approved early release and that is due to happen on Monday. I also note that it was me who agreed for you to go. Now, and this is the fun bit, I can also disapprove it and I can do that in the blink of an eye."

Terry heard Martin snigger from his cell. Obviously Martin knew where this was going.

"As a result of you wanting to poke a number of items up my arse this morning, and I believe that you requested me to poke at least two documents and my adjudication penalty firmly up there, I seem to have lost the will to let you go home to Mummy and Daddy. I think you can stay with Uncle Terry for the next few months. How does that grab you?"

"Governor, please don't do it, I need to go home, please! How about I tell you where the mobile phones are hidden?" The boy was not feeling quite so cocky now he realised his release was in jeopardy!

"Let me guess son, are they up my arse as well?"

A huge laugh came from the other cells.

"I don't like grasses son, if you want to inform on people, that's your business, just don't do it to me." Terry stood up to leave.

A shout went out, "You tell him boss, grassing bastard."

Terry turned to the other staff and whispered

"Get the information off him, I'll be back later."

The little rat had tried to save his own skin. One hour later two mobile phones sat in Terry's possession and two very pissed off prisoners wondered how he had known. Honour amongst thieves never happened.

CHAPTER TWENTY THREE

Tanya made two cups of coffee and passed one to Stephen, he looked up from reading the morning paper just long enough to thank her.

"What are you reading sweetheart? You seemed engrossed." She was a bit put out because she wanted a few minutes to chat together before he went out to work.

"Chief inspector of prisons has published a piece, he states that the service is in crisis. Apparently all of the cuts made by the government have come back to haunt them, violence and self-inflicted deaths are going through the roof." He placed the paper down, after all these years he had learnt to read Tanya.

"Is he right?"

"Spot on, the service is falling to bits around our ears; it's hard work keeping it together."

He hunched his shoulders in that sort of '*what can I do about it*' manner and took a sip from the cup. It tasted good, must be a new brand he thought.

"My mum is coming over mid-morning", Tanya continued, "She wondered if she could stay overnight. The twins are excited as she has promised them a play in the park."

"Sounds great, shall I pick up a take away on the way home? It will save cooking."

"Sure, see you later, stay safe sweetheart."

Stephen picked up his briefcase and kissed Tanya as he opened the door and crunched his way across the gravel to the car. He was deep in thought about improvements to the prison and how to deal with Mr Heard who seemed determined to corrupt anyone who stepped into his path. How on earth he had persuaded the chaplain to act in such a foolish manner was beyond him, but the fact that Heard had somehow acquired his address details was a real worry. His other concern was how to side step the pathetic Paul Parker who was intent on derailing any progress. Apart from that, things seemed to be going well.

Tanya was busy sorting out the washing when she heard the sound of a car driving across their gravel. The doorbell rang and a silhouette could be clearly seen through the partial glass door. She opened the door and gave her mother a kiss on both cheeks before enveloping her in a hug. The twins scampered from the playroom and they squealed as they saw Grandma, wrapping themselves around her legs.

"Hey you two, give Grandma a chance to get in! Coffee mum?"
Tanya offered as she led the way to the kitchen

They had a relaxing hour chatting about nothing in general, whilst watching the children dancing around the garden and studying every insect that they came across.

Tanya's mum stood up and took her empty mug over to the sink.

"Right love, I am going to keep my promise to take the children out to give you five minutes to yourself. We'll go over to the park and maybe for an ice cream if these rascals are good!" She smiled fondly down at the twins who were jumping up and down with excitement.

Tanya nodded and gave the children a kiss.

"Now be good for Grandma, no running away from her."

She could hear giggling as the trio left for the walk to the village park. So lucky to have mum help me out she thought.

The park was a fancy affair, banks of slides, climbing bars, individual roundabouts which looked like upturned umbrellas and swinging hammocks which just encouraged children to lay back and swing in the sun. A beautiful sand play area sat in the far right corner and the children had insisted on Grandma bringing a bag of tools, just for the sand pit. She had shovels, rakes and moulds in which every shape and object could be constructed.

An hour whizzed by in this park which gave adults as much fun as the children. The rope climbing area was perfect for all of them, not much of a drop and a soft rubber landing for anyone falling. The more adventurous child could climb to ten feet, three year olds could not go above a few inches but they didn't need to. It was fantastic fun and with the promise of an ice cream afterwards the twins were in their element.

As this was the perfect village, with a good shop, pub and church, it attracted a few visitors, either Sunday drivers or those searching for the village life style. The man in the black car sat in the lay by watching was neither. The cigarette smoke drifting from the quarter inch gap at the top of the driver's window was the only clue that the car was occupied. The gentle click of the camera as it took photo after photo, the buzz of the phone as text messages were passed to and fro were heard by no one. Nothing seemed out of place, nothing to alert anyone to the danger within. Just someone sitting in a lay by having a break, watching every single move of those in the park.

The cigarette butt was flicked out of the window and fell onto the pile already building on the road. The driver got out and ensuring that his hat covered his features, he locked the door and set off on foot. The mechanical bleep from the car and the flash of the lights were the first indication that someone else was around and it made one of the children look up before they were quickly distracted again by Grandma sliding down a rope.

"Grandma, you're crazy" they shouted which made everyone in the park laugh. Well nearly everyone, the man sitting on the bench didn't raise a smile.

"Ice cream time!"

Grandma and the twins marched off in the direction of the shop whilst the man climbed back into the car as his eyes followed them. He looked at his watch, almost time to end his surveillance for today. He had little to report back to the boss.

CHAPTER TWENTY FOUR

It was Friday lunchtime and Stephen had allowed his mind to wander a little. He was looking forward to a lazy weekend, family time, he also hoped that Tanya's mother, however much he loved her, had alternative arrangements for the Saturday and Sunday so they could have the weekend to themselves.

Terry and Martha were chatting in the duty governor's office, the room next to Stephens, both eating a packed lunch and reminiscing about their experiences in various prisons. Stephen liked hearing these conversations, he didn't have many years under his belt and enjoyed listening to how things used to be. Terry's stories in particular often had him laughing out loud. The prison service from the 1980's seemed a lot easier going than today's business. For one thing ninety five percent of Terry's stories would have resulted in him facing misconduct charges. The other five percent would probably have been police prosecutions!

His phone rang with a request from the healthcare unit for him to pop down to speak with a prisoner who was insisting on an urgent meeting with the governor. Although he wasn't usually at the beck and call of all prisoner requests to speak to him, it was on his 'to do list' to pay the unit a visit this morning as it had proved to be a very testing place for the past few weeks with high numbers of very unwell mental health cases pushing the staff to the limit due to four of these prisoners being multi staff unlocks. The main person causing the concern was an enormous black prisoner, staff called him Green Mile after the Tom Hank's film and the resemblance to the character in the film was evident. A heavily built man standing at more than six feet six inches, he seemed to be as wide as two people, arms and legs the size of telegraph poles and a neck that wouldn't fit into any shirt collar that Stephen had ever seen.

He had a quick temper which turned to violence when presented with the opportunity. Although he had only been in the prison for less than a week, he already had a very big reputation.

Stephen stood outside of his cell door.

"Boss, I need to chat with you, are you the Governor in charge of this place?"

Stephen nodded and confirmed that he was indeed the boss.

"Can I speak with you in the office, it's important?"

Stephen told him to wait for a second while he consulted the staff about his behaviour. Staff informed him that 'Geen' had been calm all day. However they didn't know much about him other than the obvious, he was flipping massive! He returned to the cell but remained outside the door. Green mile stood up and moved his huge frame towards the door, regarding Stephen through the open panel.

"How are we treating you in here?" Stephen asked the man mountain.

"Like a King Governor, it makes me want to book in for next year as well! I'll give you good reviews on trip advisor when I am released!" Green proceeded to give a huge belly rolling chuckle displaying a dazzling row of white teeth with a glistening gold crown displayed proudly to the right of his front teeth.

"I can't take you into the office, but I can chat for a second here, what can I do for you?" Stephen knew better than to agree to a one to one confrontation with a prisoner he didn't know.

"It's what I can do for you, boss, people outside want to hurt you. People that I know want you dead, boss, just thought that you should know." Green's smile had disappeared and had been replaced with a look of genuine concern.

"They had better join the long line I'm afraid" Stephen joked. He had been receiving threats against him and his family since he started in the prison service, it went with the job.

"Oh no boss, they have been in line for a long time, they're tired of waiting. Just thought I would tell you my ex employers are spending a lot of time and effort thinking about you!"

"Really, and who would this ex employer be?"

"The Broods, boss, I think that you may have already met them. Now, I know I'm no angel but I support no violence against women and kids so just wanted you to know to keep your family safe."

A chill swept over Stephen's body as he nodded in acknowledgment towards Green before walking briskly away from the cell, head buzzing. Would these people ever stop?

Stephen pushed open the health care office door and slumped into a seat. Head in hands he just wished he could make this all go away. With a sigh he signed the unit documentation before his thoughts moved on to Mr Heard. He didn't dislike many people; Mr Heard was an exception to the rule. Stephen hated him as someone who had also threatened his family, but the Broods, now they scared him.

He gathered his thoughts and left the Health Care Unit. He took a short cut through Segregation where he chatted to the staff before making his excuses. On the way out he had to walk past the cells and as he did, he heard Martin walk towards his door and tap on the viewing panel.

"Governor" it was almost a whisper. "Give my love to Tanya and the twins, I look forward to meeting them one day."

Stephen snapped. Just for one second, he felt the hot flush of anger rage through his body, but he said nothing. He knew that if he showed any weakness, it would be instantly recognised and exploited by this individual.

"Governor, that anger you are feeling, I feel that before I kill! You see, we are not so different after all."

Stephen turned and left for his office livid. Why this monster should be allowed to terrorise him in this way was disgusting. Why was he still here making these threats? He decided to phone the Deputy Director of Custody and ask for Martin Heard to be moved,

he shouldn't have to put up with this. He then changed his mind. It was pointless, and there were no other prisons who could take this man. They were joined in this game for a little longer. Terry and Martha were still in the office when Stephen walked past on his way to his own office and they could see that the spark had gone out of him,

"You ok boss?" asked Terry

"Yeah, just that bloody Martin Heard, he's getting into my head" Stephen replied as he closed his office door. Tanya really would have a sense of humour failure if she knew about this latest threat to the family.

CHAPTER TWENTY FIVE

It was Tuesday the following week when Terry drove in to work. It was mid-July but felt like Autumn. What the hell was going on with these seasons he said out loud to himself? Chris Evans chatted away on Virgin radio as he put another child through the regular ordeal of telling the nation what they had just done for the first time. He admired Chris greatly, a brilliant example of what was right about our country and that hard work paid off. If Terry could bottle some of that talent, he would never need to take this long drive in to work again! It hadn't helped his mood that this was the first day back after a long weekend. Four days of fun and now back to the grind stone.

As he drove he wondered what may have gone wrong in his absence. There were always odd dramas that needed to be cleaned up. This had always seemed to be the pattern of his life – clearing up other people's problems.

He strolled through the gates and picked up his prison keys. He walked in to the administration corridor and said good morning to Stephen through the open door of his office. The boss seemed happy enough with his career on the way up. Terry wondered how far up the ladder Stephen could go. In all his experience, he could honestly say that Stephen was the best governor he had ever worked for. In fact, if it ever came to it, he would risk his life for him. A thought that may come back to haunt him!

To Terry's surprise, the wheels hadn't fallen off in his absence; things were more or less how he had left them four days ago. The thing that he had noticed, however, was that Martha had become very interested in Martin Heard's reports, there were no reasons for her interest other than a ghoulish curiosity. As Head of residence, the pile of emails he had waiting for him when he turned his computer on testified to this. He would have to call her in but would speak with Stephen in the first instance.

"I'm worried about Martha, she seems to be spending a lot of time discussing Martin Heard" he told Stephen when he saw him after the morning meeting.

"Yes, I've been made aware" Stephen continued, "Bloody Martin Heard, I've told her about it, I've made my thoughts on this perfectly clear, so let's keep an eye on how it goes, hopefully she will heed my warning."

Terry nodded, relieved that he didn't have to have a meeting with her. He would have only upset her as tact wasn't his strong point when discussing silly decisions made by others.

"Okay, I'm just going to go around the wings and see what's going on." He left the office and walked in to the central area. A prisoner stood at B wing gate.

"Are you a governor?"

To Terry this was always the opening salvo of a complaint against some poor member of staff or a request for something the prisoner already knew he couldn't have, but let's all still play the game Terry thought!

"I am, but not the person in charge, I'm the head of residence."

"Yeah, you're the one I've been waiting to see."

Terry smiled and thought yeah, of course you've been waiting just for me, shame you didn't have a clue who I was.

"I need some more tobacco, everyone I ask just keeps ignoring me, my mum's just died and I'm stressed. If I can't get some tobacco, I'll hurt myself. Since my mum's death, my head's been all over the place."

"What's your name son?" Terry asked.

"Phillips, Brian Phillips."

Terry told him to wait by the gate, he would be back in a moment. Five minutes later, Terry returned.

"Okay Brian, sorry about your mum, when did she pass away?"

"On Friday, I'm screwed up boss; I need a smoke to calm myself down."

"Well, I'm sorry she passed away on Friday, but very happy that she recovered enough to visit you on Sunday. I thought that type of occasion was strictly for Easter son. Now fuck off and stop wasting my time."

The prisoner disappeared with a now accepted 'stick it up your arse' catch phase. Terry loved his new IT system, he could check any information on any prisoner in less than five minutes. With a smile on his victorious face, he continued his tour of the wings.

The day flew past with a list of emails to get through and the prospect of Martha making a terrible decision in regard to meeting Martin Heard, it was sounding obsessive. If she did, he would spend no time in making attempts to corrupt her, a system called conditioning whereby a prisoner trains a member of staff to comply with all their demands. Martin Heard was an expert in this dark art. He would spend weeks if not months picking his victim; he would deliberately be rude or aggressive towards the target then one day act nicely. The staff member would be so shocked that they were not the subject of abuse anymore that they would do anything to keep in the good books. This was when the prisoner started asking for things that they should not have. Because the staff member didn't want to go back to the abuse, they would comply. The demands would become more extreme until they became illegal. The trap had then been sprung.

Terry could see that this was in the process of happening with Martha, through her own making, they needed to stop it now. First point of call was reporting his concerns again. This was completed via a staff corruption form; he then spoke to the security manager and arranged a full staff training session on Conditioning and Manipulation. He would make sure that Martha was on this training session.

Before he could catch his breath it was time to go home, another blur of a day but very productive none the less.

CHAPTER TWENTY SIX

The alarm clock woke Terry up at 06:00, the positive feeling from the previous days productivity had long melted away. He was feeling very tired and demotivated, a day at home with Jo seemed a far more appealing idea. His lovely wife had other thoughts though.

"Come on get up old man, go into work and be brilliant. If you don't get up now you will be late".

He grumbled but climbed out. The heating hadn't kicked in and the room was freezing. He ran the shower and wished that he were back in bed. However the cold air hitting him as he stepped out dulled any thought of lust. He dried quickly and got dressed, checked that he had his wallet and phone and kissed Jo goodbye.

Jo had waved Terry off for work from under the duvet as he exited the bedroom. She missed him while he was out, and looked forward to his retirement as she walked up the stairs into her small office later that morning.

When Terry had been promoted to the dizzy heights of a governor grade it came with a house move. They had settled on a small three bedroom place in an up and coming market town, not cheap but hopefully the last move they would need to make. She had felt at home here instantly, with the closeness to the shops and the school, but still keeping the countryside all about them.

Jo had set up a small jewellery business, working from home; she was very arty and made small bits from non-precious metals. It made a little money, enough to pay for exciting weekends, plus it kept her busy, feeling useful. She hated the whole little wife at home vision, she was her own woman who wanted to have her own life, and she was good at what she did.

They had not been able to have children, she guessed that was just the way God had planned their lives to pan out, but they did, however have a deep love of children, so at an early stage in their life together they decided to try their hand at fostering. They were natural parents and sometimes this left Jo feeling a little sad that they couldn't raise a family of their own, but at least they could still enjoy the youth and fun that children brought into a home.

At first they had been gifted with a number of children, all had been short stays, many children very damaged and demanding. All of them had settled down with the love that Jo and Terry wrapped around them, no matter how fragile or damaged they were.

Then on one damp grey Wednesday evening a very special child entered into their lives, a little baby, only days old. The story was that the mother had died from a drug overdose after the child had been taken from the parents while still in the hospital.

They felt so blessed, a perfect baby! It felt as though it were their own baby, small, warm, delicate and they fell in love, unconditional love, the love that only a true parent can feel for a child. The child stayed with them for some time and a bond was formed, they were a unit, a family. For the first time Terry was in a functioning family, one where the child was central to life and not an inconvenience.

They felt fulfillment overflowing; it certainly overflowed from their eyes the day that the adoption was confirmed. Tom was now their son and nothing could or would ever change that. He had grown into a fantastic boy; he had the winning nature of Terry and the caring, kindly side that Jo possessed, all in all a perfect young man.

Tom also loved school, he achieved encouraging reports from the junior school and now at the age of twelve, he had settled into the senior school.

Terry and Tom enjoyed jogging on weekend mornings, and the family always had some form of adventure planned for weekends. Sometimes walking through the hills and heaths that surrounded them, Terry would teach Tom some of the survival tricks he had learned whilst in the Marines. The boys did occasionally get away with a trip to the local football, something Jo had no interest in attending with them, and called it 'their lad's day out'. With the recent promotion of Tadcaster to the Championship Tom got the chance to see a few of the football stars he liked watching on TV. Then home by six o'clock, fish and chips for supper whilst Tom would chatter to his mum for the next hour about every kick of the game!

They didn't know the identity of Tom's birth parents; it had never been an issue. Tom knew he was adopted and had no problem with this. He knew he was special as he had been chosen by Terry and Jo and to him, they were his only parents. He didn't know anything about his birth parents, he had no reason to know, and had never really asked, he had all he ever needed.

CHAPTER TWENTY SEVEN

After the escapades of B Wing Martin had quickly acclimatised to being where he should have remained in the first place. Segregation and him would always be a perfect match, that was until he decided differently.

The iron grey sky of Wednesday welcomed Martin as he stepped into the exercise yard, the sun of yesterday seemed a distant memory and the coming thunder was matching his mood. He was becoming restless, he had picked his next victim, she just didn't know it.

The opportunity hadn't presented itself for a proper introduction, however Martin had practiced his lines well. He couldn't fail, he never failed, and targets were always picked carefully, a tried and trusted plan. Vulnerability was the first quality he needed, like a lion spotting the weakest animal in the herd. The second thing he looked for was a lost soul, but more importantly a lost soul wanting to help others who were lost; this was why chaplains were normally such easy prey.

On this occasion he had spotted a high value target, he just needed to set the ambush. He looked at the sky again, it was coming, the storm was nearly ready to be unleashed, the itch returned as he signalled to the awaiting officer that he was ready to go back inside.

Once back in his segregation cell, the door opened, it was the Duty Governor, "Duty Governor visit, any problems?" Martin considered some type of meaningful conversation but the problem for him was simple, Terry had seen it all before and it was almost as if he was immune to anything Martin could say or do. The thing that really pissed Martin off most was simple, he bloody respected Terry. He was someone who really knew what he was doing.

"No boss, everything is good." He'd learned when to lay low and let the attention focus elsewhere. The door shut and the show moved on.

Martin sat on the edge of his bed; he shut his eyes and gave a long sigh. The addresses were firmly in his head, he had viewed the locations where he would kill Chris Byfield and his family through Google earth. He doubted they would have moved again since his research which informed him they had only moved in to their house a couple of years ago, as had their son, Stephen. He would kill anyone he could that was connected to this child grabbing family; he just needed to get out first.

He had considered the possibility of attacking Byfield during his visits, however since the disclosure that Martin had his home address, security had become tighter. Byfield rarely had less than six staff with him, and Martin had to be scanned with a metal detector before each visit, he was like fucking royalty, the jumped up prick!

So everything had changed. The thing that kept Martin Heard ahead of the game was knowledge, people had to second guess everything that he might do. Martin just had one plain objective, to escape from custody, it didn't matter how or when, he just needed a plan. The prison had even tried to move him on, how petty - just for threatening to kill the governor and everyone he loved! No one would take him, however, so he was all theirs, for the time being anyway.

Then the plan came to him, it was unexpected in its ferocity, but so simple.

Martin was sitting in his cell reading a newspaper, there was a new younger prisoner moved into a cell opposite his. Martin had decided that he would leave him alone, at least for the first night; he was obviously suicide risk as staff were checking on him at least every ten minutes and he could hear the conversations between the boy and the staff.

It was clear that he had run up some substantial debt, borrowing tobacco and forgetting to repay it, which had led to a number of altercations, the final one happening in the shower that evening. The lad was dragged from the landing into the steamy shower, a homemade knife was produced and with the prospect of serious injury imminent, a member of staff had seen it developing and had raised the alarm, hence the poor terrified lad sat in segregation scar free.

Then in desperation the boy asked to speak to a member of staff as apparently he was feeling like cutting himself but nobody listened to the warning so the boy then opened up his right thigh with a blade, the wound so deep and gushing it had the staff running back and forth, a code red being called over the radios. Martin knew from his extensive experience that this meant healthcare staff were being summoned as a matter of extreme urgency. Within thirty minutes the boy was being loaded on to a trolley and taken off to the nearby general hospital where he would be free, bar his close attachment through handcuffs to a burly night officer. If they could do that for a simple cut leg, what would happen if they saw the real show? An intriguing prospect Martin pondered as he stored these thoughts away for later use.

CHAPTER TWENTY EIGHT

Stephen enjoyed his weekends away from the prison, but this Sunday he had a tight knot of anticipation in his stomach and he just had to deal with the feeling. Should he lose control he would not be able to say what he intended without sounding like a nervous son. He fumbled around looking for the keys to the car, and pulling on his shoes, he took a deep breath. The feeling of apprehension wouldn't leave him.

"Sorry sweetheart , I just need to get this done, then I can relax again" he explained to Tanya.

She kissed him, "I know darling, let's just get over there and sort it out. See you later mum, we won't be late" she called towards her mother in the kitchen.

A muffled shout and children laughing met her farewells as she dashed back in and kissed the twins.

"Be good you two, I mean you three" kissing her mum before leaving them all to their games.

Stephen and Tanya drove over to his parents; Tanya's mother seemed delighted to be looking after the children which was a Godsend as with the conversation he had in mind, it didn't seem right for the children to be around.

It was a pleasant drive, but almost conducted in silence, both of them thinking about how to start the conversation with Chris. Would they just say, "Hi Dad, what have you done in the past that has made a lunatic want to kill us all?" Not the best opening!

Before they knew it, they had driven up to the end of the lane where the gravel drive welcomed them through the gate. Tanya especially loved the solitude of this house, she said that it all just seemed so peaceful with no neighbours to mow lawns or chain-saw hedges during a summer's afternoon. Stephen heard his mother shout from the rear of the house and as they walked round and past the conservatory he could see his parents sat outside by the summer house. The sky looked a bit threatening with a layer of grey cloud obscuring the sun, but it was warm which was a good excuse for a BBQ at this house on any day and Stephen could see the waft of smoke coming from the oil drum style grill.

He stuck his head through the kitchen door and could see the dishes of meat marinating in the home made sauce that he knew it would be delicious.

A cold bottle of white wine was in the chiller, and at his mother's request he took it out to the garden table where four glasses sat.

His father opened up the chat, with the normal catch up session, but he could read Stephen so well and he cut his pleasantries short. "Stephen, I can see something is wrong, what's on your mind son? I had a feeling on the phone that there were things you wanted to get off your chest, so what's the problem?"

"It's not really a question about what we can do, more about what has been done." Stephen began. His father sat forward, "Go on" he encouraged. Stephen was ready, and he was soon into full flow, "Dad, we have somebody who wants to kill us, I mean kill us all! A prisoner housed in my prison has somehow managed to get our addresses, I'm not absolutely sure how, I just know that he has, and he wants us all dead. I need to understand why."

"Oh my god, who is this man?" Stephen's mother Lucy asked as she clutched her husband's hand.

"His name is Martin Heard. He's been in prison or secure mental health facilities for a number of years, and he has a bee in his bonnet about the Byfield family!" Stephen explained. His father listened and thought deeply, he then went into the house and came out with a thick journal. "I tended to keep my appointments in here. If I have had any dealings with a Mr Heard I will have recorded it in here." He thumbed through, and then stopped, "Ah, I have it, not sure if you will want to hear it, but I have it!"

There listed in the journal was the name Heard with a few notes beside it. "Okay, let's see what I can remember" he mused as he took a sip from the glass of wine on the table in front of him.

"I remember it was a straight forward case, a drug addicted couple who were homeless had managed to have a baby. There were no options other than to take the child from them and place him immediately into care. They were in no situation to care for a child and he would have been severely at risk if we had not intervened. I understand that the child has done very well and was eventually adopted by the foster parents. I do remember that there were a lot of threats made at the time, but that was not unusual in the circumstances. Not sure what happened to the birth parents afterwards, they just vanished and we were not able to track them down. I've never given it a second thought. I was right to do what I did, we often had hard decisions to make, but they were always in the best interests of the child."

"I know Dad, just this idiot has given it a second and probably a thousand thoughts, and we just all need to be aware. He's locked up with no prospect of release, but he has some phone numbers and maybe contacts with others outside so we just need to be cautious." Stephen felt a little reassured now that he knew the background to Martin's hatred, it was easier dealing with known facts.

"Sure, we will change the house phone number and hopefully that will be that!" Chris replied, completely unfazed by the threat. As a past social worker, he had spent his working life being threatened by people who objected to the way he 'interfered' with their lives.

"I hope so too!" Stephen agreed as they all relaxed in light of Chris's calm and reassurance. They had an enjoyable afternoon, chatting, laughing, eating and drinking, the anxieties dealt with and the ghosts laid to rest. Just a story of a man doing his job, and the casualties that fell from this. After all, they would never have to meet this man would they? He was in a safe location, Stephen had him locked up behind bars.

CHAPTER TWENTY NINE

Martha curled up on her sofa, the TV whispering softly in the background. A glass of chilled white wine sat on the dark wood table within easy reach as she scrolled through the programmes on offer on channel one to a thousand and one. Nothing grabbed her interest, shame really, she loved the natural world style programme but nothing going. Even the Yesterday channel had nothing worth watching, at least five stations had documentary's about Hitler, a couple about secret world war two weapons, a dozen channels selling things and a whole raft of cops chasing teenage drivers or Australian custom officials searching for hidden vegetables! All bloody rubbish she thought.

She picked up her lap top from off the floor and flicked it on. At times like this she wished that she was on Facebook but it was all a bit dodgy given her occupation. She then had a thought, she would Google Martin Heard as he had fascinated her since he first arrived at Marwood.

A whole list of court extracts, press releases and even a Wikipedia page was available. She was fascinated by what she read and even a little excited that this man was sitting within the walls of her prison. All she had to do was walk into the segregation unit and she could meet this fascinating, exciting monster face to face! Who else could claim that right? She had seen him behind a scrum of segregation staff but they had always done all of the talking. When would she get the chance to look this man in the eyes?

Having exhausted all media coverage of the infamous Mr Heard, she then picked up and flicked through an old photo album which was lying on the coffee table next to her wine glass. Martha couldn't remember why the album was out, perhaps she had showed it to a visitor, who knew?

The first page that flopped open showed her on a small bike, she guessed that she would have been around six or seven years old. Her father was pushing her along the road, stabilisers off which must have been for the first time. Seeing Dad made her think of him, he had been a kind man who had worked down the mines in their small Welsh village. She remembered him coming home still dirty from work but what no one could see was the residual dirt in his fragile lungs. She remembered him becoming poorly, but couldn't remember him in hospital and thought he had died at home. She was only nine when he passed away and she never thought that she would ever stop crying.

Mum became very withdrawn after the death, she didn't seem to enjoy living anymore and she certainly didn't think that laughter was appropriate. This lasted for the remainder of her days, and a very subdued childhood awaited Martha.

Friends were never allowed to visit, nor was Martha allowed to stay out late, jobs needed doing and without her they wouldn't be done. She had two escapes from the world of drudgery and darkness, the first of her loves was reading, she read everything and anything, she just adored being able to escape from her world and reappear somewhere fantastic, exciting, interesting or dangerous. She would fall in love with the characters and wish them to be with her. She would imagine cuddling up beside the leading man and running away at midnight, all to escape from the endless drudgery of real life.

The other love of her life was food and her mother cooked delicious meals. She was almost always in a state of being fit to burst, and very quickly her cloths went the same way. She would never win the battle with comfort eating and comfort clothing as one led to the other.

But the additional bulk which piled around every curve of her short body led to unhappiness and more comfort eating. Bigger dresses led to smaller ambitions, so although that all went hand in hand, she knew her hands would never hold a man.

At school she was brilliant, standing out as a shining example for all students who thought that you had to be in the cool club to get by. She breezed through with top marks, seemingly effortlessly her peers unaware of the four hours studying she did each night which helped her deal with her friendless status.

She wasn't a pretty girl, her features seemed to be in the wrong proportion and the boys never looked at her. Why would they? She didn't have much going for her. At the school disco she was always the one to sit alone, she would look at the boys and smile at the one she liked but this was never followed up by a spin around the gym floor.

As she grew older and wider university became a welcome distraction and she loved the life at Durham. Groups of like-minded people could gather wherever or whenever they chose and with no love interest she focused on her studies, looking forward to the next lectures and more knowledge. She gained the reputation as being a first class scholar, and the other students enjoyed revising with her, it was fun and there were no topics that Martha didn't understand. This was her power-base and she loved the control that knowledge could bring.

There was one cloud on the horizon, she still needed to return home during the holidays and she hated this. Made to feel stupid and dull from the moment she arrived over the door step, too fat, horrid clothes, no money, it went on and on until she could scream. Get a job, get a boy, get this, get that, it was incessant, and at the end of the break they pretended that it had been fun. The day Martha had learnt of her mother's death she felt nothing but relief.

She was sitting in her room at the university when the welfare officer knocked on her door. She broke the news that Martha's mother had died of a heart attack. It had happened in Tesco where apparently the first aider had tried everything they could but it had been pointless, she had died on the spot. The woman had left the room leaving a list of contact numbers and leaflets around bereavement on her desk top. As Martha danced across the floor, feeling free for the first time in her life she brushed it all into the bin.

She did of course play the part of the sad daughter; she made the arrangements and buried the woman who had held her life back. As the curtain closed in the crematorium she looked around the small bleak room. Five people had attended, she knew one of them, her neighbour of twenty years and the other four were old friends of her father apparently…a sad reflection of an unhappy life.

With the service over, this little free dove decided to open her wings and start her life anew. The sale of the house left her with a modest sum in the will. One hundred and seven thousand pounds and it was all hers. All of that shit and misery for one hundred and seven thousand pounds, she could just picture the letter of apology her mother might have written her;

'Dearest Martha, thank you for being my life long slave and punch bag, here is the money I owe you, now lose some weight and get a job!'

She purchased a small flat in the city centre welcoming the new freedom, a feeling she loved. Once she had graduated with a first in Nineteenth century literature she decided to become a teacher and her first job was teaching prisoners in HMP Durham.

The job fascinated her, the fact that she could mix with all these dangerous but exiting men who paid her attention was a revelation for her. She wanted more of this and spoke to the Prison Governor. One year later she was standing on the landing of F Wing Durham prison as a new prison officer, on a fast track programme due to her strong academic past which ensured good prospects for rapid promotion. The other benefit to her new life was the loss of five stones in weight. She needed to pass the fitness test to join and then she worked hard in the prison gym to get into some type of shape and as always, she did it with pure guts and determination.

It wasn't long before her strong sense of ability and determination lead to her promotion into her first post as a Governor in HMP Marwood, a move which also came with a hefty pay rise. Unfortunately her desire for fitness had long since disappeared and she had gone some way towards replacing the five stones previously lost. She had taken her time to find the right house and was delighted to be able to afford her little three bedroomed cottage which she took great care in decorating. She had found a beautiful sturdy table for the kitchen and loved the look and feel of its rich wood. She had no idea how attached she would become to this new piece of furniture.

CHAPTER THIRTY

Back into the old routine was fine except now things were tighter, no more cosy chats with the chaplain which made Martin smile with grim satisfaction, he knew how Colin's life had ended and he had caused it. He was planning however. Martin always planned, and he knew his next target, he had already done his homework.

He had noticed one Duty Governor who seemed extra nervous around him. When his cell door was opened for the daily rounds, she was the one who still stood behind a group of staff, the others had long stopped this pantomime. She also developed a red rash at the top of her chest when she looked at him, he had timed it, normally twenty eight seconds from the start of the first timid glance. It was like clockwork, she was the target and he planned just how this one would play out.

Regarding his thirty nine year old unfortunate victim, Martin thought that the way in which Martha's face was composed was unfortunate; she had a large forehead, although she tried to hide this by covering it with strands of her curly black hair. She wore hard black rimmed glasses through which a set of piggy eyes stared out, enlarged by the bottle thickness of the glass. Her nose was okay, maybe her best feature, a very regular shape and size, but her lips were very large. Mick Jagger would be proud of those kissers Martin decided.

She was also fairly short, only standing at around five feet one inch, and although not grossly overweight, was carrying a fair bit extra round the waist topped off with the biggest boobs ever seen in that segregation unit. All in all, not a pin up girl, but Martin had spotted her vulnerability.

Her kindness and willingness to help would be the way in he guessed. She had the manner of a kind primary school teacher never turning her back on a bad child. This would be the key to the door he mused as he waited for her next weekly visit.

"Morning Miss, how are you this morning?" Martin waited, counting silently under his breath, twenty eight seconds later and up the rash came like the sun rising over a mountain range!

"Can I ask you for some assistance? I have a problem which has had me stumped all morning!"

"And what might that be Mr Heard?" Martha poked her head round from behind the officer standing between her and Martin flushed with the excitement of a first word with this man.

"The Times crossword Miss, I'm stuck on twelve across, and these fine people were unable to help. The answer has more than four letters you see, bit beyond most prison staff!"

Martha chuckled and held her hand out for the paper. Bingo! thought Martin.

She studied the clue, and then looked at Martin, neither was sure how it had happened but they were now face to face, no staff between them.

"The answer is Production". A look of triumph crossed her face, Martin looked at it and clapped.

"Thank you so much, I enjoy my daily crossword. Brilliant, I can relax until tomorrow." Martin held out his hand, and tentatively, she shook it.

Then she was gone, Martin had of course worked out the solution, he had done this within two minutes, but he had made her feel so useful, she would be back, next time without the staff, that was for sure. Six letters, V blank blank blank blank M, oh yes victim! Martin laughed to himself.

The following day, like a puppy sniffing around for a treat there she was, this time only one officer with her. Again she solved the problem. She felt so superior, so valued and quickly this became a habit. Gradually there were no other staff present and more and more clues to solve. Two weeks later, they had progressed to sitting together in the spare office. Martin could not believe the ridiculous nature of people, or the prison service. This was the very same office in which he had corrupted the chaplain, now he was doing the same to the kindly Miss Boswell

Martin noticed the rash had stopped appearing, her confidence was oozing and the stammer was long gone. He accidentally brushed his hand on her thigh but she didn't respond, she was too engrossed in the clues so he then put his hand firmly on her leg. She looked up, her eyes scanning his face but still she said nothing.

A knock at the door and they both looked up, Martin slowly removing his hand from her leg.

"Is everything ok Miss?" the officer looked worried.

"Yes, no problem, I could think of worse ways to spend ten minutes". She smiled and stood up to leave, then with a classic poker players tell, she touched Martin's hand and smiled,

"See you tomorrow".

Martin crashed back into his cell and fell on the bed, he was about to ruin this woman in more ways than one. He only had to wait two more days before their next meeting.

It was a Sunday morning, staffing levels were terrible, only one officer in segregation and he was needed to help serve the meal on E wing.

Martha offered to sit in the seg office alone as yet again Martin was the only prisoner held here. It was a strange transient population, sometimes large numbers of residents, sometimes only him, all dependant on the main prison population. Today it was just him.

Martha sat in silence reviewing the morning's adjudication paperwork when she became aware of a song playing on Martin's old cassette player, a Roxy Music song, an old song on an old cassette player. Whatever it was, it made Martha walk to Martin's cell and look through the flap,

"Hi Martin, I love this song" she started to sing a few words, "reminds me of when I was a child."

"Come in and dance, no one will know!" They both laughed, then surprisingly the door opened.

And there she was, vulnerable, completely at risk, but she was glowing and the rash was back.

Martin moved forward and stroked her breast. Martha knew it was wrong but she also felt that she knew Martin as no one else had ever bothered to know him. She felt safe, Martin had proved he liked her, she wasn't at risk!

"Are you sure Martha?" Martin asked, still stoking his hand gently against her breast.

"Oh yes Martin, I am sure" she replied, catching her breath with previously unfelt excitement.

They both undressed quickly, cloths scattered on the grubby floor and they fucked, quick anxious sex. Everything felt strange, it was the first time a man had touched her, the first time she had been penetrated by a man. The fact he was a killer, a vicious killer, she was temporarily blind to. Someone wanted her, someone wanted to hold her close instead of pushing her away and laughing with revulsion at her body. She lay across that broken bed while he pounded his cock into her, loving the closeness, loving the rough nature of this act. She wanted it to be rough, she'd had a secret fantasy of being raped by a strong man and she had often played with herself considering this option. And now it was happening! "Fuck me harder!" Were these filthy words coming from her mouth? She couldn't quite believe herself and what she was doing, but these words spurred Martin onto greater efforts.

"You dirty slut" he panted as he fucked her hard and came, deep inside her.

She sighed deeply, she was no longer a thirty nine year old virgin! Feeling slightly embarrassed, she cleaned the mess from between her legs with toilet tissue and redressed. She turned and smiled at Martin who lay back on the bed, a satisfied smirk on his face.

"That was nice, but not a word Martin."

Martin smiled, "Our little secret, will we dance again?"

"Martin, we'll dance so much your feet will hurt, we just need to be sensible, this could be a good thing for us both if we're careful."

She would have liked to lie next to him, cuddled up in the aftermath of good sex, but knew she needed to get out of the cell before the officer returned to the unit. She had taken a huge risk but her cherry had been well and truly popped! Who could have guessed it would be like that? She was already planning another fantasy as she left the cell, carefully shutting the door behind her so nobody could hear the lock shoot back into position.

She sat back in the segregation office, guilt and amazing self-doubt crushing in on her. What on earth had just happened? What had she just done? She got up and walked quickly back to Martin's cell. She opened the door and stood in the doorway, Martin looked up at her as he remained lying on the bed. He had pulled his clothes back on and was flicking through a book.

"Martin, that was a dreadful mistake, it must never happen again!" She threw at him.

Martin gave a small laugh before replying

"Oh, it will happen again you dirty whore, you belong to me now. My security friend Mr Peters, would be very interested in how I know where your little mole is located at the top of your thigh! Who will they believe Martha? They didn't believe poor Colin Method! I own you and you are my toy you filthy bitch. I will see you tomorrow, bring me something in to show how much you want me".

"What do you want me to bring? I can't bring anything in to the prison, you know that!" Martha was feeling terrified, sick but strangely excited. She was almost being given an excuse to have sex with him again.

"Oh Martha, surprise me you silly mare!" Martin picked up his book again. He knew he had her now, right where he wanted her. The silly bitch was gagging for it, who'd have thought it would have been that easy?

Martha returned to her office within the Offender Management Unit. She had a position as Head of this unit that nobody envied, it was a pig of a job. Terry had held the position for eighteen months and had hated it. Lots of in fighting between civilian workers who didn't give a toss how hard you had worked to become a Governor, to them you were no one important. Sentence calculations, bail, immediate releases, release on temporary license, early releases, public protection, stopping this prisoner from contacting that person outside or vice versa. This job was an absolute disaster waiting to happen. Any mistakes could ensure that your career was over and maybe even that of the Governing Governor too, that was how serious it could be.

Martha had seen one Governor lose his job. Identical twins had been sent to his prison and, against the advice of security, they were placed in a shared cell, one serving twelve months in prison for driving a car during an armed robbery, the other serving sixteen years for armed robbery.

The twelve month sentence was soon over and he was prepared for discharge.

The prison happily discharged him in the morning and at lunch time the prison received a phone call from the twin's mother. She was enquiring why her son serving sixteen years had walked through the door, packed his bags and left in a blazing hurry, and where was her other son whom she had expected home that morning.

Son number one went on the run, committed further armed robberies and shot and killed a security guard. He also shot a firearms officer in the shoulder during the same bungled raid.

Questions were asked in the House of Commons and the Governor was dismissed with immediate effect. If the correct checks had been conducted by the person at the lowest level, that Governor would still be happily sat at his large wooden desk sipping luke warm coffee. Instead he was presently sending CVs off to every security firm he could find, such was the thin line they trod.

So Martha took the job incredibly seriously.

She also realised that should she be a success in this position then Stephen would support her for taking the examination that proved she was capable of being in charge of a prison. She had been studying already, checking past papers and practicing specimen answers. The first paper was mainly based on the understanding of statistics and she could do this in her sleep. In all the papers that she had attempted she had scored higher than ninety five percent, this would have given her a top marking. She could see shapes out of percentages, it just made sense to her, recognising trends through figures was like spotting mushrooms growing on a flat green lawn, so simple.

The financial test was equally simple, the answers were there, you just had to understand what you were looking for. Martha had this sussed in less than thirty minutes.

The Job Simulation assessment was a different ball game for Martha and this would test her to the max. She lacked confidence when under increased pressure or aggression and she tended to make quick decisions, but not good decisions. She hoped that Terry would help her with this as he had recently passed this series of tests.

But that was very much in the future, she needed to sort out this department first, and of course try to sort out the personal mistake that she had just made with Martin Heard. What had she been thinking to risk her career like that?

Her head was still spinning, Sunday lunchtime and she'd had sex in a cell with a convicted killer! That wasn't how it was supposed to be! She knew that she could face prison if caught, could she trust Martin to keep it secret? She looked through his entries on the prison computer records.

It didn't look too good, he had had so many security reports over the years. She couldn't access what the exact nature of the reports were but she could guess. There followed thirty four separate entries involving attempts to corrupt staff, and dozens stating that this man should never be interviewed alone! Looks like she'd scored a real own goal she pondered.

She wondered what would happen should she stop and deny that she were involved but he knew too much to risk that. Should she just continue to see him? Ultimately she would be discovered, then what? At least four years in prison and if it came out that she had smuggled goods in as well, then maybe another four on top.

She banged her head with her hand. Stupid bitch, stupid fucking bitch!

121

Then she came upon the answer, it was written there a dozen times, this man must not be seen alone. Tomorrow morning she would reinforce this warning, persuade the Governor to issue it as a Notice to Staff so it would be read by all, and then she could just shrug her shoulders at Martin and say sorry, no more one to one meetings, the Governor would not allow it.

The only way that Martin Heard would see her one to one is if he managed to be released and turned up at her house, that would be a different proposition. The sex had been fantastic and she felt a tingle flow through her body as she relived the moment.

One more job to do before she spoke to the Governor, she was going to speak to Martin first, explain what the Governor had instructed, and that she couldn't stop it happening. But she also needed to tell him how she felt about him, how he excited her, how he stirred her emotions. She wanted to feel him in her again one day.

CHAPTER THIRTY ONE

Stephen sat back in the large leather swivel chair in his office, he looked at the notice boards on which he had listed all of the action points to take the prison forward. He was happy that apart from Paul, the team was pulling together, however he was also concerned about Martha. Numerous intelligence reports were arriving at his desk and by all accounts she was getting too close to Mr Heard. He took a yellow post it pad and scribbled a note to himself which read *Martha 0930.*

Today was going to be a good day. He had decided that this would be the day that this crumbling old prison would be put back on the map. He had spoken to a number of his friends working in various audit departments around the prison service; they had agreed to give the prison a health check. This was his own terminology for coming in, having a good nosey around, look at the compliance with processes and then give him the feedback, warts and all. This would give him a good idea as to where the progress really did sit. What he had failed to tell his team was that the audit teams were due at eight thirty with a strict brief to be brutal. If it wasn't right, he wanted to know.

The audit team comprised of Sally Cowell a fifty something year old Safer Custody lead from the central office in London. She first met Stephen when he was on loan to head office as part of the induction to prison life and they had got on so well that they kept in touch. She had been very impressed with his drive and focus and she was not surprised at all to see him achieve so much.

David Wardell was the security lead from Head Office security group, he had a vast range of audit knowledge and again admired Stephen. He didn't need to be asked twice to be part of the audit team as he hankered for a job working with Stephen at the prison. He thought that he would make a good Deputy Governor as after fifteen years in the prison service he was ready to move on.

Jo Burnell was a young twenty five year old Deputy Governor from a small young offender prison. She was on the same investigation course as Stephen at the training school in Rugby and again they found a shared interest in improving the levels of decency within prisons. They had both dreamed of running their own large prison and Stephen had made it. Jo was close but being so young, was a few years behind him.

The final member of the team was a very close friend of Stephens', Jeffrey Biscuit. He had been in the audit team for years, had seen every prison in the country and more importantly he knew every trick in the book so no one would get one over on him. Jeff was a God parent to Stephen's children, and would go on to be a lifelong friend to both Stephen and Tanya.

Never having been one to duck a challenge and laughing to himself, Stephen called Paul into the office. Their own differences were growing, and Paul had continued to be 'an arse' as Stephen would put it, but he was Stephen's 'arse' and Stephen would do whatever he thought right.

"Paul" Stephen greeted him as he plonked himself down in the chair facing Stephen's desk looking pissed off at being summoned. "I've arranged a number of auditors to come into the prison today. They're arriving shortly at eight thirty and they'll be looking at our main areas of safer custody, security, including the control of tools, and resettlement. I deliberately haven't told anyone, because at the last senior management meeting you all told me that your areas were up to speed. Let's have a reality check and see where we need to go from here".

Paul was not amused and it showed in his reply. "Really, is that the way you operate Governor, sneaking people in to check our work? It was almost a snarl from Paul.

"I can't see the issue as you personally Paul have told me that your areas are tip top! I am not so sure though and this is my reputation on the line. As good as you think that you may be, I cannot just take your word for it. This place has had a number of issues and I need to ensure we're on track with addressing them."

Paul shrugged his shoulders in a 'whatever' motion.

"And let's not forget" Stephen continued, "that although you clearly don't like me, or in fact like working for me, I expect you to be professional and to assist the auditors in doing their work." "Or what?" hissed Paul.

"If needed I'll manage your arse straight out of this job! Now you can moan all you like about me, I will stand up for my actions anywhere and in front of anyone. I have been told that you have many qualities, I have yet to see any of them for myself!"

Paul stood, "Are we done?"

Stephen nodded and Paul walked briskly out, the door shutting a little louder than normal behind him. Soon after, Stephen received a call from the gate informing him the audit team had arrived. He went down to greet them, bringing them back to his office for a quick briefing before sending them off to meet up with the lead governor for each area to be observed.

124

The team fanned out to their specific areas. Sally met with the Head of Safer Custody; she sat in on the weekly meeting in which all prisoners at risk of self-harm were discussed. This seemed very impressive, and she also noticed that the structure Stephen had put in place within the Health Care department which encouraged good working relationships between prison officers, nurses and mental health teams, was working very well.

On inspecting the documentation aimed at supporting prisoners at risk of hurting themselves, she discovered that all support and care plans were well managed, and observations and assessments on all the at risk prisoners were of a high standard. Again this was a reflection on the training programme Stephen had insisted upon, plus the robust management check lists that had to be completed every day to ensure the staff had done their job properly.

A forum with staff and some 'at risk' prisoners was also a positive experience. All in all just some minor housekeeping points and Sally was very impressed and looked forward to passing this good news on.

Jo and Jeffrey had similar experiences in the areas they visited, again Stephen's leadership had produced some excellent growth in the departments, and staff were motivated and keen to continue the progress.

They also noted how open the staff and prisoners they spoke with were. They called it a 'heads up' culture. If staff and prisoners looked you in the eye, it normally meant that they were used to being spoken to by staff and managers, and this was very healthy.

David, who had spent the day with Paul had a very different time however. The head of Security was away, and Paul was his line manager.

From the outset David had problems. The control of tools was appalling with staff having little idea in regard to where tools were in the workshops. Stanley knives, screwdrivers and scissors were handed out like sweets with no checks or balances for the issue. Staff were only interested in getting them back at the end. David was shocked, it was an accident waiting to happen, and as he watched this poor practice, Paul sat with his feet on a desk speaking to a workshop instructor who made no effort to watch his workers. Not only lazy, but very, very dangerous

David did try to suggest to Paul that things could change but Paul replied by asking him if he was prepared to leave his nice little office to help them! He seemed a man out of his depth.

The rest of David's visit was no better. Control of prisoners was very poor, wing staff didn't know where some of their prisoners were, searching was non-existent and the smell of cannabis was strong in the air. This was very disappointing and it seemed to David that Paul had no interest in improvements, and it would appear that he was attempting to sabotage Stephen's good work.

The most heinous of crimes was still to come. When questioned by David, Paul absolutely slated the work completed by Stephen. He told him that Stephen had no clue about running a prison, and that he should go back to becoming a deputy governor until he had learnt the ropes! These comments were made without a care. When David attempted to report back to Paul, in fact give him some warning as to the contents of the report he would be submitting, Paul refused to listen any further.

Although this part wasn't fully reported back to Stephen, Paul actually pushed his office door closed on David saying that he was not welcome. It was an incredible thing for such an important member of the team to do and David had never witnessed such arrogant and rude behaviour.

Meanwhile, at precisely nine thirty Martha appeared at Stephen's office and knocked on the pine door,

"Morning Stephen!"

"Morning, come in" Stephen replied as he turned away from his computer screen. Martha stepped into the office and took a seat at the large round table just inside the door of the office where they held the morning senior management meetings. Stephen stood from his leather chair, gently closed his office door and joined her.

"Martha, I will get to the point, I have had a number of worried staff contact me during the past two weeks as they feel that your relationship with Martin Heard is a concern. It has been reported that you are seeing him on a daily basis alone, and that you have been insistent with other Governors that you will conduct the segregation rounds. Now I know how hard you work, and that you are a kind person who always sees the best in everyone so I am suspending my judgment on what I am hearing until I had the chance to speak with you to hear your side". Martha fidgeted in the chair, only a small movement but Stephen noticed it.

126

"No, it's not like that at all Governor and it embarrasses me a bit that anyone thinks so. I have helped him a lot, and in turn he has behaved. There has not been one incident involving Martin Heard since I became directly involved in his case!" "That's true Martha, but he is also an excellent manipulator of staff. Have a look at this". Stephen pushed a file in front of Martha, which contained reports of a number of staff sacked from the prison service or secure hospitals as a result of Martin Heard.

She read through, her eyes drinking in every word. She stopped and read one report twice, Heard had had sex with a male nurse before the nurse was caught bringing a phone into the hospital. The nurse was sacked and sent to prison for two years, a prospect she didn't relish for herself! She closed the file and looked at Stephen. "I'll bear it in mind Governor, but you needn't worry about me, I'm not an idiot".

"I know that Martha, but nor is he. From today the only contact that you will have with Mr Heard will be when you are Duty Governor, and then, as in other interactions with him, you will video the conversation, is that clear?"

She nodded, stood and left the office. She had no intention of any further involvement with Martin Heard whilst he was in prison, however she was not going to be dictated to by the Governor. Who did he think he was? She was an experienced member of staff and she would see who she wanted and when she wanted. At least he had removed her dilemma by insisting she did not see Martin on a one to one anymore; that had played right in to her hands.

The day flew by for Stephen, a myriad of meetings, spreadsheets and a sorting out of various staffing issues. However at four thirty a knock at the door made him raise his head from the screen.

The audit teams were back with a quick and dirty feedback. Jeffery took the lead. "Okay Stephen, we have looked at the areas suggested by you, of course we don't have time to present the complete feedback to you, that will be sent over later in the week. However we have a number of recommendations from these area and we have a brief overview here which we would like to discuss with you". Jeffery handed Stephen a short handwritten document.

"Sure, thank you for your time, how did it look?" Stephen was keen to get their opinion on how things appeared. "In brief, and based against last year's audit reports, the establishment has made great strides. We find your prison to be a decent safe environment with improvements in all areas, in fact we would say dramatic improvements. The only areas of concern during the visit were the areas managed by your Deputy Governor. We found him unhelpful, and his procedures were of poor quality. There were numerous examples of noncompliance with standards, and a number of repeat non compliances. As a team, we did try speaking with him."

"What did he say?" This would be interesting Stephen thought.

"Nothing, that was the issue for us, he refused to discuss anything, just said that he was too busy to meet us". Jeffery looked apologetic.

Stephen nodded and continued reading the report. When he finished he stood and shook their hands, "I want to thank you all for sparing me your time. I understand how difficult it would have been to get away from your own work, and I truly would like to apologise for the actions of my Deputy Governor. I will deal with that outside of this process".

With that the team left with Stephen's secretary to be escorted out of the prison. Stephen pondered the report, it was excellent work, and showed extensive progress from the team, in fact better than he had anticipated. The team had been brutal in the auditing, and still the processes stood up to it. But Paul, now that was a different kettle of fish, one which was soon to be boiled.

Later that evening as Stephen sat watching television with Tanya, the children tucked up sound asleep in bed, Jeffery rang on the house phone. They chewed the fat, talked about past holidays together, and family issues. Once the pleasantries were over Jeffrey told Stephen that he had some very important information, something that he felt that he had to share from the day's activities, but hadn't wanted to mention it where others may hear back in the prison.

"Stephen, I have always been incredibly loyal and honest with you and I know that you realise that. With that in mind I have to tell you that you have a member of your team who is trying to destroy you, and your reputation. Your Deputy Governor is a class A turd Stephen, get him out of your prison as quickly as you can possible arrange it, he'll destroy you and everything that you're doing." Steven moved out into the kitchen where he could concentrate without the distraction of the latest crime drama being shown by the BBC.

"On top of the poor quality of his work, the lack of loyalty towards you and his appalling manners, I have been made aware that he has established a very close working relationship with the Chair of the prison union." Jeffery continued. "Between them they are plotting to have a vote of no confidence in you and they are trying to push the Deputy Director of Custody to have you removed. I have just emailed you on your private address some copies of emails sent from Paul to the union chairman, plus his replies. Just don't ask where I obtained these Stephen, need to know basis only, it's just lucky that most of the staff respect you!" Now dear boy, I have presented you with the silver bullet to suspend and sack your deputy governor for lack of trust, how you do so is up to you, just act quickly before the damage is done". Stephen thanked him for his support and they rang off so that he could fire up his laptop and read the emails Jeffery had sent him.

He was right, Stephen could hardly contain his anger and lay awake long in to the night deliberating how he was going to deal with his deputy. However events about to occur would mean that that fish would have to wait a little longer to be fried!

CHAPTER THIRTY TWO

The next morning, Martha visited the segregation again and in spite of Stephen's warning, asked staff to escort Martin Heard to the office. Her routine had raised a few eyebrows and staff were talking. They thought it could be the Colin Method thing all over. However Martha was a good actor and she convinced staff that as Lead of Offender Management, she needed to see him during the course of his sentence and in private.

They entered the spare office again where a short awkward silence was broken by Martha gushing "I loved it Martin, I want more of it, I will do anything to spend time with you, have sex with you. You don't need to threaten me, I am a willing partner but we can't do anything whilst you are still in here, it is just too risky for me and for you. I will just have to be patient and wait for your release."

She had hardly slept the last couple of nights, with what had happened going round in her head. She was terrified with what she had got herself in to but at the same time determined that now she had found someone who wanted her, whatever his reasons, she wasn't going to let it go. No longer was she the only one amongst her friends and work colleagues who had no one in her life, she could now contribute to the "my boyfriend" conversations - they just didn't need to know who she was seeing!

She slipped her hand into her pocket and pulled out a packet of Rolos, "See I love you so much I'm giving you the lot!" They both laughed. "This is going to be difficult though, the governor is stopping all one to one meeting with you, I will need to bide my time between visits to you so please be patient".

Martin looked at her, weighing up the information. It sounded as though it may be true and not just an excuse to wriggle from the hook.

"Martha, I am going to trust you with a secret, can I trust you?" Martin was smiling inside, this was like taking candy from a baby!

"Yes, of course!"

"I am getting out of here soon and I'll need a place to stay. Will you look after me?"

"When will that be?" she asked, the fact that she knew he was not due for release for many years to come, if ever, didn't register in her brain. All she could think of was the fact she would be like everyone else with someone to love her at home.

"I'll be out soon, and will come and find you, don't worry." Martin would promise her anything, he wasn't planning on her being around for long.

"And Martha, I will need one more thing, I have a list of items that I will need when I do get out, can you get them for me and leave them at this place for me?" He passed a note to her with precise instructions of where to leave the items.

"Of course I will, you can rely on me. I'll be waiting for you to come and visit me!" Martha smiled.

"Let's just take this casually from now; we can't afford any last minute mistakes. If we get this right, we could spend the rest of our lives together, no more contact till we are meeting outside, okay?"

She nodded; this suited her fine, no more risk to her career but still an opportunity to be with him again. "Just keep me in touch with how you are doing, send me a text to let me know that you are safe, please".

This time it was Martin's turn to nod. He rose from his chair and returned to his cell.

CHAPTER THIRTY THREE

Martin Heard was indeed a man with a plan, a long strategically thought out plan.

Some clever thought had gone into researching Stephen Byfield in the ten years Martin had been away from prison. The mental health unit had inadvertently given him access to the internet. The guilty staff member was sacked, but that was too late to take away the information that was already filed in Martin's head.

Every detail in regard to the Byfield family was memorised including the address of his parents. The bastard Chris Byfield who had taken his child was intensely researched, even the recent change of address. Google earth had especially good views of both houses. Martin considered that Stephen's would be the easier to enter, the windows were old and the doors were older. One push and they would fold open, easy!

Pictures of family, especially Stephen Byfield's wife and children, and then, also obtained from the magical internet, phone numbers and specific address details, he had the lot. Stored in his computer brain, stored for revenge, they would all die, he just needed to work out what degree of pain to inflict. Chris and Lucy were going to have a very tough time of it!

The big break for Martin however was through the good Colin Method and his Salvation Army contacts who disclosed the precise location of his son, Tom Davies. It was positively amazing what you could find when you were looking for an exact bone marrow donation, as they had been told, and so speedily! Two weeks was all that it had taken, and now it was stored within Martin's brain for later use.

The planning of the last few years had culminated in Martin's readiness for action. He had festered in this shit hole of a prison for long enough. As he had informed Martha, it was time to get out and tonight was the night! Martin waited, playing with the blade in his mouth. Timing was crucial; he didn't want to bleed to death after all! He heard the commotion of the shift change over outside his cell and thought *"Okay folks, show time!"*

Staff coming on for the night shift opened Martin's observation flap to check on him, only this evening they could see nothing. The blood sprayed onto the glass prevented this. Staff cried for assistance and the door was opened. It seemed as though they were wading in a sea of blood! Martin sprawled on his bed, back against the wall and head slumped, blood everywhere and his arms opened up, like the work of a suicidal artist

Health care staff detected a pulse and called a code red on the radio, this was only called so nurses knew someone was bleeding to death. The ambulance was summoned attending under a blue light and Martin's lifeless body was loaded onto the stretcher, handcuffed to a member of staff on each side.

The police were waiting and escorted the ambulance to the hospital which was only a five minute drive from the prison. Everyone of importance was made aware; Stephen was phoned along with the Category A section and the deputy director of custody. No chances were taken.

Armed police awaited the ambulance and Martin was rushed into the resuscitation area of the accident and emergency department. Doctors worked on him for twenty minutes in their efforts to stem the blood flow. Eventually they succeeded, the rumour being that there was not much in it, it had been very touch and go.

Maybe touch and go for the staff, Martin knew exactly what was happening, he kept his eyes closed and waited, his time was near. Although he had lost a lot of blood, he was now being transfused and regaining his strength at a fast rate. He was an old pro at this and knew exactly how much risk he could take. The old scars on his arms testified to this.

CHAPTER THIRTY FOUR

Sally Arnold's alarm clock went off at five thirty that afternoon waking her in time to get ready for her final nightshift of the week. She actually quite enjoyed doing nights, settling the patients with their final medications, dimming the lights and the quietness of the ward after the bustle of the day. No visitors, no porters wheeling patients up and down to theatre or for scans. Just the occasional call bell, and actually time to sit and talk to patients who needed the comfort of another human being. The form filling, low staffing aspect of the day time meant there was rarely time for any interaction with her patients and that is what she had come in to nursing for six years ago.

At twenty four, she was a pretty, bright vivacious girl who always had a sparkle in her eye, and was a favourite of her patients. She was efficient, but caring, everything a nurse should be.

As she got up to shower, her fiancé Jake walked in with a cup of tea for her. They had recently moved in together as they planned for their wedding next year. "Last night darling" he said as he popped the mug down on the dressing table. "I can't wait to have you back in bed with me at night time...I've missed you!" He wrapped his arms around her, gave her a big hug and kissed her. "Silly billy, that's it after tonight, a whole month before I have to do nights again" she replied as she reluctantly pulled away and walked through in to the bathroom.

While she showered and got dressed, Jake cooked her supper. He loved doing this for her before she went to work, it was almost a reversal of traditional roles and made him feel he was supporting her in what was an exhausting time. Night duty wasn't easy for anyone, turning your body clock upside down. As a mechanic, his work was strictly day light hours only and he was usually home around the time Sally had to get up for work.

Dinner finished, Sally put her coat on and gave Jake a quick hug. "See you tomorrow darling, last night for a while. Don't forget next week we're meeting with the caterer for the wedding, have a look through the menu choices she left us and see what you fancy." She kissed him and hopped in to her Ford Fiesta. Jake waved till she disappeared around the corner, shut the door and sat down to look through menu choices. Roll on next year when they would become husband and wife!

Another thing Sally loved about night duty was that there was always a parking space! Sometimes for a day shift, she would have to drive round the car parks three or four times before finding a space, even with a parking permit. She walked in via the accident and emergency department and through to the short stay ward next door.

"Evening Sally, you've got an interesting one tonight!" She was greeted by the day shift staff nurse. "One in from the prison, suicide attempt, nearly succeeded too. Don't know what he's done to be locked up, but he has two guards chained to him at all times!"

"Oh what fun!" Sally replied "That should add some drama to the night". She said good bye to the day shift and set about settling her patients. She allocated herself the prison patient, a Mr Heard, as the staff she had on with her that night were quite inexperienced and she didn't want them scared or falling for any tricks.

Martin lay in the short stay ward next to the accident and emergency department where the lights were dimmed, and the officers handcuffed to Martin settled down for a long night. Martin could feel the changes, could feel a relaxation in the tension around him.

The armed police escort had been stood down, this was looking to be a long drawn out affair and security was purely down to the prison now.

He touched the blade with his tongue, the blade hidden in the skin flap made inside his cheek, an old African trick shown to him by another prisoner in the young offender estate so many years ago. It worked, it was not detectable and it was lethal. It was always present, a weapon at the tip of your tongue.

All he needed now was a young nurse to make a mistake, come too close, show too much Florence Nightingale, not enough common sense. She would wish that she had decided to clean up some drunken spew rather than hope her face could be stitched back together as Martin planned to make her the bride of Frankenstein during the next few minutes.

Then she appeared, checking his blood pressure and ignoring the senior member of prison staff standing at the foot of the bed. The very staff who were here to stop Martin from doing just what he was about to do.

The Prison Officer on his right had changed the handcuff for an escort chain. This was a longer chain attached to Martin on his left wrist and to the officer on his right, as obviously this man was left handed. The chain itself measured a few feet in length, enough for the officer to sit back comfortably during the long night shift.

135

The nurse came close, a pretty little blonde. Martin thought that he heard her name, this was a bonus, Sally! She had a slim figure, she wore a blue surgical top with baggy blue bottoms and somehow she made them look good. She also sounded nice, a friendly almost cheeky tone as she introduced herself to the officers. Come closer my lovely, you may be pretty now but no one will ever look at you again, Martin thought. I hope you have someone who really loves you Sally, it could be a long time before anyone else will have the guts to view my handy work. She would never forget this patient, that is if she lived! Poor Aunt Sally, I am about to knock you down! Martin could feel that special itch and it was about to get a medical scratching.

He could hear some smart arscd comments shared between the officers and her, probably about him, as he lay there, feigning sleep. Then she was there and so was Martin, blade dislodged and ready for action. He felt his arm touched as she took his pulse, not a flinch, just wait, three, two, one and action!

The escort chain was whipped around the young nurse's neck in a heartbeat, the blade out and her left cheek opened up for all to admire. Sally screamed with the pain of the blade slicing through her flesh.

"Ok boys" he said to the two male officers, "Cuffs off, or Florence Nightingale loses both of her eyes!"

He then opened the right cheek; Martin inspected the work, two identical five inch cuts, and gaping open in a lovely juicy style, "Well, what do you say?" he demanded again, brandishing the blood stained razor-blade.

The cuffs came off and Martin was free.

Dragging Sally with him, the blade now to her throat, they both crashed through the back of A and E and out onto the street. A passing car was stopped as Martin stood in the middle of the road in front of it. The driver tried to object, but when one of Sally's eyes was removed with a flick of the blade, the driver threw himself out of his car and was left in the gutter as Martin bundled the now almost unconscious Sally in to the passenger seat before throwing himself behind the wheel and accelerating down the road. A now unconscious Sally flopped against the passenger door, the front of her surgical top dark with the stain of blood running from the gashes on her face and her empty bloody eye socket.

The car disappeared into the traffic and was gone. Martin was gone and all hope for his future targets was fast disappearing.

CHAPTER THIRTY FIVE

Phones rang off their hooks in office blocks across the country. Stephen knew what lay ahead for him, the consequences of a Catagory A escape and unimaginable horror for the politicians. The head of the prison service would certainly face a public enquiry and was probably finished, and Stephen, his career was in serious doubt. But worse still, Stephen knew that this man was aware of every aspect of his life, knew his family, knew his address and wanted them dead. All in all, a terrifying prospect.

Stephen phoned his family, he had to prepare them for the imminent police invasion and he had to get the message through."

Fuck, fuck, fuck, what do I do, I don't want to be here, but I have to give leadership, I want to go home, but the police will cover every aspect, what do I do, tell me , tell me, tell me" he muttered to himself as he dialled his own home number and waited for it to be picked up.

The phone was answered by Tanya,

"Stephen, what the hell is going on? We are been moved, the police are everywhere and the children are crying. I don't even know where we are going. What have you done?"

This was the first time Tanya had questioned Stephen and he felt the doubt climbing through the phone line.

"I'll sort it, just trust me. Go with them and you'll all be safe, I'll get to you when I can".

The phone went dead, Stephen sat at his desk, head in hands. How could this have happened?

The answer came to him in the form of Julia appearing in his office ten minutes later. She stood in front of his desk, not stopping to take a seat.

"Let's get this straight Stephen; you need to understand where the heat is going to fall. I am the one who took this man from the secure hospital which was against the advice of the Prison minister. I just thought we could make a difference. You couldn't have prevented what happened, all protocols were followed. I have taken the blame and today I may need to resign. I could be finished, it was my shout and you are still safe to do your job. Do me proud Stephen, do not let me down. Unfortunately I let you all down badly, the nurse, the staff, all of you. The scars the nurse will wear will haunt my every dream and the fear the staff felt will run the length of my spine for eternity. Can I live with that? I don't know, only time will tell. Good luck Stephen and be brave, you will need to be."

Then she turned and left before Stephen could say a word.

CHAPTER THIRTY SIX

Chris and Lucy sat in the lounge watching Dragons Den when the phone rang. "Hello" said Chris. No answer, the caller had hung up.

"Who was that darling?" Lucy was captivated with two men pitching their idea for a self-cleaning barbeque.

"God knows," he replied, sitting back down. "Wrong number most likely."

A distant dog barked, the bearer of bad news was trying to warn of the coming storm.

An itch was growing, it needed satisfying, and the only way to stop this sat in a room less than twenty yards away. Martin stood in the summer house of the thatched cottage, hammer and chisel in his hand. He had a plan, one that even a top stone mason could not match and the itch to act was overwhelming. He had been out of prison for a matter of hours but couldn't contain himself any longer. He needed to act, he needed vengeance and he would have it tonight.

He stood as the lounge curtains were pulled shut, still some lights on, and movement in the kitchen. Then a blinding light as a car moving slowly up the narrow road turned towards the house. Where the hell did that come from? This wasn't in the plan! He retreated into the darkness of the summerhouse and listened to the faint conversation. He only caught the first few seconds before the door was closed on the dark night.

"Hi Dad"

"Stephen, is everything ok? What are you doing here so late? Are Tanya and the children alright?"

"Let me in and I will tell you. Tanya and the children have been taken into police protection. I don't know where they are at the moment but I will find out in the morning. Let's have a drink, I sure need one, and I will fill in the blanks for you".

Behind the closed door, Stephen and his father moved down the hall and into the kitchen where Lucy was making a cup of tea.

"Dad, things are a bit sticky. I have had a high profile escape, it's the prisoner who has all our details, Martin Heard. I think that he'll be coming for us all. He blames you for all of his problems, and with you comes the rest of us. You need protecting for a few days as I'm sure that he will then make a good get away. Once gone I am positive that he will not want to return, but we do need to be on our guard. I can sort your security out, in fact it is been sorted and that's why I am here."

Chris took a bottle of red from the wine rack and proceeded to open it whilst nodding at Stephen to continue. "Tanya is furious that they are in police protection again but what can I do? It's not exactly my fault. I have arranged the same for you and Mum, they will be here within the hour."

Chris raised his eyebrows but again said nothing. "Just let them do their job, you will have some short term panic alarms and a copper sitting outside the house for a bit. I am sure that it is nothing to be too concerned about". Stephen, who was shattered with all that had happened that day took a large mouthful from his glass of wine.

"Stephen, I am not having any security around our lovely home, I can look after Lucy. I am sorry son, they will all be turned away. Thanks but no thanks."

Stephen could feel his father bristling with anger. He should have known that all offers of help would be rejected.

"Anyway just think about it" Stephen gave a last ditch attempt at persuading his father. "Can I sleep over here tonight? I will drive up to join Tanya and the twins tomorrow; it'll only be an overnight stay. The children will think that it's an exciting adventure hopefully."

"Of course, how the hell did this man get out of your prison? How could that have happened?" Chris couldn't believe someone so dangerous had been allowed to escape.

The story was retold in sorts by Stephen and the violence used to manage the escape was discussed. It would be all over the press soon enough and plans to take a holiday away for a month or two were also bandied about. They could go to a small Greek island for a while, relax, let the police catch this man. After all, for someone with no fixed address to keep at large for any length of time was impossible wasn't it?

A national police operation was underway. A tracker had been employed by the police; this was a civilian survival expert who would guide the police to the areas where characters such as Martin would hide. They would go for food, warmth and to avoid being recaptured, but eventually they would be tracked down just like the chap in Newcastle a few years ago - the one who had killed a policeman to escape. It would be settled within two weeks. If they flew out tomorrow he would text them when it was over.

"Afraid we can't do that Stephen" Chris replied, "we have a number of things planned. If Martin Heard is silly enough to come calling we will deal with that. I will not be terrorised from my own home. Now, let's have another glass of wine and some supper if we still have an appetite."

The summer house door blew shut in the breeze, its occupant long gone.

CHAPTER THIRTY SEVEN

Martin crept out through the fields avoiding the barbed wire which had ripped the bottom of his trousers earlier.

He had picked up the parcel left by Martha behind a bin in a lay-by on the A38. He had asked for clothes and money and he needed to move quickly as he also knew that every ferry port and airport would be on high alert. Martha had left these items and she had also placed some biscuits and a small hand written note. It just said *"Don't forget me!"*

He had long ago changed cars, the vehicle so badly stained with Sally's blood was burning in a country lane and the car that he was driving now was stolen a little later. Two young lovers had the shock of their lives as Martin slammed his hands onto the rear window and they had fled in fear. Martin had allowed them to live, the car was perfect. He figured that he would have around an hour before the police put two and two together.

He found his way onto the M5 and drove for around thirty minutes before stopping at a service station. He made his way around to the hotel at the back where a number of guests were staying the evening - lots of people who wouldn't notice their car was missing for another few hours.

Martin continued into the night in the new car, driving north through to the Scottish borders and on to an old fishing village. He had heard from a Scottish prisoner who he met some time ago that this particular village had a healthy obsession with money which meant they would smuggle anything in or out of the country. This prisoner supposedly worked there and had his own boat or he used to. Martin would take his chance that he had been released and was still around.

The man no longer lived there. A local said that he had sold up and moved to the city. The local, a boat owner himself was interested in what Martin was proposing and at first light the "Endeavour" sailed out and across the Irish Sea, Martin curled up below deck.

By the time the car was found it was just a shell. Martin had left it with the keys in the ignition and the local lads had seen to the rest. It had been spun up and down the hills and glens until it ran out of fuel before it was torched. All in a nights' work for some!

CHAPTER THIRTY EIGHT

The cattle farmer drove his old battered Land Rover around his vast expanse of rented fields which provided plenty of work for a farmer to do. He had noticed a couple of lame cows in the bottom field, they needed an injection of his special drug combo. One shot normally sorted them out, it was shit for everything else, but for bad feet, it was class in a glass.

He drove into the bottom field and was surprised by a scarecrow which stood on a post in the far corner. He couldn't remember seeing this yesterday, and there were no crops to protect. Bloody village kids he thought as he drove over to pull it down, and then stopped. He opened his door and vomited onto the churned mud outside before raising his head and looking again.

A grotesque site greeted him, a slim blond girl, naked apart from the caked blood on her body. Her throat opened up like a dripping red moon and the stake that held her up impaled through her body. She stood there like a vertical hog roast, violently slain, one dark hole where an eyeball once sat, the other eye staring blankly. He could sense the horror of her last seconds, and then the killer touch, a crown of thorns around her matted blond hair, a crown of thorns made with barbed wire

Police combed the area -not a single clue - but they didn't need clues, everyone knew what had happened and they knew that it would happen again. They had to catch this man and stop him. If the police thought that this was a hard task, then Martin had made it impossible. He knew how to vanish, it was a life skill.

With a twenty four hour head start, Martin sat in a Dublin bar, a cold Guinness on the table in front of him. He could have been anyone, he was invisible again. He was teaming up with a travelling fairground which needed a hand, no questions asked. Martin knew the trail would go cold, no one would have a clue as to his location and security could not be maintained on his targets for ever. He had waited years, he could wait a little longer.

CHAPTER THIRTY NINE

Lucy parked her car in the multi-story car park and caught the lift to the lower level of the shopping centre. She enjoyed these self-indulgent days, especially on Fridays with the weekend to look forward to laid out before her. Chris had treated her 'just because she was fabulous!' He felt very blessed to have such a beautiful wife and organised a hair and nail appointment followed by some clothes shopping. He had declined the offer to go with her and instead visited the golf driving range to straighten up his tee shots. Rails of promising designer clothing at discount prices littered every inch of available store space which added to the excitement of the shop.

Lucy looked at her watch. She had ten minutes before her hair and nail appointment, better get a move on. She left the centre and entered the heat of the sun; it was a glorious day, the wall to wall sunshine that had been promised by the weather man the week before. The tattoo shop on her way attracted her attention, she wasn't sure why, but this urge to have a little discreet tattoo on her shoulder had started to appeal to her. Chris would go crazy but she guessed that she could talk him around.

She popped in, "Hi, if I wanted a small tattoo done on my shoulder how much would it cost?" Before she had time to breath a heavily tattooed man had found the ideal design and a spare space in his cluttered diary. She took a deep breath and booked herself in. A tingle of excitement ran through her body as she thought how naughty it made her feel. But fifty pounds seemed a good price and next Thursday she would be a tattooed woman!

Dashing into the hairdressers she considered cancelling the tattoo appointment, but couldn't help talking to the hairdresser all about it. she felt so impulsive, how would she tell Chris? Hair and nails done she felt fantastic as she noticed her reflection in the shop windows as she passed. She looked good, people told her that she had the body of a lady ten years younger and today she was seeing that.

Shopping for clothes was such a hassle when she felt frumpy. Today feeling sassy she whizzed around and purchased a number of figure hugging outfits. An item or two of cheeky underwear and Chris would agree to anything. Trap set!

On the way home Lucy stopped off at the Waitrose supermarket for a few bits for supper and bottle of chilled wine. All Chris's dreams could come true in one evening! She was exciting herself. By the time she pulled back into the drive she was an unstoppable woman and feeling a million dollars Lucy had become a force to reckoned with, this was indeed a perfect day!

Looking from the kitchen window she noticed how fantastic the garden looked in the sunny afternoon, and thought it would be lovely to have Stephen and the family over for a meal that weekend, and she could tease them all about her forthcoming branding! They had all had such a scare over the last couple of weeks with that horrid man escaping, but there had been no sightings of him at all so things needed to return to normal. They couldn't let him affect their lives forever. She sent a text over to Tanya inviting them all; Stephen never seemed to answer text messages. Within a minute an answer popped back, they would love to come over, could this day get any better?

It had been a dream of Lucy's to own a home in such splendid isolation, the nearest neighbour, almost half a mile away at the far end of the leafy lane. The garden completed the perfection of the house, a beautiful four bedroomed thatched cottage. A border of roses and peonies ran along the front of the house and along the side of the gravel driveway, which was entered through a solid five barred gate. An archway entwined with honey suckle led between the double garage and the side of the house through to the back garden where a wide, velvet like lawn, boarded with beds filled with delphiniums, hollyhocks and all manner of plants providing an artist's pallet of colour, spread out leading the eye down to the summer house, positioned at the end of the garden, just before the post and rail fence which separated the garden from the open fields beyond.

When Chris retired from his life working within the social services department it seemed that the three bed semi situated close to the busy A29 road would be theirs for ever. Then unexpectedly, he was left a windfall with the death of his Uncle Jack, a successful trout farmer who made his millions selling fish to upmarket shops. Although they had always been very close, and to some degree Chris had felt like a younger brother to Jack, he could never have expected to be left such a generous amount, enough to buy this dream home, and still have sufficient to buy their only son Stephen a lovely cottage as well. Such a funny feeling, to work hard all your life just to make ends meet, and then at fifty six, suddenly become a millionaire! It took some adjusting to. Good old Jack!

145

With the oven on and supper cooking, she found Chris sitting in the lounge watching Sky Sports golf. It was lovely outside but he was sitting watching golf, typical! She cuddled up to him and pulled out a holiday brochure she had picked up in town. "Sweetheart , shall we look at a nice little spring break for next year?" Chris grunted, he had just watched Justin Rose miss a three foot putt, " Yes, that sounds nice" he replied distractedly.

"But I was thinking about asking Stephen and Tanya if we can take the twins." Chris looked at her and smiled, "That sounds fantastic, let's get on it".

"And I am having a tattoo next week!" Chris looked at her again, this time he didn't smile quite as much.

"That doesn't sound as fantastic, what are you thinking about? Is it a done deal?"

"I will cancel the appointment if you like, I just thought that you would be happy that I am happy!"

With logic like that Chris knew he was beaten and returned to the golf.

CHAPTER FORTY

Stephen sat in his kitchen, life had settled back into some type of routine. It had been two weeks since the escape and the police protection had evaporated in the same manner as always. There was even talk that Martin Heard had managed to flee the country, no clues could be found and his trail had gone cold. Things were strained at home, cracks had developed, but some good news was to follow.

"Stephen, we need to talk". Tanya turned and leaned against the sink, facing him.

"Sure darling, what's the matter?" He looked up from the paper he was reading.

"Do you remember a drunken conversation in Greece over a couple of bottles of cheap local wine and what happened afterwards?"

Stephen sensed what was about to be said. He jumped up and grabbed hold of Tanya and howled, "Am I going to be a daddy again?"

"Sure thing sweetie, confirmed today, no stopping this little bump happening!"

This was a blessing, the best news that had happened for a while and they went to bed that night with their unity restored.

"That bugger nearly broke me" said Stephen "Never ever again, I am so sorry. I was so scared, I nearly lost everything." He pulled Tanya in closer, his hand caressing her slightly rounded belly.

"No you didn't Steven, we are here for the long haul, all five of us."

Paul Parker was waiting in the Governor's office when Stephen walked in the following morning. He was a little taken aback at Paul's cheek. How dare he sit in his office before he had even arrived! He tried not to look pissed off.

"Now Stephen, your way has well and truly failed" Paul began before Stephen had even had a chance to sit down. "Julia has gone, your little Cat A prisoner has gone, and our own Chief Exec has resigned following a request from the Home Secretary. So I think all in all, you are in the shit!" He waited a second before adding "Old son!"

Stephen felt a wave of weariness wash over him, too weak to fight this man, too weak to stand up for himself. Parker knew this, he could smell it. This was his chance and he intended to take it.

"Now Stephen, I think that you know who Julia's temporarily replacement is, my old friend Brian Cox. We served together as officers, we play golf together Stephen, he was my best man! No more bullying from you old son, no more fucking performance management for me. Any questions...... old son?" He walked out without waiting for an answer and sat at his own desk, the smell of victory filling his repulsive nostrils.

One thing that Paul hadn't smelt, hadn't even thought of was the depth of support that Terry would offer Stephen; he had just made the assumption that he would do what most people do, switch alliances. Terry had been in battle before however, and the sound of swords clashing didn't scare him.

The dynamics had certainly taken a temporary shift. This was natural given the escape and the politics practiced by Paul. The very lowest form of management was destabilising the man in charge and Terry despised what he was seeing. He approached Stephen's office.

"Boss, can we talk?" Stephen turned away from his computer screen and faced Terry. He looked tired and somewhat resigned. His confidence had taken a severe knocking over the escape of Martin Heard.

"Sure Terry, we haven't chatted for a while, how are you?"

"Well that's part of the problem Stephen, you used to tell me how I was, you didn't need to ask, you just knew. Now the jam has been taken out of your doughnut! Listen to me, the escape was not your fault, the death was not your fault but this place falling to bits will be your fault boss. Get a grip! We need you leading this prison as you know you can".

Like a bear out of a winter slumber these words soaked into Stephen's foggy brain. He knew Terry was right but should he admit it? Stephen tossed a mental image of a coin in his mind, heads he would take the advice, tails he would ignore it. There it was, heads!

"Terry, you are a man of the highest integrity, and maybe even a mate, and you know what, you are bloody right, I've been a selfish idiot, thinking of myself. Let's get the team together, let's get busy!"

Stephen phoned Brian Cox, and had a long chat around his plans for development and changes within the prison before the team rolled into the office.

"Afternoon all, I need a quick Senior Management meeting as I need to know exactly where we are. I have a visit from Brian Cox next week and I want us all to show him what we're made of and how we've dragged this place in to the twenty first century.

The team fed back, it wasn't all bad, but performance had dipped. Stephen put action plans in place to address all weaknesses and it was great to have him back firing on all cylinders. Paul Parker sat watching, thinking and looking forward to Brian's visit, he was sure it would result in more shit to throw at the boss.

It was as though a phoney cease fire had developed between Paul and Stephen, no sniping, no back chat but Stephen knew what was coming. When Brian Cox was here, Paul was going to open up on rapid fire.

A week later Brian sat in the office with Stephen, the first time that he had done this since his appointment, all other visits having been low key and with Paul.

"Stephen, Julia will come back into this position, she is just on a short break while the investigation happens"

The muffled voice outside of the office stopped the conversation dead,

Paul came busting through the Governors door without even knocking. He ignored Stephen and slapped Brian on the shoulder. Stephen thought that the trap was ready to be sprung and he waited for the venom to leave Paul's nicotine stained fangs, but it didn't come.

Instead, Brian simply said

"Deputy Governor, don't you think that it would be good manners to knock on the door before entering? We may have been talking privately about you, now try again dear boy!"

Paul stood up like a scolded school boy and left. He didn't return, he just sulked his way through the rest of the morning in his office knowing the tide had changed against him.

"I never liked that golf club anyway" Brian joked as he and Stephen got down to business. "Let's talk about your improvement plan, it sounds very good. One more thing, thanks for the phone call last week, I didn't realise what a two faced git that man was! If he continues to be an arse, let's get shot of him, no skin off my nose." And so a mutual respect was born.

Stephen had little sleep thinking about Jeffrey Biscuit and Brian's advice regarding Paul. They were right, he was the common denominator in this problem, the real fly in the ointment. Things had just been so busy that Stephen had failed to see the damage caused. In the milky light of dawn he had a moment of clarity.

The next morning, Stephen phoned Brian Cox and after thanking him for the support shown the previous day he explained that he would have Paul Investigated for his unprofessional behaviour.

"Well done Stephen, I thought for one minute that you hadn't listened to my advice, now sack the little shit".

Still laughing to himself with Brian's words ringing in his ears Stephen asked his PA to request Paul Parker and the Head of HR to attend his office immediately. This would be a meeting without coffee.

The head of HR rushed into the Office,

"Is there a problem Stephen? It sounded important!"

Sue Dickens was out of breath. Stephen had a vision of her dashing to his office at break neck speed.

"Yes I am about to suspend Paul Parker!" He then briefed Sue about what had happened and she quickly phoned the HR help-desk to gain some advice. This was a situation she had not had the misfortune of coming across before in her career in the prison service. "Okay Stephen" she continued once she had come off the phone. "We're on firm ground, they have sent a specimen letter through, and it should be on your email system as we speak".

The system pinged, and there it was.

"Ok just place his name on it. We're charging him for gross misconduct, failure to ensure security, and performances of duties. Other charges could follow, they have also given us a case worker as this looks like it could be a drawn out process". Stephen looked at the documents; it was straight forward. "I'll take notes of the meeting that we are going to have with Paul. It is important that we get this right, we don't want him accusing us of putting words in his mouth". Sue officiously sat at the table with her pad and pen at the ready; she would ensure all procedures were followed to the letter.

Fifteen minutes later Paul Parker arrived at the office, he looked confused when he saw Stephen with Sue. "What's up?" he queried.

"Take a seat Paul" Stephen gestured towards the table and chairs by the door. "We have some concerns that we need to discuss with you, do you want to have anyone present at this meeting?"

"Are you shitting me? No I don't need anyone!" Paul was immediately on the defensive as he sat down in the seat closest to the door, across from Sue.

150

The allegations were spelt out to Paul in all their glory, along with a letter of suspension. Paul sat looking at Stephen and Sue. "You pair of wankers, you are loving this, you bullying bastards. I bet you couldn't wait to see me go!" With that fanfare Paul was escorted from the prison with his day about to get a whole lot worse. As they paraded through the gate complex, it was made clear to gate staff that Mr Parker would not be returning to the prison without the approval of the Governor. Paul made no comment, his face was crimson. In the car park Paul threw his lunch box into the back of the car and as he was closing the door he spotted Terry leaving his car with his sports bag.

"Terry, the fuckers have suspended me, the two faced twats have kicked me out!" He was looking for some support but Terry offered little. He continued to walk past Paul's car towards the gate.

"Oh I see, you are all cozy with the Governor, you don't give a shit, you pompous little prick!" Paul spewed insults in Terry's direction. The bad news for Paul was that Terry realised that this was the one part of the car park not fully covered by CCTV as the camera had gone down last week and was awaiting fixing.

He put down his sports bag, walked back and punched Paul straight in his dirty mouth. Paul fell backwards but Terry wasn't finished yet. He grabbed him by the jacket lapels and pulled him close.

"Listen to me you little shit, I have hated you since the day you arrived, you are a poisonous man who I am glad to see the back of. Now go crawl back under the rock from which you came, and if I ever see or hear from you again, I will not be so gentle!" With that Terry picked up his bag and reported for duty. He strode through the gate and past the Governor's office. "Terry!" It was the Governors voice. Terry stopped in his tracks. He saw Stephen, leaning on his door frame, big smile on his face.

"Paul has left us for a while, I wondered if you would like to be my acting Deputy Governor in the mean time?"

Without a seconds thought Terry agreed. "One thing boss, Paul had a small accident in the car park, no one saw it but will that make any difference?"

Stephen rolled his eyes, "Terry, I don't want to know! Now get into the Dep's office, we have work to do."

CHAPTER FORTY ONE

When thrown out of the prison by Stephen a few weeks ago, Paul Parker had returned to his pokey little flat, a one bedroom place above a carpet shop. He lived alone and had no family that he could count upon; his attitude towards anyone who cared for him drove them away quickly. He was obnoxious to everyone he met, he drank far too much on a regular basis and he had an ability to mess up any relationship he may have had with an unsuspecting lady who usually walked out when his roving eyes and wandering hands were uncovered.

He had rented this place since his enforced move to Marwood and he had given up his last flat although it wasn't much better.

From the first day of his suspension he had picked up the whisky bottle. Although still on full pay, his love for booze and a punt on the horses usually took all his money long before pay day. He could be described as a sad little man.

On more than one occasion he had returned to the flat from the pub with a bruised lip or black eye; the locals disliked him. He had his place in the pub which others would say as far away from them as possible was always the better option. His inability to shut his mouth when drunk normally meant someone else shutting it for him and last night was no different. Only this time they took his wallet and phone. This sad little man had become a joke.

He looked into his mirror and didn't particularly like what he saw staring back at him. Apart from phoning into the prison every morning at ten o'clock as per the conditions of his suspension, he hadn't spoken to anyone else.

The investigation into his conduct was in full flow, the investigating officer was a young female Governor. Paul had thought that he could intimidate her but his plan had failed spectacularly. She was much brighter and a lot smarter than Paul and she had tied him in knots. Before he had even realised what was going on, he had admitted everything.

His full disciplinary hearing date had been set, three weeks away. Stephen was not able to hear it, but was giving evidence against him. A Deputy Director of Custody, Susan Link from the Central region, was the hearing authority and Paul knew that she was mustard. Oh the irony, he had spent his life giving women a hard time and now his fate rested in their hands.

The last three weeks sped past, mostly in an alcoholic blur. He smelt bad, looked ten years older than he was and he arrived for the hearing unprepared. He had asked various old friends to represent him but everyone had declined. The word was out that he was past his sell by date.

The hearing began with Susan Link opening up procedures, everything was being recorded and the lead from human resources was with her offering advice. Susan looked a little pitifully at Paul.

"Mr. Parker, do you have anyone to support you?"

"No Susan, I can do this alone."

He was steam rolled on every point of law and each piece of evidence was proven; he had nowhere to go and he knew it. The biggest kicker for him came when Stephen gave his evidence, he had still hoped that he may be a little sympathetic but not a chance. He gave his evidence slowly and surely, he used the words disloyal a number of times and when summing up Stephen described Paul Parker as the worst member of staff he had ever had the displeasure to work with.

Susan called a break to the proceedings after all evidence was presented; she sat alone for a number of minutes before calling the human resource lead into the office.

Paul was then asked to come back into the room.

"Mr. Parker, I have heard all the evidence presented, do you have any further points that you may wish to raise?"

He didn't, in fact he had given up caring.

"Do you have any mitigation for your actions?"

"Not really, it just didn't work out, I wasn't given a chance."

"You have been given a number of opportunities to progress and develop while working within the Prison Service but you have failed to grasp these. I find all the charges against you proven and as a result the only punishment that is available to me is dismissal. This is with immediate effect."

"No surprise!" Paul knew he was finished.

"I will send you the appeal paperwork Mr. Parker; you may wish to contest my decision."

He thought for a second, he was done, sacked. He also knew an appeal was futile, no point at all.

Head still fuzzed from the booze from the night before, he couldn't think of one sensible comment to make, but suddenly found tears in his eyes.

"Susan" he stood as he spoke, "please reconsider, I will do anything to keep my job". He found he was crying uncontrollably, "Please Susan!"

She stood and collected her belongings, then looked up at the pathetic man stood in front of her.

"You have had too many chances Paul, you are a liability".

And with that his career was over. He returned home, a two hour train ride. He looked around at the young people sat near him. They were all chatting either to each other or on mobile phones to friends or family, their lives still in front of them. He caught the smell of an unwashed body and looking around he realised that he was smelling himself. How had his life come to this point? How could he have behaved in this manner? He was a horrible man and he knew it, he had nothing, he had never had anything and it was nobody's fault but his own.

He looked at his reflection in the train window. He looked and felt seventy, he was dying in front of his own eyes. The train pulled in to his station and with a heavy tread, he walked down the street, past his flat and into the pub.

CHAPTER FORTY TWO

The family sat in the sun, children running in and out of the summerhouse, BBQ hissing and spitting. With the continued good weather, Chris had pulled out all the stops, dinosaur burgers for the children and some little skinny sausages that they loved to put in a bun, curly fries were in the oven and small bottles of cherryade so full of E numbers they would fly home! They had also prepared four large T Bone steaks from the local farm shop which were glazed in his specially made secret recipe BBQ sauce.

White wine and fizz chilled in the freezer while the tall glasses held by the ladies never seemed to empty. Cider cans for the boys, so cold they almost frosted their fingers; it was simply a perfect afternoon. It was soon noted however that Tanya's tall glass was filled with non alcoholic elderflower sparkling water.

"Are you not drinking today Tanya?" asked Lucy

"I can't really, I'll stay on the water."

" Tanya, is there something you want to tell us?" Lucy persisted

"Maybeee" she replied, glancing at Stephen. "Early days yet!

The garden erupted and corks popped as Lucy and Chris delighted in the news of a third grandchild.

The smell of the meat wafted across the lawn as Lucy prepared the salad and as she topped it off with a sprinkling of pine nuts, four massive king prawns were butterflied and laid on the grill, garlic butter drizzling from the shells.

They eagerly ate these as another tall glass was refilled.

"You know that you can all stay over this evening, we have nothing arranged for tomorrow" Chris suggested.

"I think that we will Dad" said Stephen, "Is that ok with you sweetheart?"

Tanya nodded, "I thought that this may happen, I know my Stephen, once the BBQ starts and the booze comes out. Just in case I popped a small overnight bag in the car!"

Stephen howled, opened a cold cider and chased the children. They ran in and out of the summerhouse, around hedges and back again.

Soon they were all sprawled out on sun loungers, fit to bust. A couple of chicken legs lay on the grill looking slightly lonely, the twins put them out of their misery and gobbled them up as they continued to dance and charge around the manicured lawn.

Two bones went whizzing over the rear fence, it was too late for Stephen to say anything so he just lay and baked in the sun...a perfect end to a perfect day.

CHAPTER FORTY THREE

Terry woke up late for work, the alarm had not been set. He felt grumpy and his mood seemed to match the leaden sky which had replaced the glorious sunshine of the previous day. He could see through the window the persistent rain he had listened to all night. He wasn't sleeping well at the moment, nothing was on his mind, he just couldn't settle.

He padded downstairs and into the kitchen, the dishes that he had asked Tom to clear up as a brief alternative to playing X Box were still sat there smelling of the curry Jo had prepared the evening before. A flash of temper flew through his head. "Tom, don't forget the dishes" He called out, not expecting any reply, "Your only job was to put them in the dishwasher" he then heard himself say "Lazy bastard", very softly but it was building. The rage that had come and gone throughout his adult life was building up for eruption.

Terry fully knew the script, he would keep finding things wrong, small things, things that didn't matter, a pair of shoes left to trip over, recycling left for him to sort out, bloody X Box games everywhere, then he was in full flow. "Get your backside down here, I am not your slave, you get these things cleaned up immediately!"

Here we go, full flow again, third time in as many weeks, the last time had been about the TV not tuning itself in properly. Pathetic really but he seemed to be less able to control these abrupt mood swings.

Jo lay in bed listening to the tornado approaching back up the stairs, "Get down there now and sort it!" Terry opened Tom's door, "Look at the state of this tip. My bloody God, sort it out!" The tornado continued to twist and turn as Terry closed Tom's door with a bang and thundered back into their bedroom. "Terry calm down sweetheart, I will make sure it's sorted, you just get yourself ready for work" Jo pleaded as she watched him with concern. There was no stopping it as he banged and crashed toiletries around the en-suite bathroom. Not until he had showered and sat on the bed to pull his socks on did the storm abate.

"Sometimes I worry myself Jo, I just blow, it's like I can't stop it building up, and it's getting more intense the older I get". He gave her a rueful smile; "I am glad you know me so well sweetheart, I don't know why you put up with me!"

Jo turned over in the bed, she was beginning to wonder if she did know this man sometimes. It was as if a switch were flicked for no reason at all, but she would stay supportive, she loved him to bits and knew there had to be a reason for these mood swings. She didn't know how to raise the subject with him and sometimes she felt as though she was walking on egg shells, Terry was such a tough man with a strong character. Nothing could knock him down, but this, this worm in his brain was trying its best.

She though that he may be under pressure from work, or that money issues so close to retirement may be haunting him. She thought a lot of things but she was way off target. He leaned over and kissed her goodbye. "Sorry I'm a grumpy old git!" he smiled ruefully as he left the bedroom.

He climbed into the car and thumped the wheel, 'Why have I started the day so badly? There was no reason to be so cross with the world' and so he pondered his own thoughts all the way to the prison.

Terry's mood had lifted slightly as he arrived at work. He stopped off in Stephen's office and had a quick chat before phoning Jo, "Sorry sweetheart, I just woke up in a bad mood, but Tom still needs to tidy that pit of a bedroom! I'll see you both this evening."

"I wish that you were here, you will never believe what just happened, I walked into the kitchen and there was a massive spider, the size of a dish! I nearly screamed my head off!"

"What did you do, apart from scream of course?"

"Tom raced down, he picked it up and put it outside, and guess what, he spotted the dishes and sorted them straight away, it took twenty seconds, so you need not worry your head my darling!"

They both laughed, "Okay, back to work then, see you later." Terry replaced the receiver feeling better. These moods seemed to go as soon as they came. His phone rang again almost immediately, it was Stephen.

"Terry, we have a 'Veterans In Custody' meeting today at ten o'clock, all prisoners who were in the armed forces are invited, I hoped you could attend on my behalf".

"Of course, how many veterans do we have? I only know of three or four" Terry replied as he mentally went through those he could remember.

"Twenty four Terry, an amazing number! Feed back to me after the meeting as I'm interested in what comes up. Most are Iraq and Afghan vets, but some are Northern Ireland and Falklands, just like you mate!"

Just after ten o'clock, he sat surrounded by a group of likeminded souls, all former service people, many of whom had fallen on hard times and were in custody through their resulting circumstance, drinking, drugs, homelessness and desperation. The stories were very similar, discharged or thrown out of the army, the only family they really knew, having experienced scenes so horrific that they couldn't discuss them, along with the accompanying visions which kept them awake at night. A number had triggers which powered thoughts through their heads for no reason, speeding them into despair, depression and beyond. All had friends who had taken their lives when discharged, strong proud men crushed and reduced into rummaging through skips to find food to stay alive.

One man told his tale, tears flowing from his eyes as he spoke of his lovely family, his beautiful wife and two children, left at home to fend for themselves, all because of one stupid night. A night that he could never erase from his mind, one stupid argument, one stupid punch because his temper had boiled over and countless lives ruined, a man with medals for bravery in both Afghanistan and Iraq, a Captain in the Parachute Regiment, a leader of men. Everything was gone because he had lost his temper and killed a man with a single punch. Lost his temper and he didn't even know why it had happened. It was only later that Combat Stress told him that war had made him like this; he was suffering PTSD, he was ill, not criminal. Why hadn't he been helped earlier? Why had he been allowed to roam the streets like a weapon with a defective safety catch, where was his help?

Terry listened and realised that the man speaking wasn't the only one crying, he wiped his eye and hid the evidence.

He hurried back to speak with Stephen after the meeting. It was all now blindingly obvious what was happening to him. "Mate, I need help, everything that has happened to me is biting me firmly on the arse! I'm reliving the bloody Falklands on a daily basis and it can't go on." He explained his feelings and the loss of temper for no reason, he explained the sleepless nights and his despair that appeared like a thunder cloud on a summer's day.

Stephen listened, he said nothing as Terry spoke but he listened and understood and a trust and brotherhood were formed that day. Within a week Stephen had arranged help for Terry. It was their secret as apart from the counselor no one else knew of Terry's weekly meetings.

CHAPTER FORTY FOUR

The dirty smell of diesel seemed to coat Martin Heard from head to toe. He gagged as the boat hit another large wave. Life in a small Irish fishing boat was no fun. This little thirty footer was stuffed with fishing gear and stinking water and like a filthy little green cork, it bounced from one wave to another. Martin sat on an upturned fish crate, his backside was numb, but there was no space for him to stand. He was jammed into a small corner and he was taking valuable fish storage space. This meant a loss of profit, something not lost on the crew as they reminded Martin on every available opportunity, and these were hard men. He had paid a lot of money to sail back unnoticed to the UK and he had the feeling that these fishermen would have rather tossed him overboard as crab bait, so he just shut his eyes and waited to hit the coast.

It was a journey that seemed to know no end, hour after hour spent on natures roller coaster, until at last a voice shouted down to him,

"How you doing down there mate?"

"How much longer?"

"We are coming into harbour now, we are stopping over in the port of Weymouth. That's your cue to jump ship!"

The relief was fantastic, Weymouth was a shock though, he thought they were heading to the Scottish coast, but no drama, it didn't matter.

The boat chugged into port, He took a peek, colourful houses and shops came as a pleasant sight and the smell of fresh air was a blessing. As he jumped out on to the jetty, the smell of lunchtime fish and chips drove him wild but no time to eat, he needed to leave this bit of paradise quickly.

He left the harbour and headed to the train station, around a fifteen minute walk and well sign posted. It was good to stretch his long legs, and to see that no one paid him the slightest bit of attention. The six months between his escape and his return to England had diminished the publics memory of the incident and his horrific crimes but he didn't want to risk the chance of someone recognising him, hence the longer hair and well established beard. He took an old scrap of paper from his wallet, Martha's address and number. He just hoped she was still in the Martin Heard fan club. He had sent her one letter from Ireland with instructions for his return but had supplied her with no return address.

He phoned her, three rings and it was picked up,

"Hello?"

"Hi it's me, just getting onto the train, is everything in place?"

"Martin, it's great to hear from you! I received your letter so I have two weeks leave booked; we have the place to ourselves! I have drawn out some money for you, is four hundred pounds going to be enough?" Martha sounded genuinely pleased to hear his voice.

"Perfect, expect me when you see me." Martin replied thinking she was one of the more useful contacts he had made. "And I have some clothes for you, I also have a little surprise, hope you don't mind?" Martha continued unwilling to let him go now he had made contact at last.

"As long as it's a good surprise, as you may have gathered, I'm still a wanted man! I just need a couple of hours sleep and I am good to go."

"Oh good, see you soon". Martha put the phone down feeling like a giddy school girl. Her infatuation with Martin had seriously clouded her judgement, and she had blocked the atrocities he was capable of from her mind. He wouldn't harm her any way, he loved her, surely? Why else would he risk coming back to see her?

Martin put the phone into his pocket. He knew that she was a nice lady and if he had the emotional ability, he would have felt a little guilty about how this would end. They were similar in many ways, both rejected through their lives, both feeling that they didn't belong. Oh well, he thought callously, business is business!"

The journey was hazardous; Martin's profile had been splattered around the world, a serial killer on the loose with wanted posters stuck in airports and train stations. He needed to be low key, pay for the journeys with cash and no disagreements with petty ticket collectors or gobby teenagers. He put his hood up, pretended to be asleep and ensured that his face was covered from curious gazes. This proved harder than it seemed as Martin didn't smell too good. The trip in the fishing boat had left its own scent on him! At least he had a seat by himself, but that made him more noticeable, which was not good.

The train stopped at Birmingham and he had to change trains and platforms to continue. He had around twenty minutes before getting onto a much slower branch line train so took the opportunity to buy a cheap pair of jeans, a fresh tee shirt and another hooded top. The rest would be ok, he still smelt, but not of an Irish fishing boat, he could pass as a labourer on his way home. He boarded the next train and hood pulled up he searched for a good seat. The train was filling up, not the best prospect but people were too distracted with their own insignificant lives to start thinking about last month's Crime watch or a poster campaign that had torn and faded in the elements.

He propped himself by the window with a sliding door that kept opening and closing behind him and slightly to his right. The air coming through would help disguise some of his bodily smells, although the squirt of deodorant and fresh clothes had seemed to work their magic. A young black lad, around sixteen years old flopped into the seat next to Martin, he had ear phones on and was listening to music, loud music. Not a glance was exchanged. Absolutely perfect, thought Martin, no contact no chat. He looked up at the electrical display screen showing which stations the train would stop at. He counted seven names before his station flicked onto the rolling screen. The old diesel train pulled out, engine complaining with screeches and rumbles as it passed through the city outskirts and into more rural areas.

The graffiti on the bridges had stopped, must be a better class of area mused Martin and as the bumpy line occasionally threw his head left and right. Through half closed eyes he noticed that the passenger numbers had fallen. Rap boy was gone, he hadn't even seen him leave. He had a free seat beside him so no prying eyes to spot his face. The train rumbled on, Martin was unsure as to what would happen when he arrived but he trusted Martha to have not alerted the police. Too many awkward questions if she had, for example, why had she placed four hundred pounds into his account and how did he know her address?

He wasn't going to have sex with her either, memories of her fat white body didn't exactly fill him with anticipation. He would play the tired card and promise to perform in the morning. You never know, he may even manage to get an erection, after all it had been a while.

The train continued through the corridor of grassy embankments and then the sight of open fields and cows followed. "Tickets please!" The conductor walked down the row of seats. He reached Martin and took the ticket from his outstretched hand. Martin heard the ticket clipped and placed back into his dirty grip, hardly a second glance and not a word spoken, perfection!

The train jolted to a squealing stop, Martin looked through the window and realised that this was his station; he jumped out and gained his bearings. There were no ticket collectors at the gate and Martin was able to walk straight through. He passed the small commuter car park, around twenty cars with parking permits on the windscreens and then into the lane that ran left to right from the station entrance.

Notices outside offered fun days out in London or Birmingham, tickets two for the price of one, summer specials to visit the London Dungeons or the wax works. A local lad had brightened the place up with the obligatory scribble, 'Birmingham FC, shit on the Villa!'

Even in such a lovely place as this village, petty people still want to mess things up. He thought that it might be fun to catch this person in the act, Martin had met them before. They were the type who would urinate on him as he slept in a shop doorway, or try to steal the few pennies that he had begged for one final shot. He hated them with a vengeance; it made him feel itchy for retribution, but all in good time.

From Martha's text it was clear that he needed to turn right into the lane and continue down the one road. He didn't want the circus of her turning up to meet him, people could see that and it would have been out of the ordinary. Even though this was rural England, CCTV still ruled. The hood stayed up and he strode off.

Forty minutes later he was there, a sweet little house, a semi-detached red brick with an established wisteria climbing its way across the front above the upstairs window. He had phoned her again an hour before he arrived and he knew she was very excited at the thought of seeing him. It really was a shame she was just a pawn in his game, maybe he'd put a bit of effort in to ensuring her last few days on this earth were some she would remember in her after life! He walked briskly up the path, it had been a two mile walk from the train station and it would seem that he was a forgotten man. No one paid him the slightest bit of attention so he would enjoy this while it lasted. It was amazing what the public forgot in the short space of six months, six months of him travelling in the back of beyond working the fairgrounds of the Irish Republic. His longer hair and stubbly beard finished the more rugged disguise.

The door opened as he reached the door step and Martha stood there in casual cloths, a massive smile on her face. "I have been so excited, I couldn't wait!" She flung her chubby little arms around him and hugged him around his waist. "Phew, you stink of something, not sure what it is, get upstairs and shower. I have surprises, and your longer hair and little beard, they suit you!" She gabbled as she pulled him in to the hallway and shut the door

"Is it Rolos?" Martin asked as he glanced around the small space, eying up his accommodation for the next few weeks.

"No you cheeky bugger, now get up those stairs!"

He took off his dirty trainers and Martha took them at arm's length and plonked them straight into the outside bin. He then walked upstairs followed by Martha chattering excitedly behind him. He stripped and climbed into the shower, the hot water cascading down his aching fish scented body. It felt fantastic and he briefly allowed himself to relax and enjoy this basic pleasure. His grubby socks and boxer shorts followed the fate of the trainers.

He could have stayed in the shower all afternoon but no chance with Martha around.

"You must be shattered" she said as she poked her arm round the door with a fresh towel. I've made up a nice bed, you get some sleep and I'll wake you at six. I have something planned for this evening!"

This was good news for Martin, he felt very wanted, in fact he was starting to rather like Martha. She had made him feel very special. What a predicament, he never trusted those who were kind to him, in his experience it had never lead to anything good.

Sleep quickly overcame him, a long blissful sleep. For the first time for as long as he could remember Martin relaxed, let down his defences and succumbed to the comfort of a soft down duvet and pillow.

He was woken by a gentle voice whispering in his ear. He opened his eyes, Martha was sitting on the bed, "Wake up sleepy head, it's six o'clock."

This domesticity was getting surreal and it was going to get a whole lot worse.

Martin yawned and sat up, "So, what's this surprise of yours? I'm intrigued!"

"Don't be cross, but I had something booked for this evening and if I hadn't gone, my friends would have come around here to see where I was and I didn't want that yet, so it was easier just to go."

"Go where?" Martin asked

"Salsa dancing!"

Martin couldn't quite believe his ears. Was this woman for real? After the care he had taken to protect his identity during the trip here, it was madness to expect him to attend such a public event. She surely didn't expect him to go with her? But Martha did. In her excitement of having a "boyfriend" for the first time in her life, she had been unable to stop herself from mentioning the fact to the friends she attended the dance class with.

"I was thinking about what you said in your letter, about needing to have somewhere to stay for a couple of weeks without being recognised. Sometimes the best disguise is to be there where people least expect you. I've told my friends you are staying for a while so we won't be disturbed. Once they have met you tonight as my boyfriend, no one will think twice about that being what it is. You look so different anyway, everyone just thinks that we are together, they are happy for us and not in the slightest suspicious".

Martin thought about his options. Who would ever think that he would be right under their noses with one of the governors from the very prison he had escaped from? Besides, the sheer absurdity of him, the infamous Martin Heard attending a salsa dancing class with one of his victims appealed to him in some perverse way. "I'm not happy, but I can see the benefits to your story for us being undisturbed for the next couple of weeks" he told her, "let's do it."

Martha's surprise didn't end there however. Martha left the room to go downstairs to prepare something for them to eat before going out and Martin climbed out of bed and looked around for his clothes. His jeans and tee shirt weren't in sight but on the chair were a pile of men's clothes and lots of them, in all colours. He didn't see one thing that he liked; they looked like the clothes worn by someone who would find Martha attractive!

He got dressed - red cord trousers and a flowery patterned collared shirt; he couldn't have made this shit up! The glow of appreciation on Martha's face as he came down the stairs said it all, he knew he looked a complete freak, but what a great disguise – anyone looking for Martin Heard would not give him a second glance! And off they went, Martha's Ford Focus trundling down the road on the way to pick up Nathan and Trisha, her dancing partners.

Introductions were made, apparently Martin and Martha had met on line, he was a builder from Kent here for a couple of weeks; she had made him learn the script before they left.

Nathan gave Martin the once over as they got out of the car,

"Hi mate nice to meet you at last, Martha has been chatting about you for months! I was beginning to wonder if you even existed except our Martha here has had such a spring in her step since she met you! Have you danced before?" Nathan was oblivious to the fact he was conversing with one of the country's most notorious serial killers

Martin confirmed that he was a novice and in fact hadn't danced for a long time. The couple seemed very nice; they didn't give him any cause for concern and just seemed happy that Martha was so content at last. They posed no threat to him...they would live.

Throughout the evening Martin remembered that he was the long distance boyfriend and carried on with this make belief. He held her hand and kissed her when he thought others may be watching, he gave nobody reason to doubt that he was a bricklayer from Kent.

The dance class took part in a village hall; there were only seven people present plus the instructor, so only a few strangers to deal with. Martha was very keen to be involved so he was spun and twisted for the next hour. He hurt, he was aching, he was sweating like a pig, and he was happy! The session had been a total hoot, he was a natural and Martha and her friends were actually fun. For the first time in the last seven years Martin felt content. How unexpected.

"All aboard, Nandos next stop!" Martha instructed as they piled in to the car like a bunch of students. The short drive to the town took less than ten minutes, he was so hungry following all that exertion and confident in his anonymity Martin was happy to continue the charade.

They huddled around the table, chicken in different flavours and degrees of heat were presented and dispatched, gallons of soft drinks were swallowed and the ice cream factory took a big hit.

The car drive back home took a little longer, it was carrying at least another two stones in weight and again the car was filled with the sound of laughter. Martin was even getting used to people taking the piss out of him, he was actually enjoying people poking fun at him, the fact that he didn't need to react with violence, the fact that it was friendly felt refreshing, the burden of having to get the retaliation in first had gone. There was no expectation that he had to teach someone a lesson for disrespecting him; it was the first time in his deprived and depraved life that he had experienced normality

Soon they were back at Martha's, just the two of them having dropped Nathan and Trisha back home. They fell through the door, Martha giggling with happiness and kissed, kissed because Martin wanted to kiss, not because he was playing the role of loving boyfriend. They carried on upstairs and in to bed where they made love, not the cruel sex of in his cell but the coupling of two people who cared for each other. Momentarily Martin loved this life, he was wandering in an alien environment, a land of love and caring, something he had never before experienced.

The feeling that Martin had hoped would last forever lasted another ten minutes, then it was gone. As Martha lay next to him in an innocent replete sleep, the voice in his head that popped up like a voice from sat nav, was back and it was directing him loudly. It cautioned the kindness that had been shown; it instructed him to treat this with mistrust. 'You are about to be hurt, make a U turn when possible.'

Then a cruel thought cut through the fog of the evening, it was a very clear thought, it swept over every inch of his body. It warmed him, it smoothed his brow, it embraced him, it was his real lover, the evil within. '*Remember who you really are dancing boy!*'

CHAPTER FORTY FIVE

They awoke the next morning, the violent, insistent voices in Martin's head having eventually let him fall in to a deep dreamless sleep. The bedside clock told them it was eight thirty.

"Are we alone for the next two weeks Martha?" Martin enquired as the voice of the last night stirred in his head.

"Yes we are, have you anything planned?" she asked coyly

"I do have one surprise, I just hope that you like it!"

Martha giggled and ran to the bathroom in anticipation of a repeat of the sex they had the evening before. Martin checked his bag, the tools were there, the Birmingham shopping centre had been a godsend.

Martha crashed back into the bedroom.

"TADAAAAA" she shouted in circus fashion with her arms held wide, before noticing the bed was empty. She glanced round in confusion as Martin appeared from behind her and plunged the needle into her plump white neck. Darkness and unconsciousness swept over her instantly.

Martha came too, a thundering pain in her hands and feet. She was very groggy and confused and in a world of pain, a shuddering pain.

Martin viewed his DIY handy work, Martha was screwed to the upturned oak kitchen table, large screws had been drilled through her hands and feet thus attaching her firmly to the wood of each leg. It felt horrific to Martha, it looked lovely to Martin.

He took a CD from his bag and slipped it into the player on the bench. What a lovely touch…. Roxy Music, all the greatest hits!

Martin danced around the kitchen as he spoke to Martha,

"Martha, I love to torture, I love to kill and I do love terrifying people! Today I am going to do all three!"

Martha was drifting in and out of consciousness, "Why Martin, why me? I thought you loved me."

"That's the kicker Martha, I don't fucking know, I guess that you were just too kind, I hate kind people." He spun his body around the shiny tiles, the tiles that were about to be awash with blood. The pain was intense, but still Martha battled, she just hoped that she could make him stop,

"Martin, I just don't understand" she sobbed, "Who are you really? I don't understand, I would have given you everything."

He pulled up a hard wooden kitchen chair and straddled it, the high back of the chair facing Martha. "Who am I? Please let me explain. You know me as Martin Heard, a bit of a rogue, your misunderstood bit of rough. I am in fact Martin Heard the vigilante, some say psychopath. I was left to fend for myself since my junkie mother was hacked to death in our home, a home filled with drug addicts, a home where apparently I could be abused for the price of a fix, and believe me she had hundreds of fixes.

Left on a blood soaked floor at four years old, maybe younger, telling mummy to wake up, but knowing that she couldn't. They never found the killer, I did hear that the police hardly bothered to look, after all, she was just a dead junkie. And then the joy of care, I was fucked stupid for years, but then again it felt normal. At least these people smelt clean, I could smell the soap and the aftershave those monsters wore.

And when I became old enough to realise that old men shouldn't be doing these things to me, I ran away.

That's when the violence kicked in, beaten daily. Apparently by the age of thirteen I had suffered one hundred and thirty nine placements, all failed. I spent the last three years before running away in a home as no one else would take me. I was told that I wasn't a bad boy, there was just something different about me, I guess now it would be called multiple personality disorders, or in short I was nuts. I knew this, but I also knew that I was bad, pure evil, I'd been told that enough times in my life! The kinder you are to me, the more I want to hurt you, hence your predicament at the moment. You were very kind, lovely in fact."

Angel eyes from Roxy Music played, and Martin sang along for a few moments.

"Oh yeah, where was I? I grew up, met someone , lost them, lost a child, you know every day shit, boring. My one chance of having normality, stripped away by that fucking Stephen Byfield's father, which left me alone. A child ripped from my grasp. They broke two of my fingers taking that beautiful baby away from me, a child who now lives in a stranger's family showing school photos to uncles and aunties, a fucking made up family, State sponsored child theft! The child was mine, that life should have been mine, and the bastard Byfield took it from me. And then my angel, the girl I wanted to grow old with took her life, she couldn't live with the loss of our child, couldn't live with the thought that she had failed a young innocent child. She lay on a urine covered stinking car park floor, spewing and convulsing in agony. Then she died in my arms. Fucking Byfield, honestly, I will gain some comfort from his family's deaths, they will be slow, painful, but very, very worthwhile!

169

Oh excuse me, I have digressed! But when did Martin Heard turn into a cold killer? That is a good question. My first victim was a thirty plus year old junkie, living in the city centre multi story car park, second floor. On the first floor was Lisa, an alcoholic who hated everyone, the second floor was ours. Then one day, after I had an especially cold, wet bad day, I decided that I was jealous of a man who I didn't even know personally, he used to buy drugs with me, but he was cleaning himself up and I couldn't. He had a place booked in a hostel, I had nothing and worse still, he had a family who loved him and wanted to help him. They kept coming looking for him and offering all kinds of support whereas I had nothing. So all in all, Mr unknown victim had the world at his feet. I just ended up with his dead body at mine. I killed him with a single stab wound, and nobody cared, no one looked for the killer, no one even spoke to me about it. I even went to his funeral; I sat there at the back with five other people sitting crying at the front. I guess they were the family, and I felt good. So I just stole his future from him, I guessed if he had everything, it might just be my turn to have his luck. Of course it didn't happen, but so what? And then I acquired a taste for death, and using people, yet again hence your discomfort, and here I am! I guess I am in the last years of my life, in my thirties and people want me dead, how the very fuck dare they?" Martin let out a sardonic laugh and pushed the chair over, he was done with talking.

He threw a glass of water into Martha's face, "Stay awake sleepy head, look what I can do with my new drill!" He went to work on her knee caps, an hour of home improvements later and the job was done, she had lasted for thirty five minutes before death took her away from the show. This had disappointed him, but still, he finished the job in style. When this one was found in two weeks time, hopefully by Byfield, he would appreciate the hard work and effort needed to present such a work of art. In the meantime, this house would make a good temporary base. How stupid was he to have thought even for a second there was a normal life for him....that was never going to happen to someone with such a thirst for revenge!

CHAPTER FORTY SIX

Stephen sat in his cottage garden, a small inflatable pool had been blown up for the children, and it sat nicely on the freshly cut lawn, its blue and white pattern stood out boldly from the lush green grass. Although it was still only spring, the water cast sparkling images as the unseasonal sun shone through it, reflecting from the plastic bottom, a pool now showing the signs of grass cuttings as the children dashed in and out. A couple of buckets of hot water from the kettle had made it bearable when the twins had insisted on getting the pool out so early in the year.

The last of the spring flowers in the bed bordering the patio looked and smelt delicious, the three steps leading down to the grass were made from the local stone and had cost Stephen and Tanya an absolute packet. Established shrubs flanked the borders and led down to a small orchard, a mazy path leading the way. The twins thought that the garden was magical with its hidden nooks and crannies between bushes and the fruit trees. Tanya's mother 'Granny' had told them that there were fairies that lived at the bottom amongst the raspberry bushes and they spent many afternoons down there looking for them. Stephen's father 'Papa' had promised them a tree house in the large oak which offered shade to the left of the lawn. He had recently bought the wood for this and it lay to the side of the garden shed, waiting for Stephen and Chris to begin the construction. It may have been magical, but it took a lot of effort to make it this nice. It was a real labour of love for Stephen and Tanya and her mum most weekends, just not this one.

The leafy trees towards the bottom of the garden stood around fifty meters from the patio, a nice size, and a good reason for them to buy the house, it was a real selling point.

Apples, cherries, plums and pears had grown in abundance, the crop was fantastic again last year and the fruit bowl had overflowed. The children loved to scamper down and ask Mummy or Daddy to lift them up to pick fruit; it was their little paradise, almost the ideal home. Maybe the one that they would settle in, but Martin Heard's knowledge of the address had taken some of the shine from the place, which is why it was only almost ideal.

To the back of the garden stood fields, stretching far in to the distance until they came up against the foot of the Chiltern Hills sitting in a blue haze against the horizon. There was one small farm house a few hundred yards away with the sound of a tractor chugging away as it moved feed amongst the fields of cows surrounding it. Today, not a cloud could be seen in the sky as they lay on the sun loungers sipping long cold drinks, what could be more perfect? This time last year it had been snowing! Even the advancing baby bump looked happy, ripples of joy could be seen every time the baby moved, another few weeks and this peace would be shattered for a while, but in the best way possible!

Stephen looked at Tanya as she lay in her bikini top and shorts, new sun glasses resting lightly on her perfect face. He looked and couldn't stop looking, she was perfect. He was such a lucky man, nothing and nobody would take that away, not even that monster Martin Heard where ever he may be hiding.

CHAPTER FORTY SEVEN

Martin sat in the lounge of Martha's house, he was growing tired of the smell coming from the kitchen, but knew that at least one willing victim would be coming from the prison to see why little Martha was skiving.

They would just find her hanging around minding her own business! He was growing a little bored of this house as well, itching to get out and find some fun, whatever that entailed. He had spent a couple of days on another project which was also coming to fruition, but all the waiting for action was wearing thin. Checking on the calendar on Martha's computer he estimated that her two week holiday was due to end tomorrow and when she failed to turn up they would phone. When they receive no answer some prison screw would visit and try to huff and puff the door down. They wouldn't have to try too hard because the kitchen door was open, just a little push and in they would pop.

He planned through what he might do to the unlucky visitor, if he did anything in fact. It may be in his interest to leave now and get a head start on everyone again, but that would not be fun, and he had prepared some toys that needed to be used, he might as well just stay put.

The letter box rattled and Martin looked through the netted curtains, it was the postman and as he disappeared back down the road Martin picked up the mail. One from the bank, one from Virgin Media and a two for one offer from a local Pizza shop. Boredom made him open the bank letter, it was a statement and he saw she was a rich little bitch with over one hundred thousand saved in this account. He searched for her cards and soon found a purse with a couple of twenty Pound notes, some small change and a host of plastic cards. She had also been a silly girl, in the back of the card holder she had left a four digit number, her P.I.N for the bank card.

Martin drove out leaving the ruins of Martha's life behind. He had used her car a few times and it was spotless inside and smelt a lot fresher than the house. He had placed his own insurance policy inside the glove box, just in case of a rainy day. He headed for the nearest town and soon found a bank where he tapped the numbers in and out came the cash. He tried twice and received two hundred and fifty pounds each time. Pocketing the money and card he headed back to the car, stopping at the nearest supermarket to buy a few items for the evening meal, nothing that needed to be cooked, even he couldn't stand too long in the kitchen. He bought cooked chicken breast and some pasta salad which would do for his last night in the house.

He was concentrating as he drove around looking for the signs that led back to the village when suddenly a blue flashing light appeared in his rear view mirror, and the police car overtook him and showed him the police stop sign on the rear window of the car. Martin took the large knife from the glove box and placed it under his seat. The policeman appeared to be alone, if he asked too many questions he would have to die.

He sat watching as the young police office walked towards him, he was taking note of the registration number and spoke into his radio. He stood for a second while the answer was relayed to him. He then came closer, five paces, three paces and then a tap on the window. Martin pushed the button to slide the window down.

"Yes officer, how can I help?"

"Is this your car sir?"

Martin thought for a second, "No it belongs to my girlfriend, she is not well so I have been sent out to buy provisions, no rest for the wicked!"

"What address is it registered to sir?"

"I'm not sure, it's in a village called Cum-Stanley. There is only one road, sorry I don't know what it's called"

"Or what number it is?"

"No I'm afraid I don't, I just drive in and out, sorry!"

"Can you take the keys out of the ignition please sir and step out of the car?"

The officer was going to be dead in less than ten seconds, Martin reached down for the knife, he looked front and back, no witnesses to what was about to happen.

The officer's radio suddenly burst into life, he listened and looked at Martin.

"Sorry sir, I have been called to another job, get that rear light fixed or next time you will get a ticket!"

He turned and sped off hunting for the shop lifter or whatever it was that had passed as a more serious crime.

"Lucky little copper" mumbled Martin as he slid the car into gear and drove away.

He hurried back through the front door although no one seemed to notice anything that happened around here and threw the keys onto the small table in the hallway, he wouldn't need those again until tomorrow.

As he sat eating his cold supper, in the lounge in the dark, he watched through the window, just biding his time, waiting, patiently for the next stage of his revenge.

CHAPTER FORTY EIGHT

The Monday morning meeting in Stephen's office was a dull affair, the weekend had proved to be an incident free one, just a couple of self-harm attempts and staff shortfalls.

"Who is Duty Governor today?" he asked the assembled group

"Should be Martha, but I haven't seen her. I'm sure her annual leave is over as she told me that she just had the two weeks." replied Terry

"I'll give her a ring" Stephen replied. "It's not like her to not turn up. Can you cover the duty until she gets in Terry?"

"Sure boss, no problem!"

Stephen tried to phone but received no answer. He tried the home and mobile numbers and he then checked the computer for her home address details. She lived around half an hour from the prison, in the same direction Stephen needed to go that morning as he had a meeting planned with the health care providers.

Terry was working on a staffing issue when Stephen walked in, "Terry, I am out all morning in Birmingham, I'm planning to call into Martha's home, see what's going on. Did she say if she was going away? I've tried both her phones but there's no answer, not like her at all!"

"No it was all very last minute, she just asked for two weeks off. She only asked three days before the leave start date and she was excited but a bit coy about her plans. I think that she had met a boyfriend or something, anyway that's the impression I got, she was acting like a teenager! Wait a minute," Terry suddenly remembered, "yeah, she said that she had planned to meet an old boyfriend."

"Okay, this could be interesting, hope she hasn't gone to Vegas to get married!" Stephen quipped as he walked out of Terry's office and down the corridor. He prayed that he didn't find them in a compromising situation as knowing Martha as he did, it wasn't a very savoury thought!

He left the prison stopping briefly at the gate to speak to the gate manager, "I'm out on a meeting, Terry's in charge. Do me a favour, if Martha comes in during the next hour, can you ask her to phone me on my mobile? I'll be back in some time this afternoon."

The car swept out into the morning traffic as he headed out into the main stream but quickly joined a small two lane 'B' road to cut out the throng of the morning commute. The new green leaves on the trees and brown corn fields made a splendid sight, the differing shades of the green trees spanning out to his left made him wish that he could paint. How relaxing that would be, just sitting at a canvas, putting this magnificent countryside view into a splash of oils! The satnav instructed him to turn right in half a mile; he was in such a trance considering the prospect of art lessons that the command to turn off made him jump.

He looked at the display, only two and a half miles to Martha's home. He would have around ten minutes to chat with her, to find out why she hadn't turned up for work, then he needed to get going. The meeting was set for ten o'clock and his watch showed just after nine.

"You have arrived at your destination!" he was informed as he pulled up outside a pair of brick semis. Stephen looked out at the house, a modest place; he guessed three bedrooms and definitely in need of paint. The garden was looking a bit unloved, the lawnmower needed to get busy with the grass being ready for its first cut of the year.

The scene seemed odd, Martha's car was parked in the drive and the curtains were closed, every curtain. Martha lived alone as far as he was aware, and why would every curtain need to be closed in the middle of the day? A paper was stuck in the letter box and recycling was spilling over the edge of the crate. The other houses had placed their recycling crates and bins outside in the road and these had obviously been collected earlier.

But the car, why was it sitting there, unless Martha had gone away in someone else's car, or could she be ill? Stephen had spooked himself; he always thought that he would be a good detective!

He rang the doorbell, no answer. He rang again and thought that he saw the bedroom curtain move and did he see a shadow behind the half glass door? This detective thing was getting to him, but something just didn't feel right. He just knew Martha was in, he wasn't sure how he knew, but he knew.

A sense of determination crept in, if Martha was hiding from him trying to get another day on holiday, he would find out.

"Martha, it's Stephen" he shouted through the letter box but still no answer.

He walked around the side of the square brick building and tried the rear door which obviously led to the kitchen. Unexpectedly it opened. The smell hit Steven immediately, the smell of decay and rotting flesh. It was disgusting; he had never smelt such a stench. It hurt his eyes and made him gag before vomiting on to the step. The noise of the flies was incredible, swarms of bluebottles everywhere. Disturbed by the opening of the door, they had risen from their frenzied feeding before alighting again on every raw surface. It was then he looked up and there she was, at least he assumed it was her, in a horrific crucifixion position, naked and unrecognisably mutilated. Her stomach had been carved open, organs spilling onto the floor, the top of her head sliced open and flipped back so that her skull was exposed, shining like a white beacon. Her hands and feet had been screwed onto the legs of the table, her face cut beyond recognition. He spewed again and fumbled for his phone. This was a scene from anyone's worst nightmare, and he needed to summon help, not for poor Martha who was beyond any mortal assistance but to help find who had performed this hideous act of cruelty. Before his shaking fingers had finished dialling, a slight movement of the door behind him made Stephen spin around and come face to face with the monster who he knew wanted to perform the same acts on his own family, just as the hammer hit his head and darkness surrounded him.

Stephen slowly came to and opened his eyes. A splitting headache jumped right through his immobile body as water dripped from his face onto a blood soaked shirt. He could barely focus, the pain stabbed so deeply right through to his soul. As his half opened eyes began to focus, he saw he was still in the rancid kitchen tied to a wooden chair with hands and feet restrained, and standing almost regally in front of him was Martin Heard with an empty cup in his hand.

"Stephen Byfield, how positively refreshing this is, we manage to meet on neutral ground at last! You'll see the roles are slightly different in this world, my world. It is you who is restrained and not me, a situation I much prefer. Now who makes the rules?"

Stephen looked at the upturned table, Martha was long dead, but she was still a witness to what was happening in this little kitchen. Her eyeless face seemed like that of a grotesque doll, she had died such a painful death. Stephen summoned his wits about him and demanded "Why did you do this, why kill such an innocent person? Your fight isn't with her, it's me, me and my family, you sadistic bastard!"

"Yes I am, well done! Well observed! Just look at that slut and imagine what I am going to do to your mother this afternoon Stephen! Sadistic bastard, yes, that arouses me!" he smiled. "I have something to share with you Stephen, something that I both love and hate in equal measure, but I will share it with you. I want you two to become lovers, share my history."

He produced a syringe, carefully prepared with good quality heroin, "Meet my little friend Stephen, melt into the splendour of your mistress and enjoy the feeling!" He rolled up Stephen's sleeve and placed the needle easily, effortlessly into Stephen's vein. He introduced the liquid with one steady push into his body and instantly Stephen felt it, the warmth and comfort melting into his brain. He relaxed back in the chair and let it flow through him.

When Stephen woke again he was no longer in Martha's kitchen, and felt momentarily relieved to be away from the revolting sight and smell. Martin had driven him to his new surroundings in the boot of Stephen's car, a dark dusty barn where there was no noise, no sound of traffic, just the sound of bird song from outside the somewhat derelict building. The headache was back with a thumping intensity which was hard to ignore. Looking around Stephen could see this was a disused building, its solid concrete floor was filthy and the asbestos looking walls and ceiling had seen better days. Some old farm equipment and hoists stood idle to one side, and at the end sat his car. He could smell animals, but could hear nothing which made him think that maybe the place was used in the winter to house cattle, in which case, someone could be around. It was the only thought going through his mind and as if mind-reading Martin's voice answered him.

"Stephen, the nearest person is around two miles away, shout all you like, no one will hear. I, however, have work to do, I am due to be an unexpected evening guest at your parents! I would have been there for lunch, but they were out. The good news is, I have seen them come home! They seem such nice people!"

He then handed Stephen his phone. "Work will be missing you should you not return. Phone your secretary and tell them that you will need a couple of days away for personal business. Any nonsense on the phone and people will die, understand?"

Stephen nodded and made the call, he would not be missed for days.

"Now phone your wife, tell her that you are away for the next two nights, a prison in the South is having a major disturbance and you are needed. You will be unable to take your phone into the prison but will phone her as soon as you can".

He made this call, Tanya protested and seemed to find this explanation strange.

"Just trust me sweetheart. Everything will be ok, trust me please" Stephen pleaded with her.

Although this was so strange she listened to what he said. "Okay darling, just phone me when you can and please keep safe".

The irony of this last request was not lost on him. He couldn't have been in any more danger if he tried.

Before Stephen could react to what he had just heard and said, his sleeve was rolled back up, "Medication time!" The needle again slid into his arm, heaven awaited and he drifted off into a deep dream.

CHAPTER FORTY NINE

Martin was proud of his homework, days of watching, hour upon hour of research, sneaking into places that the average person shouldn't be going but it had gone like clockwork. He was exhausted after his exertions with Stephen but still had a lot to accomplish that day. He looked at his watch; three fifty pm, perfect timing!

Life suddenly surged back through his body, the adrenaline buzz hitting him like a line of coke. He pulled up the hood on his sweatshirt and walked with a purpose down the street, straight past Terry's driveway. Not a glance in, he didn't want to give anything away, didn't want to make anybody suspicious, not just yet, that was still to come. He smiled as he thought of what lay ahead and scratched his itchy stomach.

He saw the school signs warning drivers to slow down, the council had introduced a twenty mile an hour speed limit. Great idea he thought, keep the kids safe!

Cars double parked everywhere; it was a scene of total chaos. Although he had completed two dress rehearsals for this act, today was just a little busier than the past attempts.

Then he realised why the extra traffic, there was a school football match on. The screams of parents from inside the school gates had given it away. This could screw up his plan, but wait, when one door closes another opens he mused to himself and walked onwards.

No one gave him a second glance as he walked through the gates; there were dozens of parents from the other school so no one recognised him as a stranger. He slipped straight in. The school was a small affair, possibly two hundred children with a single story building. It looked like a 1970s design, no character just a simple concrete block.

The sign stated it was a Church of England school, the head master's name Jason Douglas and apparently it was a good school or so the signs outside of the gate boasted. Good OFSTED results, whatever that meant.

The football field lay in front of him, parents screaming for their child to shoot, run, tackle, anything, just do anything. As normal the kids just followed the ball. Martin laughed at how futile it all was.

Then he saw him, Tom, standing on the far side of the field, deep woods behind him. Only twenty feet behind him, deep, dark woods that could hide a number of sins. He recognised him easily, he had seen him getting ready for school a number of times that week.

Martin walked around the pitch, shouting for the opposing team. Then he strode behind the goal and on to the same side of the field as Tom. He took his time and edged closer as he pretended to follow the game. A ball rolled off the pitch and Martin chased it giving him the opportunity to be within an arm's length of Tom. As he threw the ball back in to play, he glanced over at him, the closest that he had been to him since the day the police broke his fingers as he tried to hang onto his child. He wanted to smell his hair, touch his face, but he couldn't. He couldn't give himself away. If the boy ran, his plan was over.

"Which team are you supporting?" Martin asked, offering Tom a weak smile.

"My school of course, Northwood"

"What's the score?"

"Don't know, I'm just waiting for my mum, she's here in a bit, don't like footie really".

"No nor me, I have just come to see a nephew of mine, I haven't seen him since he was a baby. I hoped to see a teacher to show me who he is as I'm a bit shy to be honest, teachers still scare me a bit!"

"Me too, what's his name? I might know him".

"It's Tom Davies, is he here?"

Tom looked at him, he laughed "Yes it's me, are you my uncle?"

"I am Tom; I'm your Uncle Martin!"

"How come Mum and Dad have never mentioned you?" Tom asked with suspicion written all over his face.

"I'm what you might call the black sheep of the family, Tom, did a few things I'm not proud of in my youth but that's all behind me now" Martin replied giving an embarrassed looking shrug.

The pair chatted for a few minutes while Martin thought about his next move, the chance coming seconds later.

A football whizzed past them and disappeared into the woods, Tom ran after it, eagerly wanting to get the game going again. "Can't find it!" he shouted.

A fresh ball was kicked into play as Tom continued to look.

"There it is!"

Tom looked around to see who was behind him, it was Martin.

"Where? I can't see it"

"Just there, about another twenty paces in front of you, look it's there!"

They walked further into the woods, the pitch now out of sight, the sound of shouting becoming distant.

"This is a cool place Tom, can you show me more?"

"Sure I will show you the badger set, hardly anyone knows that it's there so don't tell anyone Uncle Martin."

"Don't worry Tom, no one will ever find out, I promise you that."

Jo stood at the school gates, she had walked around the pitch a dozen times looking for Tom, she was frantic, speaking to everyone, anyone. Where was Tom? Had anyone seen him?

She knew that he wouldn't walk home by himself, maybe he was in the school building.

She didn't notice the hooded figure walk past her, they didn't even exchange glances.

She checked the school doors, all locked except the small toilet, she shouted from the door, still no response.

"Tom!" her frantic cry had caught the attention of the teacher in charge of the team, he ran over to her.

"Everything okay Mrs Davies?"

"No it isn't, I've lost Tom, he should be here!"

A tug on her jumper made her look around

"Hi Mum!" It was Tom.

"I was so worried, where have you been Tom? I was looking for you everywhere!"

She grabbed him and engulfed him in a giant hug. "Tom, you gave your mum a scare!" the teacher smiled before turning back to the game.

Jo felt a bit silly on the way home, she had over reacted maybe. Was there anything to worry about? Surely he was safe at school playing with friends.

"So where were you sweetheart? I was a bit frightened when I couldn't find you."

"Showing Uncle Martin the badger set, he is very nice, he says he can show me loads of other places like that.Why didn't you tell me about him?"

"She froze, "You don't have an Uncle Martin, Tom. What did he look like?"

"Like a man! He knew dad, he said that he liked him and they had met up a few weeks ago after a long time as he had done some daft things in his past. He told me to tell him that he would see him again soon, then he left. We didn't even find the ball mum!"

Jo looked over her shoulder and walked a little quicker.

CHAPTER FIFTY

Later that afternoon a rattle of the letter box and a swish signified the arrival of mail hitting the floor and sliding across the tiles. Jo left her office and walked down the carpeted stairs to pick it up.

The single white letter instantly looked important as it sat looking invitingly up from the black and white tiled porch floor.

Even before she picked the letter up, there was a sense that there was something important about it and what lay inside. Jo walked through to the kitchen and made a cold drink, mixed fruit berries and plenty of ice. She looked for a postmark, it had none and was obviously hand delivered. Who on earth would send such a letter? How strange, she wondered why anyone would want to write to her rather than knock at the door and speak to her.

She mused over those she knew in the village as she climbed back up the stairs to her study where she opened the envelope and pulled out the folded letter.

She stood frozen to the spot. It read:

Dear Jo,
It has taken me some time to locate you, mainly due to the change in address, however I have you now.
I have a proposal for you, it may be of some interest should you choose to take it.
You have stolen my child, we are both aware of that. I am also aware that my child has been kept warm and safe, I thank you for that. He looked like a happy child when I met him at school. However, I now intend to take back what is mine. Should you try stop me, I will kill you both.
I am aware that your husband has knowledge of my past history, oh how I laughed when I saw who was caring for my child! What a lovely coincidence, I feel almost related to you!
Anyway, I will be coming to visit you to take my child, you can do one of many things, let me list them for you:-
1, Tell the police = You die
2, Try stop me taking my child = You die
3, Make me a cake and stand to one side= We all live happily ever after.

I will leave it up to you, I have been watching you all. I love what you have done to the house, very classy, but your jewellery isn't to my taste! While you were out last weekend I had a good look! Give Terry my love, and one last thing, check your knife block, the missing piece will be used without mercy should I need to.

See you soon,
Signed
Daddy

Jo darted downstairs and locked the doors. She closed the curtains quickly and then looked at the knife block. The large carving knife was missing, in its place a photo of the family leaving the home taken two days ago.

Jo slump to the floor and phoned Terry, he couldn't hear what she was saying for the sobbing. He left work immediately and drove home at break neck speed. He was needed.

CHAPTER FIFTY ONE

Terry made some phone calls on the way home, people from his past who would always come when called. A warm glow came over him as he pulled into his driveway, one of pride that a number of people had dropped everything to meet him, people he hadn't seen for years, and the other, the heat associated with the anger he felt. He had understood from the call that the family were at risk, someone had broken in and left a message. He didn't know who or when but he would find out soon enough.

Jo unlocked the door as soon as she saw his car pull in and Terry ran from the car towards her.

Terry held Jo tightly in his strong arms as she sobbed and tried to tell the story. Terry led her into the lounge, sat beside her on the sofa and told her to start at the beginning, not leaving anything out. After she had recounted the whole afternoon from not being able to find Tom to discovering the missing knife, she begged him not to call the police. Terry agreed for the moment, read the letter himself, cursing under his breath. Tom came downstairs from his room to ask what was for supper and was surprised to see his dad home so early.

"Hey dad! What's up? Why are you home and has mum told you about me meeting Uncle Martin?"

Terry didn't want to scare his son but knew he had to make him aware of the danger. 'Yes, she did Tom and she's right, you don't have an Uncle Martin. I know who this guy is and he's not a nice man, I don't want him near you. Now, I've got a few old friends coming round to make sure he stays away from us, so go back up stairs and play one of your computer games for a bit while we talk."

Tom didn't need telling twice that he could play games instead of doing his homework so grabbing a couple of biscuits from the kitchen, he thundered back up the stairs to his room.

Over the next hour the doorbell rang three times, three times a different man shook Terry's hand and then hugged him. They all now sat in the lounge, a hot pot of tea doing the rounds.

The men asked questions and Terry told them all he knew. They then stood as one, as if a silent command had been given. One of them spoke.

"Give us an hour Terry, stay here with Jo. We'll be back for more tea, and get the chips on Jo, we'll be hungry by then!"

The men fanned out, one in the front garden, one in the house, the other in the rear garden.

"Who are they Terry?" Jo asked as she hugged him tight.

"Old friends Jo, you don't need to know, you could say we have an unbreakable bond".

An hour passed, the men seemed to have been everywhere, and then they were back. Sitting around the lounge the men made notes and spoke quietly to each other. Jo realised that she didn't even know their names, but guessed that she wasn't supposed to know.

"Terry, we know how this man got in" reported the guy who had headed for the back garden. "He came through the back field, I have traced his prints. He climbed the fence in the far right corner and popped the lock on the back door. Not a professional job, bit messy, looks like he used a heavy tool, possibly a chisel."

The second man then added, "He has hidden in the undergrowth across the road, looks like he staked you out for a while, plenty of rubbish, and the dirty git even had a crap! Poor operational drills, he's obviously just an amateur."

Terry was not amused, "Yes, but what he lacks in stealth he makes up for in ferocity, this bastard is a brutal killer!"

They all nodded, "Yeah you need to leave, take everything and leave. It's too vulnerable here, I have a safe house for you" the first man continued.

The third man then added his input. "He's been in the loft mate. Two holes are drilled through your ceiling, he has installed a camera in every roof space and he's been watching your every move. Cheap shit and he needs to be close to watch the link, but he has installed it himself".

He produced a pile of electrical equipment on the desk.

"It's shit now!"

"Ok to sum up Terry, this bloke is all over you, there is no doubt he will kill you and your family if he is not stopped" the first man confirmed.

Jo let out a gasp,

"Sorry Jo, it's just what it is." The first man gave a glimmer of a smile and shrugged his shoulders,

"Go fetch your son from upstairs, pack a bag and come with me, you will be safe with us."

That is exactly what they did, and in record time. The next thing Terry, Jo and Tom knew was they were sitting in a warm car driving up the M6, heading for safety.

Tom looked at his dad, "What's happening dad? This is weird!"

"Tom, just trust me, you are on holiday with some of dad's mates. Just promise me one thing, no phone calls, no one must know where we are. Give me your phone mate, trust me."

Tom nodded and handed it over, he knew when dad was serious. Jo did the same.

"I don't trust myself Terry, keep it till it's over."

Three hours later they sat in a large house somewhere in the Lake District, easily protected. Any cars could be seen from miles away. They were untraceable and they were very safe, with two of Terry's friends bedded down for the night.

"You guys get some rest, leave the security to us, no one will get near you" they were reassured as they settled for the night.

Martin Heard vaulted the garden fence, he carried the tool kit in his left hand and he knew this route well. The kitchen door opened with ease and he was in, the cameras had failed him which was no surprise, cheap ebay shit.

Silently he crept into the kitchen then realised that something was different, something was wrong. He turned and left, hurdled the fence and was gone. The house was empty, he had sensed it, different smell, things had been hurriedly packed. They had gone, hidden. His search had to start again, he kicked at a broken tree stump and cursed his stupid letter. He should have just come in unannounced, a big mistake. No more show boating.

Terry awoke early the following morning and he cuddled Jo and Tom,

"Listen, I have got to sort this out, I need to go back and find this man. I will do it and I will finish him, that's a promise. You're going to stay here, absolutely safe, no one will get near you; these guys are a lot better than Martin. I will be back when the job is done, just hold on and no phone calls. If anyone knows where you are, you are compromised, understand?"

They both nodded.

Twenty minutes later, reassured by his two friends that Jo and Tom would be safe, Terry kissed Jo goodbye.

"Please be careful, I want you back sweetheart. Remember I love you." Jo hugged him tightly.

"So do I dad" Tom announced, throwing himself into the group hug.

Terry winked and left.

CHAPTER FIFTY TWO

Terry phoned into work and spoke with the operations manager and they agreed the police would have to know that Martin Heard was again at large. He explained the situation as he drove the car down the M6 as he knew that Martin would be looking for the family. He had arranged to stay in another safe house, he was well trained in anti-surveillance drills and he also guessed that Martin would not be difficult to spot. No doubt some simple telltale signs would give him away.

He arrived at work to find Stephen's office was a hive of activity with three police officers waiting for him. Stephen was absent. When his secretary explained to Terry that Stephen had phoned her saying he would be away for a while, he found it strange. Normally they would have spoken about any absences and Stephen hadn't mentioned anything at home was wrong when they had last spoken. He hoped all was okay with Tanya and her pregnancy, he would give Stephen a ring when he had a moment. This would be a difficult day, instead of getting on and catching this bastard he was sitting giving statements with police officers milling about searching his house.

They were not impressed that someone had got there first, he couldn't give a shit but kept silent and a quick apology soon soothed the frayed nerves. The police then wanted to know why Terry had left his family alone.

"No offence but you lot can't be trusted with anything! I'll look after my family where I know they are safe!"

The Inspector laughed, "No offence?" he laughed again, "I would hate to see you being offensive!"

Terry shrugged and grinned.

After an age they left and Terry found himself alone in the office. He shook his head wearily and talked to himself hoping to find some reason. I've been caught up in fuck knows what, my family is at risk and he's making threats to steal Tom as he thinks he's the frigging father! He will kill Jo and me in a heartbeat, and for what? Looking after an abandoned kid and giving a child a new life, unbefucking lievable!

CHAPTER FIFTY THREE

Chris and Lucy Byfield awoke to the sound of bird song, the wood pigeon sat somewhere towards the end of the garden and tried its hardest to drown out the morning call of the other birds. A blackbird shouted a warning as it flew from the oak tree, telling anyone who could be bothered to listen that danger was close - how ironic!

Blue Tits and Great Tits swung into action, nervously pecking away at the bird feeder, eyes open for lurking dangers. A crow cackled a large shout from across the farmer's field and a green wood pecker dipped and rose as it headed towards an old dead tree stump.

Lucy pulled the duvet back and placed her feet on the lush carpet. She stretched and yawned, "Come on sleepy head, let's get going, plenty for us to do!" She padded off towards the shower.

Chris ignored this plea, he would wait until it was an order, and he figured another five minutes would do it. Lucy came back and turned the light on, she was covered with a fluffy white dressing gown, her slim figure still evident, a short blue towel was wrapped around her wet hair, "Come on lazy!"

This was the order he had expected, he looked at the clock, seven forty three, still very early.

"Remind me, why so early?"

"We're playing golf with Jane and Andy!"

"Yes at nine O'clock, I booked a later tee so we could have a lie in!"

"I need to warm my back up, come on, let's get there early and hit some balls on the driving range."

He got up and showered, Chris loved golf and quickly got himself ready.

"I'm wearing my shorts to play in today, bugger the rules about long socks only, it looks silly, ankle socks and my new white golf shoes, I'll look just fine!"

He was talking to himself as the hairdryer ensured that anything that he said would be lost.

They both ate a bowl of creamy porridge before loading the clubs and trolleys into the boot of the red VW Tiguan, a perfect vehicle for golf equipment.

"Chris, you forgot to close the summerhouse door, it's open, must have been open all night" Lucy pointed out as she looked across the garden.

He pulled on his shoes and walked across the wet lawn, he had been sure that he had closed it, must be old age creeping up.

Martin crouched in the summerhouse watching this hated man walking towards him, this wasn't the time to kill, it wasn't the scenario planned in his head. The kill would be too quick and he wouldn't be able to do what he had planned. He hid behind a large chair, like an adult playing hide and seek with a child, knowing that you were far too big to hide in that space and anyone looking would spot you.

If I'm seen I will kill him thought Martin, just means plan B will come in to play.

Chris shut the door without checking inside, and without locking it. Then he walked back to the house whistling some nameless tune. Martin overheard him speaking to Lucy, explaining that he couldn't find the key, but he was sure it would be fine. How wrong he was.

Jane and Andy were also in the driving range area, everyone had had the same thought, which was to warm up and beat the opposition. Chris thought that he and Lucy were competitive, these two were like professional golfers, they all laughed about how seriously they were taking the game.

As they played Andy and Chris chatted, "What are you doing since the early retirement Chris? You're still in your fifties and as fit as a fiddle!"

"I've been doing some consultancy work with the council, not a lot different to the old job. I can just pick my hours, plus the pay is better than I used to get. It's fun but I'm looking around."

"How about coming in with me? I have started a little property firm and I need someone who is good with people."

"And someone with a few pounds to buy the first house!" Chris laughed.

"Yes, that too, we could go fifty/ fifty, six week turnaround, around thirty thousand profit, that sounds okay doesn't it?"

Chris considered it and hit a nine iron into the heart of the green, "I'll give it some thought."

He sank a twenty foot putt and the four of them moved to the next tee.

"Lucy, Andy wants half of the retirement fund to renovate a house, what do you think?" he laughed.

"I think that we are winning by three holes and if we win this, it's all over!" She then smashed a five iron three feet from the flag on the par three fifteenth hole. The others failed to even hit the green, Lucy's putt gave her a birdie and the match.

Sitting in the clubhouse eating a light lunch they chatted about the match. Chris and Lucy had played well and the prawn salad and glass of wine tasted all the sweeter for it.

"Andy, I will give it some thought, just no promises." They shook hands while the ladies chatted before loading the clubs back into the car and driving home.

"It seems such a shame to go straight home" Lucy mused, "Shall we have a drive to that Garden centre we passed last week? They may have some plants on offer."

It was a fabulous afternoon, browsing amongst the plants, planning for another border to go around the summerhouse, and having a cream tea in the café, "This is what I hoped for in retirement!" stated Chris.

"Yes sweetheart, but you are starting to get under my feet, the part time work is not keeping you satisfied, I can tell that. Why don't you think about Andy's offer?"

"I have thought about it, we have some extra cash, I may just help him with the first and see what happens." He looked at Lucy and smiled, he was excited about this prospect.

They drove back through the lanes, the tree branches looking as though they wanted to pat the top of the car as they drove by, twigs and acorns sat in the road and the telltale signs of mud from tractor wheels finished the truly rural scene.

They were soon home, flushed from the victory and a little full from the cream tea.

"Chris, I thought that you had shut the summerhouse?"

"I did!"

Lucy tutted. "Leave it to me, if you want a job doing properly do it yourself!"

She strode down the lawn and shut the door, opened and shut it again, "It all seems fine, can't understand why it was open!"

She walked back into the conservatory and snuggled down next to Chris, „We were fantastic this morning weren't we?" They kissed and Chris took her hand and led her upstairs. He didn't have an afternoon nap in mind!

They surfaced from the bedroom at around six o'clock, both like a couple of teenagers. It had been a while since the afternoon had been taken up in such a romantic manner.

"Chris, shall I prepare supper?" Lucy called from the kitchen. "I fancy making the sweet 'n' sour pork that you love, I have two packs of belly pork and we've burnt enough calories I think!"

Chris loved this meal, just what he needed. He grabbed the paper and sat back in the big leather chair in the lounge. "Sounds brilliant, do you need a hand?"

"No sweetheart, you just relax and read, I'm fine" Lucy replied, pouring herself a glass of wine and turning on the radio to listen to the Archers while she cooked.

Lucy chopped away and fried the pork making a delicious supper and half an hour later every bit was eaten, bellies were full and they were a bit tipsy from the wine.

"What a lovely day my darling man!" She always called him this when a bit merry.

"Just perfect my darling" he replied as he leaned over and kissed her on the tip of her nose.

Washing up completed, they crashed onto the deep inviting sofa. T.V on they watched their favourite programme of the moment, 'The Great British Bakeoff'.

As Paul Hollywood talked about soggy bottoms and good bakes, Martin Heard crept back into the Summerhouse, tool bag in hand. As the programme ended, Lucy yawned and stood up. "Come on sweetheart, I'm shattered, shall we go up to bed? I think that I'll be asleep in seconds!"

They locked the doors and turned the lights out before going upstairs. The bedroom still looked ruffled and still smelt a little of that afternoon's sex. They climbed into bed, too tired to read or talk for long.

"I love you Lucy". Chris yawned.

"Love you too, now go to sleep!"

They turned off the bedside light and cuddled up. Just as they were dropping off to sleep Chris rolled over. "See you in the morning sweetheart".

Martin checked his watch, forty five minutes from now.

CHAPTER FIFTY FOUR

The summer house seemed very still, apart from the comforting patter of light summer rain tickling the roof. Martin looked across the garden, this was the third time that he had hidden here and it was cozy, almost familiar. The cushioned couch had been a godsend for him as these long periods of observation would be tedious without the comfort.

The house was in darkness, the last light turned off thirty minutes earlier. He had learnt from experience that you had to leave at least forty five minutes for the homeowners to go to sleep deep enough that a serial killer sneaking up the stairs wasn't going to disturb them.

He picked up his bag of tools and walked over the dark damp grass towards the house. The conservatory door didn't resist the pressure from the chisel; it popped open, silently and effortlessly. He slipped off his shoes and walked over the tiled floor, through the lounge and stood at the bottom of the carpeted stairs. He listened, no sounds at all.

His heart thumped with excitement as he stood on the first step, not a creak. He slowly made his way up and onto the landing. His eyes were now used to the dark and he could see a number of doors, the one to his left was closed, it could be a guest bedroom. The next door was ajar with a soft light coming through from the window showing it to be the family bathroom. Martin looked in; it seemed very pretty, white toilet set and a large walk in shower, the type which could take two people with ease.

The next door was closed, but it was the door at the end of the landing which took Martin's eye, the master bedroom!

He reached the side of the bed in three strides and hit Chris on the side of the head with the hammer, rendering him into immediate unconsciousness. Lucy woke and seeing the dark figure loom over her, screamed. Martin subdued her with a punch directly to the face followed by the glint of a massive serrated knife blade, and she shut up.

He reached into the tool bag and took a rope out. Chris was quickly tied up, hands secured to the top of the bed facing directly down its length whilst his feet were tied to the end of the bed. He was naked and uncovered, Martin wanted him to feel vulnerable.

Lucy was dragged from the bed and was forced to stand at the foot. She called Chris's name and as he came too, his eyes opened wide as he took in what was going on around him.

Martin said " Hope that you are settled, lay back and enjoy the show, I know I will, your wife still has a good body so this could be nice for both of us!"

He began by cutting her silk pyjamas from her body then he tied her arms to the bed end and laughed.

Chris was begging, Martin could tell through his gag that he was begging. He was going to have a front row seat!

He kicked her legs apart and forced her over the bed end. She couldn't resist with the blade resting on her throat. He undid his blue jeans with his spare hand and kicked them off, his boxer shorts going the same way.

He whispered into her ear, "Bitch, you are going to be fucked hard but first you are going to suck my cock! If you are a bad girl, you both die, if you are good, you live, your choice! She nodded.

"Okay Chris, you bastard, let me allow you to watch your wife having some fun!"

He knelt on the bed only inches from Chris's tied feet, and twisting her head around, he forced his erect penis into her mouth. "Suck Bitch" he instructed as he untied one of her hands. "Grab my cock and suck!" Lucy closed her eyes and sucked for her life and that of her husband. As she sucked Martin looked at Chris and winked. He allowed her to taste his cock for another minute before climbing back off the bed and retying her hand.

"Not bad, made me feel very horny, Chris, she is good at that!" Martin could hear the sound of sobbing, they were both crying, "Oh come on you two, good sex and I may spare you both!"

He again spread her legs as she was thrown over the bed,

"How rude of me, I haven't introduced myself, My name is Martin Heard. Chris, you stole my baby, made my girlfriend take her own life and then forced me back into heroin addiction, but I suspect that you guessed that?"

He nodded, Chris had known from the first second who this person was and so had his wife.

"Funny thing is, at this moment I am in the process of turning your son Stephen into a heroin addict and he seems to be taking to it very well! Then while he is addicted, you can take his children from him, just as you did to me! Anyway introductions over, I have business to attend to!"

195

He drove his cock hard into the woman as she screamed. This only added to his frenzied excitement and he fucked her hard for the next few minutes before removing himself and focusing on her backside. He forced himself into her and fucked her harder. The thought of how much this must hurt passed briefly through his mind although this time he never took his eyes from Chris who lay there with his eyes firmly shut, unable to bear seeing the agony Lucy was being put through. "Great fuck Chris, look what you are missing" Martin gasped as he took his cock out and ejaculated into her face. "Bingo!" Satisfied he then tied her to a chair, facing Chris. He smacked her gently on her cheek to bring her out of her semi-conscious state. "You remember what I said about living?"

She nodded, barely able to focus.

"I lied!"

He took the chisel and hammer from the floor, lined the chisel with her beautiful white teeth and smashed. She tried to spit the teeth out, gagging as she swallowed fragments. Chris kicked wildly trying to get free, Martin turned to him and smiled, Smash, the chisel ended the job, a bloody mess stood where her mouth once sat.

The knife then was reintroduced, a crazy pattern was etched into her smooth skin, blood flowed freely, it was clear that Martin was in a blood frenzy. He hacked and slashed her head, cutting off whatever got in his way. Martin again turned to Chris, he held both of her ears aloft, like trophies. Chris hoped that she was dead and felt no pain but if she wasn't dead what happened next sealed the deal. Martin kicked the chair down so her back was flat on the floor, slid the knife into the base of her stomach and opened her up. He reached inside and pulled her organs out resting them on her chest, a filthy vision. Chris looked, wild red eyes surveying the scene, his brain melting inside his head. He no longer cared if he lived or died, he just wanted Martin Heard dead, no matter what the price.

Martin looked down at the lifeless body. "Well Chris, that would appear to be the first thing off my bucket list! She was a good fuck Chris, gave very good head, and died like a fucking bitch. Now you can live a life of pain just like mine!" He pulled his own clothing back on and walked out, leaving Chris tied to the bed, the mutilated body of his wife on the floor in front of him.

CHAPTER FIFTY FIVE

Martin strutted back into the dusty barn. Stephen looked at him, knowing where he had been, but hoping that he was wrong. He had wafted in and out of reality and consciousness for the last day or two thanks to the regular heroin top ups Martin had forced upon him, and had lost all track of time

"Stephen, I have had such a pleasant evening, your parents are lovely, such good house guests and so accommodating. Your mother was a scream, such a naughty girl! Anyway, I gave her your love!"

Stephen sat staring at Martin, hoping upon hope that it was lies.

"Got you a couple of presents, recognise this?" He produced a framed photograph of Stephen's wedding day which he knew had had pride of place in the bedroom. "And secondly I thought that you may like to hold your mother's night clothes, very sexy! Sorry about the blood, it was very messy." Stephen looked at the pile of bloodied silk Martin threw on the floor in front of him and knew his mother was dead.

Martin then rolled up Stephen's sleeve and again the drugs took effect quickly. An uncomfortable restless dream state, he drifted in and out of sleep, lingering deep thoughts of family and children, a family home with people awaiting him, all this so near, but so very far. Stephen had begun to enjoy the regular injections, he liked the feeling but knew that it was very wrong, knew that this was not a sustainable way of life, but unable to fight the effect. He sat, tied to the wooden beam. He was grubby, tired and very hungry. He also knew in his more lucid moments that he needed to plot his escape. The headaches had stopped and he wasn't sure if this was down to the drugs or if the pain had just gone, it didn't really matter.

Stephen had once read that if you were planning to escape, you needed to do this before the hostage taker had moved you to a firm base. The routine seemed very organised with not a sniff of an escape plan. Ironic really, Stephen was now the one who wanted to escape and Martin was acting as the guard. How the hell had he got into this situation?

This was a time to be practical, his mother was dead, murdered by Martin, possibly his father too, but he was being kept alive for some perverse reason. And why was Martin so driven to grow a heroin addiction for him? Stephen mulled things over in his opiate state and then it all dropped into place.

His father must be alive, Stephen's drug fuelled state would be the final chapter before they all died, Martin included. This was pure revenge, designed to hurt everyone, "Fuck, fuck, fuck, my family! He hadn't mentioned my family! They would be next, I can't stop this happening!" These terrible thoughts in Stephen's head over that night cleared the fog. Martin was nowhere to be seen, the car had vanished again and Stephen assumed he was out hunting!

It was early the next morning and Terry sat in his office. He had just received a call from the Health Care trust saying Stephen had forgotten about the meeting a couple of days ago and could they reschedule?" "What the hell is going on? He mused," I thought that he had attended the meeting after seeing the still absent Martha?" thought Terry. He found Stephen's mobile number and rang it, but it went straight to answer machine. He then phoned Martha's home and mobile, no answer. Something was badly wrong.

He walked into Stephen's office and asked his P.A. if she had heard anything more from Stephen since he phoned in to take sudden leave. Nothing, she had tried to phone herself but was just getting the answer phone on his mobile. Terry's level of anxiety increased as he then phoned Stephen's home number, something not normally done except in exceptional circumstances. When Tanya answered, it was to express her concern that Stephen had been sent to the prison in the South the day before yesterday and had still not contacted her. She was beside herself with worry and had just been about to phone in and ask what was going on. Terry didn't want to alarm her any further by telling her he had no idea what she was talking about, but instead told her he had spoken to Stephen a short while ago who had said things were chaotic in the prison and would Terry phone Tanya and tell her Stephen would call just the minute things had calmed down. Tanya was understandably unamused by the lack of contact from Stephen but reassured Terry she and the twins were fine and would wait to hear further from him.

Terry now knew there was something very wrong and suspecting that it might not just be his family that Martin Heard was targeting, almost jogged to the car. He gunned the engine and followed Stephen's last journey reaching Martha's in less than half an hour. He pulled into the drive, jumped out and rang the bell, no answer. He went around to the back, the overwhelming smell of decay guiding him. As he pushed the back door open he uncovered the horrors, sights not seen since he had fought in the Falklands and had seen men blown up and mutilated beyond recognition. He gagged but held his nerve whilst he phoned the police. "I need assistance; there is one murder and possibly more. I'm at 5, Barton Lane, Cum – Stanley village, I am here alone."

"Ok sir, is the person definitely dead?"

"She's screwed to a fucking kitchen table with her guts on the kitchen floor, I think that she is dead! Hurry up!"

Terry stood outside while the police cordoned off the area. They had searched the house and found no one else inside, either dead or alive. He then noticed the brown briefcase lying by the kitchen door. "That's my boss's briefcase!" he exclaimed. "He's in danger, he must have been taken, he may even be dead too! For fuck's sake find him!" Then Terry realised that others were in danger, he remembered the threats Martin had made against Stephen's family. "There are others in danger, Stephen's wife and children, and also his parents, they have all been threatened."

"By who sir?" asked the police constable, struggling to keep up.

"Martin Heard, serial killer!"

The police dispatched patrols to the family homes. The horrific scene at Stephen's parents was uncovered, by an experienced officer who discovered the scene after finding the conservatory door open. He wept as he untied Chris, such sights should never be seen, a broken man and a butchered woman, forced to share a night together. Chris was insane through grief, unable to cope with the horrors forced upon him. He was taken to hospital and surrounded by sanitised care, but after the horror that he had faced he didn't want care, he wanted vengeance. He pleaded with anyone who would listen to find his son, to please find his son.

The other police car arrived at the Byfield home at the same time. The officers rang on the doorbell but again, no answer. The police sergeant walked around to the back garden where the backdoor stood open. He shouted out but received no response, the home was as quite as a morgue.

199

He walked in and called out once more in the silence. He noticed that the knife drawer was open and a large carving knife sat on the worktop. He continued into the house which was cluttered, as though it had been ransacked. He quickly strode up the stairs calling for assistance on his radio. All the doors were closed, the first two rooms he checked were empty. He crept along the landing hardly daring to breath, the last door was partially open, he pushed it, then a scream and all hell broke loose.

"Who the hell are you?"shouted Tanya, "Get out!"

The policeman explained the danger and the need to leave immediately as Tanya quickly grabbed a bag and packed. She apologised for the mess, the children had been on an indoor treasure hunt and the place had been trashed as only children can. They were then playing in a makeshift den in the bedroom and they hadn't heard a thing. The family slipped into the back of the police car and were driven away. Martin stood less than fifty meters away in the back field and watched. He picked up his tool kit and slunk away.

Terry stood talking to the police officer back at Martha's house when suddenly something clicked, Stephen's car! It was gone, it must have been taken. Martin Heard must have the car. "Hells fucking bells, I know how we can find them!"

"How?" The constable struggled to keep up with his frantic note taking.

"The car has a tracker, find the car and we could find them, quick get on it!"

The police radio whispered into the officer's ear, the car had been traced; Terry strained his ears to hear where it was, then he heard it, Folly farm, approximately ten miles away, abandoned since 2010. The car was on the move, heading in the direction of the farm."Okay" said the police constable who was now coming in to his own, "We can't get anything going for a while, we need firearms officers. Just be patient, no heroics, that will only mess things up, understand?"

Terry nodded, although he had no intention of standing idle.

He waited until the officer was distracted by the arrival of the forensic team and slipped quietly away. He knew of this place, he had jogged around that area a number of times. Folly Farm was at the end of one of the regular runs, it was an old place that had gone out of business. The barns were still used for winter storage of cattle during bad weather. It was only six miles from where Terry lived, "Fucks sake, he's on my doorstep" thought Terry.

It sat at the end of a single track road, miles from anywhere, not a place that many people would visit. The only people who would ever get near to the farm were ramblers or joggers like Terry, not an area easily reached.

He raced through the country lanes, he had to beat Martin to the farm, he had to save Stephen, and prayed he was not too late. He raced past the single track lane, he couldn't chance been spotted by Martin and he knew of a lay-by just a jog down the road where he could park and get into the farm from the back fields.

He parked up, climbed the fence that bordered the lay-by and jogged to the rear of the barn. He looked around, no sign of a car so he crept to the back wall and looked through a broken slab of asbestos wall in to the dim recesses within - nothing, it seemed empty and there was no car. Terry inched his way around to the door, he peeped in and saw Stephen bound to a beam. He ran in to the barn and across the dirt floor just as he heard a car crunch across the farm yard.

He signaled to Stephen to keep quiet and crouched down behind farm machinery.

Martin drove into the barn and slammed the car door, the smell of the exhaust filling the building. Terry didn't take his eyes from him as Martin walked up to Stephen and stood in front of him.

"Ok Stephen, slight change in plan, I had hoped to bring your wife and children over to our little home here, I had such a show arranged, but the police beat me to them and think that they are safe. Then your bastard father would have joined us after his night admiring my little dalliance with his wife. I think that he may now have understood my pain. Never mind, I can wait, I may have to hide you elsewhere in the meantime".

Terry crouched, he was within ten yards of Martin, just too far to catch him off guard. Just another few feet, another couple of feet and he could jump him, he thought as he shifted slightly on his bent legs.

It was as if Martin were aware of the danger, he looked around like an animal, staring in to the gloom around him. It was then he spotted the footprints in the dust.

He laughed, "I see we have a guest, would you like to come forward stranger, or shall I just kill him in front of you?"

Terry had no choice, he stood in clear view.

"Oh Governor, how nice of you to join the show, would you like to step forward?" Terry did this, he was moving towards Martin.

"Stop, now kneel, good boy, hands behind your head please mister governor!"

Terry did as he was told, Martin moved swiftly behind him and crunched the hammer into the back of his head. Terry collapsed, struggling to breathe, and knowing that he was in big trouble, he willed himself to keep conscious. Martin grabbed his inert body and dragging him towards the beam, tied him up around ten feet directly in front of Stephen.

"Right, it would seem that we have a drama developing under our nose. If you are here acting like a superhero, then the police will be joining the party imminently, that leaves me with a dilemma. Do I run and hide, then carry on with the plan? Ummmm no chance, I will be hunted and probably killed on sight. Or shall I just kill you and Stephen, then take my chance with the courts, you know the old mental routine? I will spend my days locked up, not a nice prospect and I won't have achieved my ultimate goal!"

He drummed his fingers on his chin as he thought, and as he was thinking Terry worked his hands loose behind his back. The knots had been hurriedly tied. Martin crouched in front of Stephen.

"Let's medicate you a little more, you are a much nicer man on heroin!" He crouched in front of him arranging the syringe, this was Terry's last chance.

He sprang forward and caught Martin by surprise, the syringe dropped on the floor as Martin struggled to gain his balance, Terry grabbed a handful of dust and threw in into Martin's eyes, he then dealt him a blow to the throat. Martin was almost out for the count, on all fours struggling to breath. Terry helped him with a massive boot into his ribs, Martin groaned and fell in a heap.

There was no stopping Terry as he gave Martin Heard a good pounding, all boots and fists, Heard's ribs cracked under the onslaught. It felt and sounded good.

Terry stood back looking at the heaving mess that lay at his feet, chest heaving with the exertion as he looked up to the lofty barn ceiling breathing deeply with thoughts of family and fallen colleagues filling his foggy mind.

It was over, the horror of the past days finished, debt paid. His family would now be safe.

The graveled yell that slammed Terry from his daydream came too late to stop the attack. Like a lion Martin sprang forward, bloodied teeth shining bright in the dusty air, his fist smashing into Terry's unprotected throat knocking him backwards gasping for breath and fighting for life.

202

Heard screamed like a beast as he crashed his boot into Terry's knee and followed it up with a savage blow to his nose, Terry's last vision was one of despair, as Martin Heard stood over him, saliva and sweat falling onto Terry's bloodied face, and then with a final blow, stars filled his head as he drifted off into an uncomfortable blackness.

CHAPTER FIFTY SIX

Chris Byfield sat shivering in the peace of the family suit in the police station. Dressed in a white paper suit he sat on the edge of the well-used sofa, face looking at the carpeted floor. He had showered a while ago to remove the matted blood from his hair but it hadn't helped, he still felt as though he were smothered and he hugged himself as he started to sob again.

The young policewoman reentered the room, she had a fresh mug of coffee and placed it on the table in front of him. "There you are Chris, I will just leave it here". She sat down in the chair opposite him, her voice made him look up, red eyed and pleading as he looked at her. She passed him a tissue and he wiped his face,

"Why us, why did he do this to us, I was only doing my job" he collapsed forward again sobbing. "Why Lucy? She was innocent, he could have taken me, Lucy was innocent." His voice trailing off as he relived the horror again.

"We don't know Chris, we only know the same as you at the moment, this animal had a grudge against your family, we will find and stop him, I promise."

He broke down again, this time the Officer sat beside him and placed her hand on his hand. Other officers watched through CCTV, nobody would swap places with the officer, it was the loneliest place and hardest place to be on the planet. She had performed really well, the Scenes of Crime Officer had never encountered a crime scene as horrific. It was a lifetime of horror films fitted into one little bedroom. How this poor man would ever cope with the sights he had witnessed that evening were a mystery, but that wasn't their problem, they needed him to be fit enough to withstand questioning, they needed the killer, they needed the clues and they needed Chris Byfield ready for interview.

Chris sat in the soulless room, CD recorder sat on the table to his left, officers sitting on either side of him. It would take every ounce of expertise to keep this moving. They needed every inch of evidence, every word said remembered, every detail re lived, they must bring him back straight into his mindset from last night. The machine was switched on and buzzed before the officers began this grizzly task, but Chris was strong and he slowly recalled every detail of the day.

He remembered the summerhouse door, the threats made to Steven and how the killer committed this dreadful act. He recalled every minute detail without a tear. Chris Byfield was a consummate professional, he held it together until the last question and then he melted. He was taken under police protection to the Woodhouse mental health unit in the West Midlands, where the staff were on standby to receive him.

Quickly processed, Chris was settled into a soothingly lit room, a calm room with calm voices, gentle people who inch by inch brought him back from his safe place, the same place that he had retreated to escape the horror of the night. He had returned there after the interview and he didn't need hurting again. Inch by inch he came out, like a young animal taking food from a stranger, not sure of the danger, unsure if it should be doing this, but something drawing it forward, and then there he was, back in the world. He sobbed, and then he spoke some stuttering words, all of which were drowned out by the sobs, but he did it. He was taken to a room and allowed to rest, a trained listener sat almost unnoticed in the far corner, just in case he wanted to speak and medication was given to ensure that Chris could rest.

The on call doctor spoke with the police, she had dealt with many appalling cases of loss, some accident scenes had been as traumatic, but the difficulty faced by Chris would be the length of the attack, the ferocity of the attack, the personal nature of the attack, and the fact that he was intended to be the long term victim and he could do nothing to prevent it happening. It was a primeval instinct that would need to be addressed and the fact that Martin Heard had made him powerless. Recovery time for such a deep rooted issue involved years of therapy, maybe he would never recover, it depended on him as an individual. What Chris did need was the rest of his family, if Martin Heard could be stopped before he reached them.

CHAPTER FIFTY SEVEN

Terry and Stephen sat looking at each other, the blood and sweat had stained their clothing and a small cut above Terry's eye seeped a stream of red across his dusty cheek. There was nothing they could do but at least the shot of heroin intended for Stephen had been discarded in the futile attempt to stop Martin from escaping. The smell of the car's exhaust still lingered within the barn and the sweaty odour of Martin held in the nostrils of both men. They were finished, spent of all energy, battered and bloody but not entirely beaten. Martin still had the upper hand and he was calling all the shots.

The car could be heard idling outside of the barn, what was he waiting for? Why didn't he either kill both men or just use his time to make a getaway, why wait? The answer soon came, the car door opened and Stephen heard the melodic beeps of the warning, telling the driver that the door was open but the engine was still running. Then a shadowy silhouette stood in the doorway of the silent barn.

"Terry, we do seem to share an awful lot of things, especially children, but have you realised where we first met?" Terry shook his head, he didn't have a clue. "April 1986, Aldington Detention Centre, you called it SHORT SHARP SHOCK. I was eighteen years old Terry, you brutalised me from the day I arrived at that place, and the sad thing is, you don't even remember me. I remember you, around twenty five years old, full of Royal Marine spirit, as you used to shout at me while I sweated in the gymnasium, and then you stood and watched as I was beaten for answering a member of staff back. That bastard broke my arm and you stood and watched Terry.

"He stood staring at the two men waiting for a response which didn't come.

"I have lived with the thought of my powerlessness from that day, I always hoped that one day I would meet one of you, in fact any of you. I wanted to make you powerless and I have made you powerless! You may wonder what I intend to do next but that will soon become clear!" He turned and left, the car door closed and the crunch of the farmyard disappeared back into silence.

They both sat and listened, amazed that they were still both alive, concerned that being alive was intended to be a lot worse than the alternative. Terry was the first to untie himself, he stood and walked the few paces to Stephen where he quickly undid his knots and then walked carefully to the entrance. Nothing, the yard was empty, so quickly they made their way through the door, down the lane and onto the road. Terry knew the area like the back of his hand so they walked at the fastest pace they could with Stephen in his weakened state until they reached Terry's house. It was empty, the family was well hidden in the Lake District but hospitality wasn't on anyone's mind. Terry picked up the phone and made two phone calls, the first to the police, and the second to his friends. The blue flashing lights of the patrol car came into the drive way, for Stephen it was a welcome sight, for Terry it was an inconvenience. He knew that Martin Heard was going after his family, he had destroyed Stephen's now it was Terry's turn. He needed to be with them, he needed to make sure that they were safe and he had stopped thinking like a soldier. He had become predictable, unfocused and an easy target, just as Martin had planned.

For two hours Stephen and Terry sat in the police station, giving statements and repeating the story over and over, each detail was milked for every ounce of information; every word spoken was analysed for hidden meaning and intent. It was a torturous two hours for Terry, he needed to be elsewhere. With the interviews over, the police doctor arrived, he examined Terry, shining a light into his eyes and roughly feeling the cut above his eye. "That needs a bit of attention, I can do it here or we can go with Stephen to the hospital. Which do you prefer?"

"Get it done Doctor, I need to be somewhere else" Terry instructed. The doctor worked quickly and so did Terry's mind. Why did that bastard want to hurt him and the family? Terry and Jo had only provided a home, they had done nothing wrong, yet in the sick mind of Martin Heard they were equally to blame, they had to be destroyed. All this carnage to cleanse one lost soul. He left the station fifteen minutes later sporting two new stitches in his already craggy forehead.

Stephen left at the same time, he was taken to a waiting ambulance where they exchanged a wave as the doors were closed. As Stephen was whisked away for a few nights of observation in hospital, Terry strode towards the taxi rank, he needed to get back, pick up a car and head north, and he had no other intentions in his foggy mind. He knocked on his neighbour's house and after a quick, selected explanation, was swiftly presented with a set of keys for their son's car. Terry was walking towards the car with the protests of a nineteen year old boy ringing from the kitchen so he shouted back over his shoulder, "Sorry, I will make it up to you when I get back." He climbed into the white Saxo and headed north.

A short sprint through the outskirts of the town and then as he signaled to turn onto the motorway, he was forced to brake hard. "Bloody hell, pull over you idiot, you will cause a crash!" A red car with a defective left brake light had stopped in the road, obviously lost. The car pulled over to allow Terry to drive past, a flash of the lights and a wave and he was on his way. If that was the worst traffic problem that he would face tonight he would be lucky.

The near miss had however shocked Terry into realising how tired he was. He hadn't eaten or slept for what seemed an age, sleep wasn't an option but food was easy. He drove into MacDonalds and hungrily ate a quarter pounder and large coke. He would have had fries as well but he only had some loose change to hand. He had managed to grab a credit card from home but didn't want to pay a £4 bill with the plastic. The smell of burger and body odour was making the tree shaped pine air freshener work hard for its money. He flicked on the radio in the vague hope that something decent would come on, not too bad for Radio Two, could be worse thought Terry as he pulled the car into the steady flow of the M6. *Now let's just keep this going and we will all be safe and sound in a few hours.*

He flicked through his phone on Bluetooth, selected a number and dialed. His friend answered and the phone was passed to Jo. "Terry, what the hell's going on? This place is on lock down with your friends, I can't move!" "It's ok sweetheart, Martin Heard is on the loose. We just had a fight and he is very pissed off. We need to be safe, that's why I am coming up so no drama, ok?"

"A fight, are you nuts? Stop making this situation worse Terry, just get back here! Are you hurt?"

"No I'm fine, just a little scratch on my head. I should be up there by ten or eleven this evening, the traffic is a bit thick but it's moving. I'll see you soon." He rang off and concentrated on his driving.

The traffic started to pile up, Terry looked at his watch, a hundred miles to go and it was nearly nine o'clock. Thinking about the events of the day and what lay ahead Terry planned the coming days. They would hide out in the cottage and wait for the police to catch Heard, it wouldn't take long, after all where could he go? He was top of the national news items with nowhere to hide.

The Saxo's fuel gauge showed quarter of a tank left which was nowhere near enough to get him there. A sign popped into view, 'Services fourteen miles.' Perfect.

The petrol station was bright and well equipped, he filled up and went to look around the shop where the supermarket style shelving led him on a maze to the cash desk. He found a T Shirt in the third row, all one size but it would do, anyway he liked pictures of the Top Gear team. Fifty five pounds lighter on the credit card he pulled back into the traffic, looking good in his new shirt, packets of sweets on the passenger seat and a six pack of carbonated drink to quench his thirst.

His white Saxo sped on, traffic now thinning as they passed the major junctions, music playing and Terry excited about getting back to his family with only around twenty minutes to go. The splendour of the Lake District was all around him, it was just too dark to enjoy. He looked forward to waking up in the morning and breathing the clear air in. It felt that with everything that had happened Terry's whole body was contaminated by that human filth. Two miles to go and Terry was searching for the small road that would take him to the cottage. It suddenly appeared out of the darkness and he barely had time to indicate before swinging the car into the lane. As Terry's lights lit the way, the red car with the broken brake light sat and watched, watching all the way until the Saxo arrived outside the cottage.

Martin Heard cut the engine to his car and sat thinking. The cottage only looked a mile away, he was on high ground and was able to follow the car lights all the way, sometimes losing them in a dip or a wooded section but always reappearing. He could almost hear the welcome that Terry received when he pulled up on the driveway, it made him feel envious of the warmth that only comes with a family. He had known when he left Terry and Stephen in the barn, they would get free and end up leading him to their families.

He waited for a couple of hours before getting out of the car, and pulled a small day sack onto his back before setting off down the lane. The cold night air bit into his face, the cold weather had kicked back in and a frost was appearing on the hill tops. He dug his hands deep into the pockets of his waterproof jacket and head down he walked across the uneven ground just thinking of the prize. Clearly the security that Martin had seen Terry gather together would still be around, but for how long? They must have families and jobs, the most time that they would give Terry would be two weeks and he could bide his time. After all, this had been years in the planning so two weeks was no time at all.

The smell of a coal fire floated across the fields, the scent of a cozy cottage. Martin stopped, slipped the pack from his back and sat on a tree stump. The cold moon illuminating him cast a strong shadow over the white fields so he slipped back into the tree line, he didn't want to be spotted at this late stage. A plastic bottle of water sat at the top of his pack, he undid the screw top and drank deeply, spilling some down his chin. He wiped it clean with the back of his hand and placed the bottle back. The glint of the large knife reminded Martin of the business that lay ahead as he fastened the flap of the pack and pulled it onto his shoulders. Surveying the scene he noticed the high ground overlooking the house and he slowly made his way around to it and found a vantage point. He could see a faint glow of light coming from an upstairs window of the stone built building. The door opened showing the silhouette of a large framed man, before closing and the shape was gone, obviously patrolling outside. Five minutes later the door reopened and he went back inside. Watching for the next four hours Martin calculated that there were two other men with Terry, they took it in turns to patrol, five minutes walk around, on the hour every hour. These people had become complacent, just doing the rounds because they had to, very predictable, just like a night patrol in the prison, patrolling like clockwork. He looked at his watch, around one hour until day break so he stood up and stretched his legs. A twenty minute walk back to the car and he was off, plan in place and revenge burning into his cold senses. A couple of hours sleep and he would return as he needed to know everything about their routine.

The view during the daylight was very different, he could see that there was only one way in and out of the house and the hills surrounding the place gave perfect points to observe it without been seen. Martin also noticed only one car on the driveway, last night he had seen two, but now there was just the Saxo, that could only mean one thing, the security had gone. Another two hours confirmed that the only people in the house were Terry, Jo and Tom.

He slipped back to the car and drove back to the small hotel in a nearby town where he had paid cash and the old lady at the stuffy desk seemed disinterested in any comings and goings. The shower in the room was dirty, the water flow weak as Martin stood thinking about his next move while he spun around in the cubicle trying to wash the suds away. He quickly ate a breakfast bar before drinking a mug of coffee, the plan running through his mind. This could involve a fight at the house with Terry, not ideal, but it was what it was, he didn't want Terry dead just yet. If he had to kill him however, he would.

Five minutes later the red car spat into life and Martin drove back to the little lay-by. He knew the routine and he was familiar with the terrain, he just didn't know how this would go. He slipped the knife from the back pack and slid it into a sheath strapped to the side of his calf. Anticipation and adrenaline were rushing through his body as he got out of the car and the familiar smell of wood smoke drifted back into his nose. Suddenly he heard a car start up, it was coming from the house. Martin melted into the hedgerow becoming one with the landscape and as a car approached it slowed to take the bend where Martin lay. There it was, the Saxo! He caught sight of the occupants, Terry and Tom, both sat upfront, the rear seats empty which meant Jo must be alone and unguarded.

The car disappeared, turning left towards the local village. Surely there was no way that the house would remain unprotected, if so, what a massive error, what a fatal mistake! Martin jogged the remaining hundred yards to the house and disappeared around into the back garden, he had to work quickly. Surely there must be more security, it couldn't be this easy could it? He tried the kitchen door, it was open. Martin crept in a few paces and stopped. He listened, on alert for anything suspicious, straining to hear any noise, then he heard it, the unmistakable sound of someone in the bath. That's why she had stayed at home, she wanted to have a bath, how nice of her to want to die clean!

211

He moved quickly but silently up the stairs and moving as smoothly as a tiger, he reached the bathroom door. The waft of lotions smelt delicious, the warm air from the bath stroked his face, the shower head was turned on, obviously washing her hair, and obviously doing so with closed eyes.

Jo felt a movement of air sweep from the door, then it vanished like an apparition. Maybe the place has a ghost she thought as the water washed over her head. She grabbed the towel and wiped her face, she stretched, yawned and opened her eyes. Martin's face was less than six inches from hers and she could smell the coffee on his breath. The punch that knocked her unconscious was brutal in its power, one punch, one outcome.

When Jo regained consciousness, the red car was travelling fast and in a straight line as though they were on a motorway. She lay in the leg space between the front and rear seats and found she was wrapped in a strong tape. She couldn't move a muscle and a strip of tape covered her mouth meaning she had to struggle hard to breathe through her nose. She struggled to get into a comfy position but couldn't, the pain from her jaw was horrific, broken fragments of teeth rested inside her mouth. She was still naked, however a bath towel had been thrown over her offering her little warmth.

The car slowed and turned off the motorway and it was then that Martin spoke.

"I can hear you're awake, lay still and you may yet live. If you try to escape I will kill you instantly, then I will go back to kill the others." The car stopped and the rear door opened. Jo could see that they were in a side road with lots of trees and the sound of animals in the distance.

"Right, I have clothes for you and when we get to where we are going I will allow you to get dressed but until then I want to introduce you to a life time friend of mine!" He pulled out a syringe and carefully slid the needle into her arm, the pain subsided and sleep washed over her.

Jo awoke once more, she felt cold but was clearly out of the car. She looked around, it was pitch black but then a voice came from out of nowhere and a torch beam lit her up. It was like she were centre stage and the audience could see only her.

"You may notice that you are dressed, you will also notice that you are in a building, it is a disused building where no one can hear us so we will not be disturbed." A match was lit and gas light illuminated the room. Jo looked at the surroundings and it took a few seconds for it to sink in to her drug infused mind. She was sitting in the centre circle of a basketball court with a wooden floor not dissimilar to that in her old school gym stretched around her. The room was small, only enough space for one court and it hadn't been used for a long time evidenced by the thick dust on the floor but still smelt like a gym. Bold writing covered one wall, it was too dark to read but it was clearly some motivational statements.

The gas light hissed but Jo could tell that there was nothing else around but silence, deep empty silence. Her eyes adjusted and the writing came into focus.

"HMDC Aldington, Motivation and commitment = Success."

Terry sprinted through the open front door of the house. As they had entered the driveway he could clearly see that a drama had been going on. The door was fully open, pools of water lay on the hard hall floor and Tom's bike which he had taken up for him, and had sat in the porch was half in half out of the house. He shouted out but heard nothing and bounding up the stairs with his heart in his throat, he rushed into the bathroom. The floor was awash with bathwater, blood mixed in with the suds and the half-filled bath of still warm water sat with smears of blood on each side. A dressing gown strewn on top of the laundry basket begged him to find Jo.

The car with its engine still running sat in the driveway with Tom sat looking on in confusion. Terry jumped back into the driving seat and thumping the steering wheel with the flats of both hands, he bowed his head and shouted "Fuck!"

"What's wrong dad, where's Mum?   Dad what's happening?" Tom began to sob. "Dad, what's wrong?"

"Stay here for a moment Tom, I'll be one second" Terry's eyes had been drawn to a piece of paper flapping gently in the breeze. It was stuck to the front door, attached by one of the darts that Terry and Tom had used last night. He tore it off knowing that it wasn't going to be good news.

Terry
Come find us.
I want my son back, you want your wife
We are waiting in the place where we first met, bring the police and I will kill her.

Terry ran back to the car and gunned the engine, "Tom, we need to find mum and I want you to come with me, just do everything that I ask, Okay?" He kissed Tom on the forehead and set off south towards Kent.

CHAPTER FIFTY EIGHT

Six hours later Terry was driving through the Kent country side, it was still at least two hours away from dawn and his eyes were stinging with tiredness and unshed tears as he drove on. His thoughts were firmly on what lay ahead until he was brought back to the present by the fuel light flashing an orange warning at him. He pulled into a garage and filled up, the elderly Indian attendant seemingly disinterested with anything that was going on.

"Pump 4 mate, do you have anything useful for cutting wire?"

The man just pointed to a display of cheap garden tools which could be bought for a discount as a reward for buying their fuel. Terry picked up a flimsy pair of secateurs and paid the bill. Grabbing his things Terry got back into the car, he unwrapped a Mars bar sharing it with Tom who had woken from a restless sleep as they entered the garage forecourt. Wondering what would happen when he reached his destination, he pulled back onto the empty road and estimated that he was only twenty minutes away from Aldington.

His mind drifted back to this small prison, it was an eclectic group of buildings, holding around a hundred and twenty young men aged from eighteen to twenty one. A short sharp shock of a system which was designed to run like basic army training with lots of exercise, discipline, room inspections, lots of shouting and punishment and plenty of aggression towards the boys. Not a place for the faint hearted. Luckily for those who had experienced these delights the prison closed in the 1990s. He focused his mind as he drove, trying to remember each detail of the lay out of the place. Gradually a picture formed in his mind of a green wire fence around twelve feet high surrounding the site, with a large sports field taking over most of the area with a cluster of single story buildings connected by a road large enough for one vehicle. This road stretched from the sports field to the main prisoner accommodation, probably only 150 meters long but with four buildings off to the right on the approach to the field.

The first building was the education complex, about twenty classrooms in total, following this was the visits room followed by the administration office and then the main focus of Terry's thoughts, the Gymnasium. All these thoughts evaporated as he entered the village of Aldington where a small road ran to the right of the village pub up a gentle hill leading half a mile to the now closed prison site. The old staff housing lay empty where the derelict prefab buildings had finally given in to the elements. Even with his mind in turmoil Terry thought that it was a sad sight.

He pulled the car into a lay-by that was around a two minute walk from the main prison gate. "Wait here Tom and lock the car doors behind me. If I need you to do anything, I will speak to you on your phone. I will not text, ignore any texts and only listen to either me or mum, do you understand?"

Tom nodded, Terry noticed a tear working it's way down Toms cheek. He ignored it and ruffled Tom's hair.

"I will be back with Mum, it just may take a little while mate, hang on in there."

Terry got out of the car and ensuring that Tom locked the doors, he headed through the trees until he reached the green wire garden type fence surrounded the sports field. He knew that this was the way that he must get in and he slipped the secateurs from his jacket pocket and got to work on the fence. Within five minutes he had made a hole large enough to crawl through and for the first time in more than twenty years Terry was back inside the prison.

He followed the fence line up to where a large double gate stood, this had separated the field from the remainder of the prison. The gate was still there but the locks had been removed long ago so Terry was able to slip quietly into the main prison complex.

He still needed to be careful; it would be a simple task for Martin to ambush him so the other buildings must be searched. The education building loomed out of the darkness, there were no doors to stop him entering, only a single passageway led from the front to back of the building. Glass crunched under his feet as he gingerly checked each room, the smell of damp hit his nostrils and the cold air made him feel wet. He pressed on, nothing. The rooms were clear.

Silently he made his way back out and onto the small prison road where the next building greeted him. The visits room was just a single large room, Terry looked in and listened, there were no sounds other than his shallow breaths and as he walked to the far end of the room he saw it was clear.

216

The Administration building stood next. Terry was about to enter when he heard music being played from the last building, the gymnasium. Terry knew that this was always going to be the final scene of the play so he walked directly to the gym door and pushed it open, just a few inches at first, but then fully open. He entered and closed the door behind him, the two changing rooms were in darkness, but a light was sneaking from under the door to the main sports hall and the music followed. Terry recognised the tune, it was Roxy Music's 'Angel Eyes!'

He stood with his ear to the door, hardly daring to breath. There were no other doors leading into the gym hall, this was the only way in or out of what was also a windowless room. Terry backed out of the gym, he needed to get focused, no emotion, keep professional. He also needed an escape route should things go wrong. He couldn't count on making the sports field if everything else went wrong, also he couldn't carry Jo through the small hole in the fence, so he needed to go back and look at the main gate.

The fourteen feet double metal gate stood tall and proud. In Terry's time it was locked with a large lock holding the gates together but they could be opened individually with a bolt that slid in and out of the concrete floor. Tonight it was held together with a chain and padlock, however Terry could see that this had been cut. This was how Martin had got in and the red car was parked just out of sight of the gate. Terry checked the car out finding it was locked with no keys left in the ignition, wishful thinking!

He checked his watch, dawn was around an hour away and he needed to get this show going so he moved back to the gym. The sports hall door opened easily, the music drifted across to Terry, the gas light hissed and there sat on a stool in the centre circle of the basketball court was Jo. Standing directly behind her holding a huge knife to her neck was Martin Heard. The glow from the lamp cast eerie shadows dancing across the walls and ceiling, a ghostly ballet dance embracing them all.

"Terry, well played, I knew that you would come. Do you remember this place? Remember what happened just here, on this exact spot?" Martin stamped a foot to make the point that this was the place.

"Where is my son?" he asked, not taking his eyes from Terry's, not moving the knife from Jo's throat.

"Ihave him nearby, he's safe; do you really think that I would bring him in to your trap?"

"That would have been a smart move, it would save a little more pain! Are you going to fetch him for me?"

"I'm not, Jo will. Take me as your hostage, let Jo fetch Tom, he is expecting that to happen."

"Come closer Terry". Terry noticed a second chair was sitting just in the shadow. Martin moved it closer to Jo, "Come take a seat."

"Only if you untie Jo, a straight swap Martin, me for Jo and then you get Tom, he will come with Jo."

"Sit!"

Terry sat on the chair, he stared at Jo and said "It will be fine, go fetch Tom, he is in the car. We parked in this place a couple of years ago when I showed you the outside of the prison."

Jo nodded, Martin the cut the tape that held her hands and legs, she stood up. Terry was then trussed in the same manner, his jacket thrown onto the floor to avoid any unexpected surprises.

Martin hissed at Jo. "Any nonsense and I will hack this man to bits, I no longer care who lives or dies, you have five minutes."

She walked on unsteady legs towards the door, Martin hissed her name again. She turned and froze. Martin was standing behind Terry and he was holding a pick axe handle.

"In this very room your husband stood and watched as I had my arm broken."

With those words, he smashed the handle against the top of Terry's right arm, and with a sickening crack, the bone crunched and splintered and Terry let out a long painful scream.

"It fucking hurts doesn't it Terry? Now go get the boy!"

Jo turned and ran; she squeezed through the gap in the main gate and followed the fence line back to where she could remember parking. They had been driving to Dover when Terry insisted that they look at the place where he had started his prison career. She was glad that she had taken note of the area. She brushed through the bushes and trees that had taken control of the fence line, it must be close now. Then she caught sight of the car and she could see Tom sitting in the front seat, the front window fogged up.

Just then, there was a cracking of twigs behind her and a large dirty hand clasped over her mouth. Frog marched on tiptoes towards to the car, Tom saw her coming from the trees, he smiled before noticing that she was not alone and his smile turned to terror as he screamed and buried his head in his hands. The passenger window smashed through, glass falling on Tom's back, the burly arm reached through and opened the doors. Jo was thrown into the back and the man leapt into the driver's seat. She looked at him, it was not Martin Heard.

"Listen to me, I am here to help. Is the man armed and what building is Terry held in?"

Jo told the man everything that she knew, he stopped her from time to time to clarify a point. She looked deep into his eyes, where she saw a deep, unfathomable darkness. He had a hard cruel face and a scar ran across his right cheek. He was too young to be someone who could have served with Terry. He was athletic, probably in his thirties, she guessed, still serving in the military, and definitely not someone who had been near to the house in the lakes.

"Who are you?"

"A friend of a friend phoned, he told me that Terry needed help, I was in the area, it's what I do."

His phone beeped and he checked the text that came through.

"Look I want to help, that's all you need to know, no disrespect to you or your boy but I don't care about you, it's Terry that I have to help. I have one hour and I have to go, just do what I say and I promise that the bad guy will not hurt you." He looked at her and waited for a response, none came. Jo just looked, it was ironic, she was in the hands of someone who had probably killed as many people as Martin Heard. He looked as though this was his business, and the only difference was that he was on their side.

"Okay, take Tom and go back to the Gym, do not turn around in any circumstances, have I made myself clear?"

Tom and Jo nodded, the terror of what they were experiencing robbing them of speech. They left the car and walked back towards the unforgiving sight of the prison. The man had disappeared back into the dark.

CHAPTER FIFTY NINE

Terry sat slumped in the chair, he couldn't move, the pain seeming to spread through every nerve ending within his body. He was finished, he felt old and defeated. He was no match for Martin, how could he beat him with only one arm? Martin was leaning against the gym wall looking at Terry, deciding what the next move would be when suddenly the door to the gym opened.

Stood in the glimmering light was the illuminated vision of a young boy. Jo stood behind him holding his shoulders. Tom's face full of confusion and fear looked at Terry and then across to Martin as he shuffled from foot to foot, unsure as to what this man wanted. His face looked familiar, it was the man that Tom thought of as Uncle Martin.

" You're the man who tricked me at the football match, you pretended to be my uncle, Dad said that you were a bad man." Tom sobbed as he surveyed the scene. He could see Terry but the light didn't allow him to catch any details.

For a full minute Martin stared at the child, he struggled to catch his breath before eventually breaking the silence.

"Come here son" Martin whispered," I am your real father, you were taken from me a long time ago".

Tom planted his feet into the wooden floor but his mum eased him forward. He didn't want to go near this man, why was she pushing him forward? His body stiffened, this felt horrific, surely he should be staying away from this man? Again he hesitated. Jo whispered into his ear and he relaxed a little, moving closer to where he could now clearly see Terry.

Tom looked at the man he knew as his father and gasped, the bone was protruding from the top of his arm and blood oozed out and dripped on the floor forming a stream heading towards the jacket.

Terry looked up at Tom and smiled. "I love you son, never forget that".

"I love you too dad."

"Shut up old man"! Martin leapt towards Terry, the knife glinting evilly in the flickering light. The blade then slid into Terry's left thigh, a small fountain of blood sprang from the wound and as he then lunged at Terry's throat, the knife flashed before dropping down with a clatter on to the floor.

Nobody heard the crack of the shot which split Martin Heard's forehead. No one saw where the shot came from or even where the shooter melted away to, not until it was too late.

Martin Heard's lifeless body lay motionless on the floor, his arms outstretched like in crucifixion, his left leg buckled beneath him, his eyes were open and staring, a thousand yard stare, looking up to the ceiling and beyond. The bullet entry hole oozed red, the blood staining the wood flooring, following the white lines of the court. Brain and skull spattered the basketball backboard forming a grotesque mosaic of blood and bone, proudly announcing the death of a monster, almost gladiatorial in its grisly statement.

The smell of cordite floated across the room, leaving the message of death in their throats, their ears ringing from the gunshot. And then silence, deafening silence, broken only by the sobs of the living.

CHAPTER SIXTY

Terry opened his eyes; he was in The William Harvey Hospital in Ashford, Kent. His right arm was stinging and his thigh felt on fire. "Terry you have been out cold for nearly twelve hours, they have operated on your arm and leg and apparently you will live!" He smiled at up at Jo sat next to his bed, Tom close beside her. "Thank God for that, I thought that it was game over! What happened? The last thing I remember was that bloody knife in my leg with my life just flashing in front of me!"

"I don't know, the only thing that I can be sure of is that one of your old friends scared the life out of me in the woods! Oh and he can obviously shoot straight!"

"One of my friends? I didn't speak to anyone, how could anyone know where I was going?"

Tom looked down at the floor, his cheeks had turned bright red.

"Tom?"

"The men who looked after us gave me their numbers, I kept them in my phone just in case. I phoned them when you left me in the car and they said they had a friend who lived nearby, I was not allowed to tell anyone, then I had to delete the numbers. Sorry Dad!"

"I think that I can forgive you mate, come over here." He stretched his uninjured arm around his wife and son and held them close.

CHAPTER SIXTY ONE

The hearse glided through the entrance to the crematorium, guarded by hedges and lawns manicured to within an inch of their lives, a sweeping driveway fitting of any country spa and golf club.

A bark echoed through the still morning,

"Atten.... shun!"

The hundreds of prison staff dressed in military style best uniform, immaculately turned out and looking fitting for this tribute to a fallen comrade snapped to attention. Headed up by their Governor and his deputy they lined the route from top to bottom, the gently sloping drive packed, shoulder to shoulder, staff standing like black daffodils nodding in the breeze as the wind of fate slowly passed them by. So still that the crunch of gravel submitting under the thick black tyres of the hearse sounded like wood crackling in a bonfire. The cry of a rook cackled through the still anticipation that only death's final journey could bring.

Staff tried but could not help staring into the emptiness of the cortege that passed them by, tear stained faces of her only friends in the world; the blank expressions of the only two people she considered as family, who only weeks ago had salsa danced the night away with Martha and a monster.

They both looked through the front windscreen of the single black car which followed, not daring to observe the tributes which were on show following their friend in one last late slow dance, Martha, their best friend. They had ensured that she would have an explosion of floral tributes, the coffin barely visible through the flowery word 'Martha' which filled the entire side window of the hearse. Something to show that she had counted, to demonstrate that someone cared, that she had mattered to them.

Some staff wept as she passed them for the final time, some grasped hands into fists at the rage they felt for the person who had committed this act upon such a lovely lady, some just happy it was not them sat in the car that followed behind.

A hushed black snake curled its way through the doors of the ugly cold building; horrid places crematoriums, looking as though any form of artistic license to demonstrate the beauty of the Lord was suddenly lost on a bored council worker. It contrasted with the splendor of the grounds, the gentle trickle of the fountain and the oriental fish which swam innocently around the pond and the summerhouse which held the book of condolence which for a price, you could have your favourite page on show. And then an ugly square building, no thought, no feelings, just cheap and functional. It was all there was. What a dignified ending, in a flaming warehouse for the dead!

The service was held by a vicar who had never met Martha, who didn't know anything about her life or loves but Stephen stood and gave a befitting eulogy reminding the staff of all the attributes of their fallen colleague. Terry moved uncomfortably in his seat, his arm and leg still heavily bandaged and still giving him some pain. He reflected on the last few weeks and all the loss and devastation they had endured before he glanced at his watch, and thought that they had another five minutes before it was time for the next sitting, before almost to the second, they would be ushered out. He made a mental note; never will I place anyone I love through this loveless, soulless service.

With everything that he and Stephen had witnessed, the horrors that Martin Heard had performed on so many innocent people, he wondered if God really did care, did it even matter? He wasn't sure.

The lack of a Godly atmosphere however, was drowned out by the burly singing of nearly one hundred fully suited and booted prison service staff, the roof was lifted by the final hymn, which raised a lump in the throat as did the music now playing as the curtain closed for the final time. The song was apparently a favourite of Martha's, often played and discussed after salsa classes during the drive home. As the vicar clumsily pressed play on the council CD player, only two people could have known the real irony of the song choice, but this seedy episode of Martha's life was lost with her death as the tones of Bryan Ferry filled the room. The paper order of service informed the congregation that this music was 'Angel Eyes' by Roxy Music.

CHAPTER SIXTY TWO

Jo drove the car into Stephen's driveway and the front door sprang open revealing Stephen, a heavily pregnant Tanya, Harry and Ellie, and behind them Chris.

Terry, his leg still giving him some pain, climbed slowly out of the passenger seat and noticed that the beginning of an extension was taking shape beside the house.

"What's going on here Stephen, wasn't the place big enough for you?"

Stephen laughed, "Dad is with us now, he's a brilliant baby sitter so we thought that we would let him stay around for a while!"

"Thanks for the invite for Sunday Lunch, it smells fantastic." Jo said as she gave Tanya a huge hug.

"Always a pleasure" chuckled Tanya, as she showed them through to the kitchen "We have all been through so much, we just need to get some closure on this sorry business."

Terry agreed, "Nothing like this must ever happen again, so many families destroyed by one man, and for what? It just didn't make any sense."

They all nodded and with drinks distributed all round, toasted Lucy, such a horrific ending for a much loved wife and mother. Chris still had a long way to go in his recovery and often woke with shattering nightmares, but it would get better if not acceptable as the inevitability of time took over.

They gathered around the table, a group forever united by the terrors they had endured, the love and warmth engulfing them, helping heal the wounds.

The black car pulled up outside the house, a tinted window slid down and a suntanned figure wearing a designer suit and expensive shades looked out over the house. He picked up his phone and dialed.

"Mr Brood, not today, Byfield has visitors."

AFTERWORD

Follow Stephen Byfield and his attempts to avoid the clutches of the Brood family in the next exciting novel, 'Resolution' due out later in 2020.

ACKNOWLEDGEMENT

I would like to thank my wife Jo for her unlimited patience in rereading High Risk innumerable times in order to pick out any obvious, and not so obvious errors. Before I retired, I quite often sat in my office while duty governor, listen to the sounds of the prison around me and have incorporated some of these moments into the novel. Jo ensured the story still flowed whilst allowing the reader to experience some of real prison life.

My thanks also go to the friends that read early drafts of High Risk and gave their honest critique as to whether it was too graphic or in some cases not graphic enough! Clare, Tom, Sam and Davina to name but a few.

The reader may be relieved to hear that I never had a prisoner quite as horrific as Martin Heard, but believe me, he is an entity composed of a number of those I had under my care over the 32 years I served in the prison service! For this reason, I thank the prison service for my 32 years of research into the evilness of the human mind!

Finally, I would like to thank Kindle Direct Publishing for the opportunity to make my novel available to you all, and I hope you look forward to the sequel.

Printed in Great Britain
by Amazon

41398422R00137